WILDE STORIES 2014

WILDE STORIES 2014

The Year's Best Gay Speculative Fiction

edited by
STEVE BERMAN

LETHE PRESS
MAPLE SHADE, NEW JERSEY

Published in 2014 by Lethe Press, Inc.
118 Heritage Avenue • Maple Shade, NJ 08052-3018 USA
www.lethepressbooks.com • lethepress@aol.com
ISBN: 978-1-59021-503-6 / 1-59021-503-6 (library binding)
ISBN: 978-1-59021-500-5 / 1-59021-500-1 (paperback)
ISBN: 978-1-59021-501-2 / 1-59021-501-x (e-book)

These stories are works of fiction. Names, characters, places, and incidents are products of the authors' imaginations or are used fictitiously.

Set in Jenson, LemonChicken, Bookman Old Style, Ming, and Courier New.
Interior and cover design: Alex Jeffers.
Cover artwork: TK.

TABLE OF CONTENTS

In memory of JOEL LANE, *a sweet man who understood horrors*

Introduction

Do readers bother with introductions? A similar question might be, do young children bother to read the wrappers on candy bars? Perhaps after half the chocolate has already been masticated and lips and fingertips are sticky, they might pause, spend a moment of distraction before the sugar rush to read the thin wrapping. I wonder if readers open *Wilde Stories* to a random story, feast on those words, and then another story, not necessarily the following but again a indiscriminate choice, and only when sated consider the introduction. Editors often sweat and bleed over proper introductions.

Another question editors ponder: How long do readers dwell on the table of contents of an anthology, let alone a "Year's Best" anthology? Writers, of course, care—the initial posting of the TOC online is often greeted with much the same excitement I suspect nervous drama students feel about whether or not they will have a part in a play.

I'm reflecting on all this because this volume is different from past editions of *Wilde Stories*. Not one of the contributors has appeared in the series before.

Back in 2008, when I started the series, I worried over its viability. How many stories would I find, how many authors wrote quality gay-themed spec fic? And when I saw that I was buying stories from the same folk, at least one individual from the preceding volume would be in the next, was the series getting stale or was the field of writers too small?

Six years later, I can state that those early fears have been proven wrong. I had to read so many stories (and the scope of what I consider speculative fiction has widened beyond the fantastical and horrific to include the surreal, the strange, the essentially outlandish) in the field, many by new authors I had yet to happen upon, many by authors I had never thought would write a story with a gay protagonist. The field is not barren but fecund.

Alas, there will be one individual I shall never publish again. Joel Lane. As with so many authors, I was introduced to the man through his writing and by asking to include him in this series. Joel's passing in 2013 was sudden, a true blow to horror and noir fiction and gay fiction. I am so saddened by the loss of a man who never failed to write something thrilling. Now I can no longer send him an email in the last months of the calendar year asking to reprint one of the stories he had written. I can take some solace that past volumes of the *Wilde Stories* series keep a mote of Joel alive, like an ember. Open those books, breathe on the page and his voice will burn bright for a brief span.

And as long as I am still breathing, I shall continue to gather the best stories of the strange and supernatural and wondrous for you, reader—though isn't it time you stopped reading this introduction? The real sweets are found once the wrapper is torn aside.

STEVE BERMAN
SPRING 2014

He responds immediately, *Closer than u think*

GRINDR

Clayton Littlewood

Soho Athletic gym.

7:15 PM. There's hardly anyone around. The café bar is empty. The only sound, the receptionist washing glasses, the manager ringing up till receipts and the distant sound of club music floating through the gym.

I try to catch the receptionist's eye. He's slim, toned, hair perfectly parted, the obligatory beard. In his late twenties. Probably from Shoreditch. He looks over. "Can I help you?"

"Can I have a towel please?"

"Sure," he smiles. "That'll be a pound."

I hand over a coin, sign in and then head toward the changing room, passing a tall, well-defined woman pounding away on the Stairmaster, the Brazilian trainer "spotting" for a client and a face I know from some club or other. I'm feeling strangely nervous, as if something weird is about to happen.

It's busier in the changing room, some guys are dressing, some undressing, a smattering of bears and suited businessmen. A surreptitious glance here, a lingering look there. The usual casual cruising that you find in a gay gym. I find a locker. At the back. Near the showers (my usual spot). Then I unzip my gym bag. Inside is an empty bottle of medication, a black Moleskine notebook, a pair of Adidas tracksuit bottoms and a grey

T-shirt with "Muscle" written across the chest, both items of clothing in complete contrast to the designer gym gear that most guys here wear (my gym etiquette is to always be unobtrusive as possible).

I'm about to close my locker when I remember my iPhone. I fish it out of my bag and as I do it vibrates. It's a push notification. From Grindr. I enter my passcode, tap the application and the sender's profile. The pic is slightly grainy, although it looks familiar. Like a gym. I tap Chat. The message reads, *Howdy! How's ur night going?*

I tap the Back button. There's no name on the profile, just a quote, "Life is short, so enjoy."

I contemplate what to do. Then a third message. *Don't block me!*

Actually, I wasn't going to. Blocking always seems such a passive-aggressive act. I have an aversion to it. But equally, if I don't block him, he sounds like the type that will plague me with messages. Fuck. Why did I even download this app? It's not as if I intend to meet anyone on here. What was it my friend Paul said, "Why don't you just put 'Timewaster' as your profile name?"

Then another message pops up, *Enjoy ur workout!*

I swivel round. Startled. Is he in here?

To my left is a Latino guy, blow-drying his armpit hair. Sitting on the bench nearby, an older guy, bearded again, in fatigues and a tight white vest, unties his bootlaces. Neither of them is using a phone.

I tap Back again. The profile reads:

```
Online
10 meters away
```

Ten meters!

I type, *Where r u?* Press Send.

He responds immediately, *Closer than u think*

I glance across at the toilets. There's no one there. He must be in the gym doing a workout. He must've spotted me coming in. I head back outside, intrigued.

I position a gym bench under the Nautilus equipment. Sit down. Wipe my hands on my T-shirt. Then stare straight ahead into the mirror, taking in my surroundings. There are five guys in here. Three working out and two chatting by the far window. None of them are looking in my direction. This makes me feel both safe and uneasy. Safe, because as I've said, I like to blend in. And uneasy because I remember a time when I'd walk into the gym and everyone would check me out. Now, no one does.

I stare at my scuffed trainers, thinking about my fading looks. I quickly shake the thought away. Clasp the barbell with both hands. Take a deep breath and push it upward in one dynamic thrust. I work out briskly, concentrating, not wanting to get wrapped up in negative feelings. After three sets I'm about to take the weights off the bar when I feel my phone vibrating again.

Not doing a 4th set then?

I scan the room. Everyone is either lifting weights or on a machine. I check the profile. It's still says he's 10 meters away! Where the hell is this guy? I type, *Come on! Where r you?*

U'll find out soon

I grin. But at the same time I'm getting mildly irritated. Now I can't block him. Wherever he is, he can see me and blocking him will just make me come across as uptight. I type, *Give me a clue?* Then I survey the oblong room again: a tattooed guy doing press-ups on a yoga mat and a stocky bear training his biceps. The bear's face is familiar. But then so many guys on the scene are these days, having seen them out and about for thirty-odd years, or having viewed them online. And now with this bear look, everyone has become one.

There's another vibration. *I'm not that bear if that's what u think!*

I press the Power Off button. Okay, I've had enough of this. I've got to finish this workout and get out of here. I've got work to do at home. Chores to be done. Plus I'm knackered. I really need an early night. What was it my boss said to me today? "Clay, you've been looking really tired and haggard lately. Are you okay?" I felt like saying, "Look, I'm just a bit rundown, all right! Give me a break!" But of course, you can't say that. Not to your boss. You just have to smile sweetly and say, "No everything's fine. But thank you for asking."

Twenty minutes later, I'm dressed again, standing in front of the mirror, applying Dax Wax to my salt and pepper hair (more salt now I admit). My skin, although unlined, is starting to sag. I open my mouth, wide. Then close it, watching the flesh fall back into place. The phase I went through a few years ago of having Botox every six months, well, I thought it'd passed and that I was finally accepting the aging process. Now I'm not so sure.

There's a vibration in my pocket. I take it out. *U're getting older. Soon no one's going to want u*

Who the fuck does he think he is? I clench my teeth and press Block. Then I shove my phone back in my pocket and march out of the changing room, the gym, down the stairway, onto Macklin Street, a self-satisfied smirk on my face. Vile queen. Well that put a stop to his stupid little game. And I make my way through the evening crowds to Soho.

Old Compton Street is a cosmopolitan melting pot. A Hogarth painting come to life. I pass a posse of G.A.Y. twinks, East End lads in Hackett tops, a group of bleached-blonde girls with pink rabbit ears, rickshaws parked outside the Prince Edward Theatre. Then I arrive at my favourite coffee shop, number 34B, on the corner of Frith Street. I take a seat inside, tucked up by the window and order a small black coffee. It's from this vantage point that I do all my thinking. My window to the world. The place I come to when I want to ponder life, my career, mortality. There're a stack of magazines in the corner. I pick one up. It's *The Clarion*. The local mag. It always has an interesting historical section and I'm engrossed in an article about Soho Square when I feel a movement in my pocket.

I reach for my coffee. Take another sip. Not in any particular hurry to answer it. I give it a minute. Then reach into my jeans pocket. It's another Grindr message. From him again!

In ur favourite spot I see…34B

I thought I'd blocked him! I press Block. Again. Turn off my phone. Then I scour the crossroads. But it's so busy, there are so many people laughing, or singing or arguing, it's like Gay Pride night. I exchange glances with a few guys. It could be any one of them. And they all seem to be looking at me, knowingly, as if they're somehow all in on it.

Normally I'd be here for at least an hour, writing in my notebook, trying to make the night last longer before it's time to face the drudgery of home and preparing for work the next day. But tonight my spell has been broken. My little oasis has been defiled. So I take a last mouthful of the now lukewarm coffee, thank the Hungarian assistant and leave.

I weave in out of the crowds, down Brewer Street, past the neon-lit bookshop, the peep shows, the NCP car park, the health food shop, turning right at the end of the street, past Third Space and the Piccadilly

Theatre, heading underground, down the stairs, the escalator, past the busker murdering *The Final Countdown*, until I'm on the Piccadilly Line platform (at the back and out of sight).

The train ride is uneventful. It's 9:15 PM. Fortunately I'm an hour ahead of the drunken passengers, with their out-of-tune singing and excessively loud voices, all breaking that Golden Tube Rule: Thou Must Not Speak. I get off at Earls Court and take the rear exit, away from the throng.

Now I'm above ground. The garish display of the Ideal Home Exhibition looms before me. It's all fake topiary, with a stately home backdrop. Tacky beyond belief. Although I've only been on the tube for fifteen minutes, darkness has already descended. I walk down Warwick Road toward Holland Road, thinking about what I have to do when I get in. I'm just passing Tesco when my phone vibrates. It's a Grindr notification. The profile pic is of a building. I tap it. Then tap Chat. The message reads, *Thought u'd lost me did ya?*

Online
10 meters away

I spin round. Panicking. There's no one there. And no one in front either. He must be in Tesco!

I tap on the profile pic, enlarging it with my thumb and forefinger. It's a pic of…Homebase. The building ahead! Oh God. He's somewhere ahead of me. Probably hiding behind that wall! Now what? I could press the Report button, but what am I going to say? That I'm being stalked on an app? That's what Grindr's for, isn't it? So guys can stalk each other? My mind's racing now. What should I do? Double back? Take another route home? The questions hit me like a stream of arrows. I'm aware too that I'm breathing much faster now and that my right eyelid is twitching. Wait a minute. This is ridiculous. Just jump a cab. What's he going to do? Run after it?

I wait until the traffic has subsided, then run across the road, doubling back on myself, turning left onto Cromwell Road, checking behind intermittently that I'm not being followed. A few seconds later I spot a black cab with a yellow vacant sign. I stick my hand out. Please stop! It hurtles toward me and pulls over.

"Holland Road please!" I say, diving into the back. "The High Street Ken end."

The driver indicates. I quickly turn in my seat, looking out the back window, still breathing heavily. The street's deserted. I sigh and sink back in my seat.

"Just past the pub please. Wherever you can find a space. Yes. Just here's fine, thanks."

I hand the driver a tenner. "Keep the change." He looks at me in disbelief, as the tip is more than the fare. But I'm not really thinking straight at the moment. I just want to get inside my flat. I slam the cab door. Run the few yards up the street, down the checkered tiled steps, into the basement. It takes me a few seconds to find my keys. I can hear them jangling in my bag somewhere… Here they are! I'm about to put the key in the lock when I feel my phone vibrating. I hesitate. Then take it out. It's another message. I tap on the profile. The pic is of a bedroom. Hold on, that's my bedroom! That's my Jean Cocteau lithograph above my bed. He's inside my flat!

I back away from the front door. Rush back up the stairway.

A short, red-headed woman is about to enter the main building with a young man.

"Please! Can you help me!"

She stops, key in the door and turns her head. The young man whispers to the woman. Then he walks toward me. "What's the matter?" he says politely.

"Listen, I know this sounds weird. But there's someone in my flat. He just sent me a photo on my phone. Of my bedroom! He's in there!" I point down to the basement.

"Do you know this person?"

"No! No, I haven't a clue who it is."

Now the woman walks toward me. "You've got to calm down a bit, Clay," she says, as she strokes my arm. "Ian'll go down and check."

I hand him the key. Once he's in the basement I turn to the woman. "Thank you. You're very kind. And I'm sorry for being such an idiot. It's just that—"

"Don't worry, Clay," consoles the woman. "Everything's going to be all right." She looks down into the basement area. "Maybe we should go down too."

"No, I err, don't want to."

"Perhaps you should've called the police."

At that moment Ian walks back up the basement steps. He frowns and scratches the back of his head. "There's no one in there." He looks embarrassed. "Whoever it was must've left."

"Ian, don't be silly. We've been standing here the whole time and we would've seen…" she stops abruptly, for Ian's glance is sharp. He nods at her when he thinks I'm not looking.

"I searched everywhere," he says. "In every room. And there's no one there. *Nobody*." He says it with finality.

And then the woman, as if delivering her verdict, says. "Oh well, that'll be that then…"

The key goes in the lock in one swift movement. I push the door open. Step inside. Shut it. Locking it again behind me at the top and bottom. I throw my gym bag on the sofa. Walk into the bedroom, shut the door and collapse on the bed. Within seconds, I'm in that world which is half dream, half sleep. NREM sleep I think my doctor calls it. I'm vaguely aware of a sensation in my pocket. But now I'm drifting, drifting. There it goes again. I think it's a vibration. It is a vibration! I jump up. Switch on my phone.

Took ur time getting here didn't ya?

```
Online
1 meter away
```

Istow's ghosts stand behind every seat in the parliament, their eyes burning bright and ambitious, while the dead of Besal roam the streets and will not come into any house.

THE GHOSTS OF EMERHAD

Nghi Vo

I stepped off of the train, and almost immediately, a young girl pressed a small blue flower into my hand.

"What's this for?" I asked. My voice sounded like rusted hell, but she smiled anyway, blithe and light. I guessed that she must have been no older than six when they signed the peace.

"For the armistice, sir," she said. "For remembrance."

I smiled at her because you smile at girls with flowers, but it wasn't the war I remembered, with the horses with their legs shot out from underneath them and the regular tinny sounds of gunfire far off. Instead, I remembered eyes as green as apples, and a promise that we would see each other again in Emerhad.

The train station was brand new, and the only ghosts that lived there were those of the rats and the cats. There was something nastier in the tunnels where the trains came and went, but I kept my eyes forward and they bothered me not at all.

I made my way through the train station easily enough, but at the gate I was momentarily stunned by the people. There were so many of them, and the noise of the city, sharp and raucous in the thin winter air, made me want to put my hands over my ears.

You've been away too long, I thought angrily. *You've lost your taste for people.*

Vo

It was better when I started walking, better yet when I got away from the new parts of the city. Emerhad was like a woman covering up old scars with beautiful scarves and charm. In the long silences of the night, however, the scars are still there and when I saw them, I felt at home.

I turned a corner like any other, and suddenly I'm away from the city that Emerhad wanted to be. The wall behind me was smeared with soot, and from where I stood I saw another building along the alley, one with a lower floor but not one above. Instead, there were only a few old rafters sticking up into the sky and a door below opened to allow a thin child with its head wrapped up in a scarf to come out into the cold.

This was the city that I remembered, and I wondered if I could hear the ghosts now.

Cities do strange things to ghosts. I know this, I've known it since I was a child and saw a man with a hole through his chest board the train in Cosmas. Kalisgrad eats its ghosts; nothing dead stays there. Istow's ghosts stand behind every seat in the parliament, their eyes burning bright and ambitious, while the dead of Besal roam the streets and will not come into any house. I did not know what to expect in Emerhad; when I had been there during the final days of the occupation, the dying were too loud, and their noise and their pain hid the dead.

Despite the familiar sights, the city was not the same one I thought I remembered. I didn't remember merchants hawking fruit imported from the south or jugglers in the streets, clad in medieval motley and pitching long knives to each other with lazy grace. I didn't remember the way the sunlight came through the clouds, picking out the tall towers of gray stone like an engraver's chisel. It was beautiful, no matter its scars, and I had never known that before.

As I walked, I thought about my time in Emerhad, of being cramped in the narrow alleys with a platoon of men and waiting, breath nearly silent, for the order to boil out like ants. I remembered the taste of horse meat, and cat meat as well, and I remembered the sound of bodies slapping the ground as they were brought to the outskirts of the city for burial.

I saw my first ghost after I had walked aimlessly for almost an hour. He was small and ragged, and at first I thought that he was one of the pick-pockets that thronged the streets. There was something crooked about the way that he ran, however, and when I looked closer I could see that his sleeve was flapping loose and stained dark with blood. He was off and around the corner in a moment and I kept walking.

I knew Iyan before the war, but that was distant and strange, like gazing through a salt-stained glass. We went to school together, we were friends, we were lovers. During the war, those words mattered less than a furtive match held to a cigarette, cold fingers pressed between bitten lips, and my own name, whispered harshly against my ear, that told me, yes, someone remembered it.

After the war, no one had anything left, not for a long time, and when I found his name on the lists of the dead in Malvo I only nodded, satisfied in a way that still puzzles me.

I went for years without saying his name. I went home to Barjaka. I finally angered my father enough that he disowned me, and I spent time with a widow who had known me since I was at school. I got married, but she had the wisdom to leave me before there was a child. I spent some months as a drunk in Istow, and then the rest of that year in Kalisgrad, where I felt lonelier than I ever had. Then one day I realized that simply not saying a name for ten years did not mean that it hadn't been on the tip of my tongue the entire time.

In the end, I couldn't stay away, not with my strange necromancer's gift, and so I came to Emerhad on the tenth anniversary of the armistice.

I realized that there were still pockets of the war hiding in the city. Like a child who knows he's not wanted, it kept to the old places and the broken places. I passed by a soldier dying impaled on the gates to a church as the drunks passed a bottle four feet away. From the street, I caught a glimpse of a sniper in a shattered window, his carelessness fatal and played out forever.

The war was here, and I knew that Iyan was, too. I walked faster as the darkness and the cold chased the people indoors. I knew that I would find him. I would come around a corner, or look down an alley, and he would be there.

They said that Emerhad was laid out by a blind Franciscan on a drunk mule. I was lost by the time full dark came on, but it didn't matter. I could hear gunshots now and when I came around a corner too fast I saw a short line of horses stabled in an alley. One turned to look at me with milky white eyes and I kept walking because I knew I was close.

Vo

When the cannons boomed, I broke into a run. I had few memories of being alone during the war, all bad, and I knew that I needed to hurry. The night sky above was clear and, with the street lamps taken for scrap steel, the stars hung crazed and gorgeous above the war in Emerhad.

I felt a hand snatch at my trouser leg, and that was a memory too, though it was not mine. Iyan told me about it happening to him during the fighting in Istow, when a comrade nearly pulled him down into the muck and the blood. I shook the hand off viciously. I knew that if I fell I would be dead, no matter if they found my bones in one of the grave pits or felled on the doorstep of a shocked baker come morning. I ran because it was a war, and I knew I had to find Iyan.

The street stretched before me, as much mud as cobble, and flickering along its length were men fighting one another with the blades of their bayonets, the first charge spent and no time to reload. I didn't know where my rifle was, but my hands were numb with cold and shock. Everything felt distant and I dodged around the soldiers. They were bearlike in their thick winter uniforms, indistinguishable, I thought, to themselves as well as to me. It didn't matter, I wasn't here for them.

I slid in the filth and the muck, hitting the ground hard enough that I could feel the leg of my trousers shred away like paper. It was well I did, because a moment later, I heard a hoarsely-shouted word of command, not in my native tongue but in Scaenen, the language of the enemy, and after my first week in the army I knew the Scaenen word for *shoot*.

The bullets tore through the air over my head, the shots loud in a way that not even cannons are, and behind me I could hear men dying and in front of me I heard the monotonous, disciplined clatter of a trained regiment reloading. I fought the urge to struggle to my feet, covering my head instead. Another burst of fire went over me and when I turned to my stomach from my side I could see the eyes of the dead men light around me like candles, flickering and unsteady.

I crawled on my belly to the shelter of a short wall. When I looked at it out of the corner of my eye, I could see that some whimsical person had set statues of the eight gods along the top, their colors bold even in the starlight. When I looked at it straight on, though, I saw that it had been half-blasted away, and the jagged edge of it bit into the night sky. I curled up next to it anyway, my hands over my head, and I shook, and I screamed into the noise. The cannons belched fire and made a wall of sound that struck me in the chest, and then I could see the long shadows of horses on the walls around me. We had lost the horses early in the war, but all the dead are dead alike, and they were screaming, their long elegant bones snapping and splintering.

I was frozen like that, the layers of the battle from one year to the next piling higher and higher around me and on top of me, and I never thought that I was trapped because I had never been anything else.

A hard hand grabbed my collar and hauled me partially to my feet. I cried out in fear but then I was being pulled along, and it was all I could do to keep my feet. I couldn't quite turn, and I couldn't straighten, and so I only saw flashes of the scenes around us, of the air gone dense with smoke, of a boot with the foot still inside it running blood into the gutter.

He dragged me away from the street into an alley, one that twisted back and forth. It would have been hell to fight there, but there was no fighting. He released my collar only to grab me by the arm, and we kept moving.

I called his name but he refused to speak. Instead, he led me away from the war in Emerhad.

We came to the mouth of the alley, and at last he turned. His eyes were as green as apples, but now there was a flickering light behind them too, unsteady as the flames of a candle, and when he grinned, there was something empty there that had never been so before.

I thought he would say something, but he only reached out to straighten the collar of my jacket, his touch rough and hurried. When his hands dropped to my breast pocket, he stole my half-finished cigarettes with his old familiar grace.

His mouth shaped the word *thanks*, and with a hard shove to my shoulder, I was out of the alley and into the street.

I caught a glimpse of his turned back, another ghostly burst of gunfire in my ear, and I staggered into back into Emerhad, into a cold night in early December. The moon was properly risen, bathing the street in frigid silver, and the only person nearby was a reeling drunk.

Not a drunk I realized, but an addict. He had glazed eyes and the sweet cloying smell of a kama smoker. Kama was the army's preferred sedative and war surplus had turned that medicine into a cheap poison.

"Sir, I'm a veteran, I wouldn't ask, sir, but I'm a veteran…"

Vo

Even bent and crabbed with pain, he was taller than me, and I could only imagine how tall he had been years ago. I ignored his words and dug into my pockets. I found a fistful of bills to give him, but I also found a crumpled blue flower.

He blessed me, staggering away down the street, and I was left holding the flower between my fingers, silent as a stone.

In remembrance, the girl had said, but I wouldn't need a reminder, not so long as the stones of Emerhad stood. The war didn't need to be remembered, the war was right behind me, down the half-dozen twists of a dark alley, and so was he.

In the end, I laid the flower at the mouth of the alley, offering or atonement or bribe, and I turned and walked away. If it was a comfort, it was a bad one, if it was a resolution, it was a cruel one.

The war ended, but there are places where I know it never will.

Danny said he hoped Craig would give him pointers about the backstroke. My son wanted that badly. He seemed to live for that possibility. When Daniel wanted something, it is hard to resist.

HOW TO DRESS
AN AMERICAN TABLE

J.E. Robinson

I must remember my son's name is Daniel. Anything else embarrasses him. Ever since he was eight and stopped answering to "Danny," he reminded me it is "Daniel," blushing mad. I don't want to embarrass him today. Of all days, Danny, Daniel need not be embarrassed today.

I didn't know much about him, except that Danny talked about him all the time, even before they moved in together. He was a senior vice president at a brokerage firm in the same building downtown where Danny was a paralegal. He didn't sound black over the phone, and he didn't sound that old. Jerry called NASD, just to check out this guy. In the twenty years since he got his license, not a blemish, not a complaint. All with the same firm.

"Twenty years!" Jerry said. "Shit! His book and his Series Seven are almost as old as our kid."

Danny needn't hear that from us. Too much in love, apparently, he loped from the elevator on cloud nine, in a building too pricy for his resources. "You'll totally love the view," he said. "We picked this place because you can see the park."

"Great."

Daniel looked back at me as he unlocked the door. "You sound like a fucking cheerleader, Mom."

Robinson

We had known—I had known—ever since he was in swimming. His event was the medley; he was good at it, a master of all strokes since the second grade. In freshman year, he was enthused he could be on the school team. He bubbled. Gone was his talk about being president. College was still in the cards, law school, too, at the time, but my son lived for swimming. He practiced strokes even while doing geometry and French.

"If I keep this up," he said, flailing the air, "I can be anchor."

Because he wanted it, I wanted it. His happiness was very important to me. It still is. Daniel can be hell when he is unhappy.

There was a boy on the team my Danny looked up to. His name was Craig. I suppose you can say Danny had a crush on Craig.

I wonder if that senior VP knows about Craig. Did Danny tell him?

"Hey!" someone next to me said as I got a pedicure. "Barb Hausmann! Remember me? My son Leo was in swimming with your Danny. Remember? How's your Danny doing?"

"Swell as melons," I said.

The question has been with me ever since. I approached Danny as he watered the lawn. He had weeded the flower beds, as I had told him, after washing the windows, and he had cleaned his hands on his chest, the mud smeared like blood.

"Did you do it?"

He didn't answer me. He simply smirked. He bent over to adjust the sprinkler. I could see my teenage son wasn't wearing anything beneath his sweatpants.

Daniel has never answered the question. I doubt that senior VP knows enough to ask.

It always will grate.

Danny was proud of the kitchen, a place compete with everything, capable of feeding the president.

"Tommy loves to cook," he said of the senior VP. "After a tough day with the market, nothing is more relaxing for him than whipping something out."

"I bet it is."

Danny laughed. He became as red as his hair. "Yeah, yeah, Mom. That, too."

He was right. There was a good view of the park, framed in a large picture window. Nearby was a picture of a cute black boy.

"His name is Hal," Danny said.

"Did you meet him?"

"We've played one-on-one a couple times. For a black kid, he could play basketball better. He plays like a white guy at Duke." Danny laughed again. "Just kidding. He lives with his mom in Jersey."

"Was your friend, Tommy, married?"

"Tommy is not the kind of guy to keep a baby-mamma in Brooklyn, I assure you, if that's what you're asking."

Setting the picture in its place on the buffet, I prayed for the kid. If this senior VP knew better.

For swim practice, Danny got himself up early. He never ate breakfast, never showered--those things he did at school, after practices. Instead, he washed his face and brushed his teeth, and waited for Craig to show up.

Craig drove Danny to school. He was a senior, an early decision to an Ivy League, I think, and had privileges. His family got him a new car to go back and forth in, one that was cheap, reliable, and safe. Leo Dolan was always in it, in the front seat.

I still see my Danny sitting in the living room, tapping his toes. He was always an anxious kid. He didn't want to miss Craig. Then, when Craig came, Danny became the third kid in the backseat. He never liked that. He didn't want my "good-bye" kiss.

After it happened, I asked my son if he wanted to visit Leo. Daniel just called Craig a jerk. That didn't make sense. Craig wasn't the one that was crippled.

This senior VP had given Danny a silk bed, large and neat. Danny splayed on it and angled his arms. "I can fall asleep like this."

"Where is his room?" I asked.

"Here, Mom," he said, patting the near side of the bed. "He sleeps right here. By me."

"Of course." I had forgotten they are man and wife. "Will you go to Connecticut or Massachusetts?"

"Why should we?" he asked. "Patterson said he'd sign the bill, if it's passed. We can marry in Gracie Mansion, if we want to. Knowing Tommy's contacts, he can swing that, by Bloomberg himself, no less. Have a cheap-o wedding; splurge on a fucking big reception."

"I'll come to the wedding. Wherever it is, be it Boston or New York, I'm there."

"Yeah, yeah."

"I'm serious, Danny," I said. "Your happiness is important to me."

"Yeah," Daniel snorted. "Whatever."

Craig was a well-known figure at school meets. Broad-shouldered and narrow-waisted, he had the big feet and long arms that marked every school swimmer. He was fair, and had freckles as numerous on his back as stars in a patch of night sky.

"Is that Craig Whisenton?" I heard a girl at a meet gasp. "He is amazing-looking!"

Like Danny, Craig was good at every event. Some thought he was a basketball player, but, at the meets, they said he never played basketball. I suppose he liked being the black kid on the school swim team. Craig was best at the backstroke. He owned the school records for the backstroke.

Danny said he hoped Craig would give him pointers about the backstroke. My son wanted that badly. He seemed to live for that possibility. When Daniel wanted something, it is hard to resist. Daniel does not take "no" easily.

"Craig Whisenton," I said to him once at a meet, "hi! I'm Barb Hausmann, Danny's mom."

"Hi."

Craig's big hands had a firm, manly shake, unlike my Danny's, and Craig did seem confident, but he was a bit shy, like every high school boy. I could see why he was big man on campus. He had the big man's way of talking about nothing. Leo Dolan waited nearby.

"I met Craig at the meet," I told Danny on the way home.

"So?"

I asked Danny how did he meet this senior VP. He took a soft look, the softest I had seen on his face in years. He seemed not to care that we were in a diner having eggs and hash. I didn't see that often, but his face brightened. He had color—not blush—but life. His eyes twinkled as well.

"We were at the deli in the lobby at work," he said. "Side by side, you know? I was getting me a matzo soup and he got a pastrami on rye, and, when my soup came, he said 'I got that recipe,' not with the deli crew hearing him, mind you. I told him I'd like to try it. I went up to his office, and then we started sharing recipes. Then, one thing led to another and then, *bat-ta-bing!*—is this making you uncomfortable?"

"No. Not at all."

"Good." He smiled. "I'll spare you the part about fucking on the first date."

I thanked him.

Daniel had big, strong hands. They hurt.

I remember Leo very well. His mom Patsey was an in-line skater, sprinting, practicing the form I heard she had honed at Colorado Springs, hoping for the Olympics. I heard she missed Lake Placid by, like, a millisecond. No matter. She seemed determined to get her Leo there, somewhere. On the village streets, Patsey raced him, urging him to stay aerodynamic, and to push.

"Oh, Mom!"

Leo went faster, his chestnut hair a reddish blur beneath his helmet, his arms managing turns. Later, in the pool, his arms reached for the wall as he did the butterfly. Long arms kept him first. In the medley relay, Leo and Craig worked together. They celebrated each time.

At meets, I saw my son's reaction as Craig and Leo celebrated. Though in the stands, I could see Daniel's eyes turn green.

Before he became fully Daniel, my son and I could discuss anything. There was a little girl that seemed to like him, but Danny was not interested.

"You will be," I said, knowing he was still not yet a teenager.

"Nuh-huh. She's got no ass—"

"Daniel!" I laughed.

"It's true. Her rear is too flat. No shape to it at all."

"Are you telling me you are one of those tits-and-ass men?"

"So to speak." He laughed as well. He had a cute laugh back then. Even today, I try remembering it, and its absence makes me sad. "I like a well-shaped behind," he said. "Like that one by the bike rack."

All I saw was a big, light-skinned black boy I later found out was Craig Whisenton. Right then, it struck me my boy really was. He was just eleven. "That's a boy, Danny."

"He'd be good, if he's a girl. That's the kind of ass I like. One that won't stop. Find me a chick with that; I'd be happy."

The phone rang. Danny answered, stepping away for privacy. I stepped away as well. I had the idea it was his senior VP on the cell phone. I looked at the artwork in the hall. This senior VP had conservative tastes. The artwork was of black people, but most were recognizable, unlike on the set of *The Cosby Show*. I could see real people in the art, and most of the art was original. Danny had no hand in selecting these; I knew it. The things were beyond his means.

"Sorry about that," Danny said when he was finished.

"Was that Tommy?"

"He just said he has to work late. Close some business. But we are doing dinner. Wanna come?"

"I don't want to be a third wheel."

"Tommy's paying. He got a charge-card account you won't believe."

Still, I declined. I had to give them their space. My son was a grown man. I never had the desire to chaperone a grown man's love life. Besides, what do you say to your only son's sugar daddy? I hadn't the stomach.

Jerry and I remember a peaceful night when we made love. It had sleeted, just enough to glaze the streets, and Danny went out before dinner to play hockey with some friends. When he came back, he was exhausted, too exhausted even to practice strokes. He was out before nine-thirty.

"This is our chance," Jerry said, offering to snuggle.

"But he will hear us."

"Not if we do it downstairs."

At Jerry's insistence, we used the extra bedroom in the basement. Danny was knocked out on the second floor; he couldn't hear, not even through the vents, if we closed them. Besides, we could lock the door.

I wore my red things, and lit a candle. Jerry put Dave Matthews Band on. We took a hit that got us in the mood for wild things. Then, when we were done, we fell asleep. We both had called off work already.

Pot, sex, and sleep do strange things. I saw myself barefoot in a field of daisies, back in school, playing Frisbee with a dog. I had not a care in the world, a real flower child, which I had been before, even if I was born a decade too late to have been one originally. In the dream, I saw my belly grow and grow, like when I was pregnant, until my belly

POP!

"What the hell was that?" Jerry demanded.

POP!

Thinking the worst, we sprang into our robes and ran upstairs. Daniel met us on the stairs to the second floor. He was rage.

"It's after seven!" he yelled, pushing Jerry and me downstairs. "I'm supposed to be at practice already! Jesus fucking fuck! *I missed him!* What in the fuck is wrong with you two shitheads!?!"

No parent, no mother, should ever fear a child, even when he becomes physically violent. That morning, Jerry and I knew to fear Daniel. He tried to kill his sister within hours of her being conceived. That monster tried to break our necks.

"Don't do that," Danny scolded, getting me to leave the personalized scratchpads by his bed alone. "Tommy is particular about his things."

"Your Tommy, does he doodle in bed?"

Danny, smiling, rested his head and looked at the ceiling. "Tommy fucks in bed. He writes poetry before we fuck."

I knew I had asked too much. Looking at me, Daniel smiled. He knew he smelled blood.

"Most of the time, though, he uses those scratchpads to keep track of his dreams. Tommy isn't into analysis, mind you. He just likes to write down his dreams, especially after we fuck. He usually gets these outer space and space alien dreams, then. Real fucking weirdo crazy shit."

I couldn't say Tommy sounded pretty screwed up. Daniel would not like that. I just said "oh."

Danny came home from school bubbling. "I made the medley relay," he said. He was excited, as was I. I was happy for him. Then I found out that Leo Dolan had been injured in an accident. He didn't die then, but he had been hurt so bad he was on life support. One of the swimming moms told me.

"Patsey must be distraught," I said. "She lived in that boy. How did that happen?"

"He wasn't paying attention while riding his bike, apparently," she said. "He went right into traffic. Patsey is holding up good, but that black kid on the team, Craig Whisenton?, he's really taking it bad."

Someone said Leo got a note, but no one said who gave it to him. I suppose that note kept his attention from the street. That sort of thing happens to kids.

The medley relay didn't win its next meet. Craig must have had his mind on other things. On the way home, Daniel was in his mood.

Before meeting for lunch, I called this senior VP. I wanted to make sure.

"Tommy Henderson?"

"This is Thomas Henderson," the whitest voice said on the other end. "May I help you?"

"This is Barb Hausmann—your friend Danny's mom?—we haven't met, but we've talked on the phone before. Remember?"

"Oh, yes. Barb! Yes, yes, I remember. How are you doing?"

"Fine, thanks. Just great—"

"Danny is not here," he said. "He went to the park for a bit. I can give him a buzz, if you want. He has his cell phone—"

"No, Mister Henderson—Tom, Thomas. You're the one I wanted to talk to." I looked at my cocktail. Hopefully, he could not smell my drink. "I was wondering, did he talk much about growing up?"

"You mean, about the swim team?"

"I'm so sorry," I said.

"I know," he offered gently, quietly. "I know."

"I'm so very sorry."

I felt his hair before he was taken away, and Daniel glared at me. I knew, but that didn't matter to me. I wanted to touch my Danny. By the time he was eighteen, he was fully Daniel. It was a horrible transformation to see.

I still feel for that senior VP. Does he know he has in his house some monster?

I have known all along.

Albertus made me a new heart, and he gave me an even more precious gift—knowledge. He taught me everything he knew. Hunger of the mind replaced hunger of the belly.

CARESS

Eli Easton

1. London, 1857

The child's mother was asleep in the chair when I climbed in through the window. I was small and light and well versed in the science of being invisible. Two, three, four steps to the bed. I placed the mechanical lark on the table, moving aside bloodstained rags and a bottle of laudanum that had likely cost this family a month's wages. When I looked up, the child's eyes were open. They were huge in her pale face and blue as the Crimean sky. I placed a finger to my lips and winked.

"Who are you?" she whispered, joining in the conspiracy at once.

"An angel," I whispered back, unable to resist the irony.

"Is this from heaven, then?" Her bony fingers reached for the lark.

I nodded solemnly.

She picked up the automaton as if it were so fragile a breath could break it. But despite the delicate look of its enameled wings, it was strong.

"I love it so," she whispered fervently. She started to turn the key. I touched her hand and put up a finger. *Wait.* She stopped.

I attempted a smile in lieu of a good-bye. But I could already see Death's hand on her in the purple tinge of her lips and the gray around her eyes. My smile felt like the white flag of a traitor.

I slipped out the window. As I climbed down the building—it was so close to its neighbor that even my short legs could meet both walls—I heard the key wind. *Snick, snick.* I dropped to the ground and scooted out to the street, the lark's song playing sweetly behind me. I'd given it a real lark's voice but the tune was *his*. I could almost see the throat and breast pulsing, see the tiny wires that made the eyes blink. *Nictitating membrane, upper eyelid, iris contracting, repeat.*

Her name was Grace, and two days later I watched them carry her from the building in a box. I wondered if the lark was in her cold, still hands, or if her parents had decided to sell it. The lark would pay their rent for a year, so it was only logical. But I knew the heart was an irregular clockwork, untidy. There were enough larks of mine buried in the paupers' cemetery to found a feathered choir. It had been a hard year for cholera and consumption.

Grace's mother, Molly, was a pretty barmaid at the Dunswood pub. I went there when the silence of my lonely rooms became too full of remembered screams. She was back at work a few days later, her eyes swollen and red.

"Aye, the Angel of Seven Dials brought my poor Grace her treasure," I overheard her tell some fellow customers. "I caught nary a glimpse of him, mind. But I'll tell 'ee this: that man has a heart of gold."

I nearly spewed out my drink of ale. I wanted to laugh until I cried.

They had no idea the sins I atoned for.

My heart was not gold, in fact. But it wasn't human either.

I stood next to the mirror, taking deep breaths to calm myself, and watched my bare chest rise and fall. *Pulse 120, 110, 95.* At twenty-five, I still had a boy's frame. Early privations had stunted me. Or perhaps my father was small; I never knew his name.

I had the gauze and bandages ready along with the three new valves, perfectly calibrated. *Inverted piston design, powered off the electrical impulses of the heart, warm from the sterile bath.* Albertus had instructed me on the method to replace the valves. It was done once a year, just before my birthday. But since the war I'd not been able to stomach the sight of blood, not even my own.

I used the tiny key to open the chest plate. Inside, the mechanical heart beat steady and sure. I could see the purple of my lung as it inflated in and out, the pink of my esophagus. Living arteries attached to gold couplings, but the heart itself was made with the thinnest plates of steel—*a pump, a work of art, the clockwork engine of a monster.*

I used a small pick to turn off the blood to one valve and remove it. Bright red spurted from the coupling, making me feel faint. My gloved fingers grew slick as I set in the new valve and hooked up the pins. I forced myself to replace the other two, despite my shaking hands.

I closed the chest plate and sterilized it. Done. The entire thing had taken less than five minutes, but darkness threatened the edges of my vision and my skin was clammy. I lay down on the bed. Since the war I'd had the urge, as my birthday neared, to ignore the procedure. How long would it take for the valves to wear out? Knowing Albertus's craftsmanship, it might take years. They might slow down before stopping entirely, or miss beats, causing me to lose consciousness. They might fail one by one. I deserved such a death, but I hadn't yet found it in me to ruin Albertus's masterpiece. Not when there was any lingering chance that *he* might come.

Albertus had made the mechanical heart for me when I was fourteen to replace the faulty one I was born with. If he'd known the horrors I would commit, the thousands of people I would murder, he might have thought twice.

I am sorry.

London, 1844

I was twelve when my mother and I stood in the queue, in the cold rain, for two whole days and a night to see him. I counted the cracks in the sidewalk and the bricks on the wall. *Two hundred forty-two to the bottom of the second-story windows.* My clothes grew wet and my teeth chattered like castanets. Hunger was always with me, a snake in my belly that coiled and bit. But by the second day, it was enraged and tormented me.

I was smaller than the next smallest boy in the line, *three inches shorter, two stone lighter.* Twelve was the minimum age, though there were boys who looked as old as sixteen. My body had always been little, but it ran hot as a furnace, and the broth and scraps of bread my mother could afford to feed me were never enough. I dreamed heady dreams of boards groaning with meats and heaping bowls of potatoes. All I understood or cared of my mother's determination to get me in to see Albertus was that it might lead to food. *A piece of cheese or an apple. Tangy apple, thirty grams.* Beyond that, I cared not.

Of course, everyone knew Albertus was the greatest machinist in London. But I thought nothing of my chances. I was no one, a lad frequently weak and ill, with pockets too mean to even afford lint. But the hope that they would feed me inside, and the fierce determination in my mother's eyes, gave me the strength to endure.

When I was finally seated at a table in Albertus's workshop, and the wondrous tools and puzzles were placed in front of me, I forgot my hunger. I forgot about being wet. My brain was caught like a gear engaging, and I reached out my fingers to touch. I'd never imagined such marvels.

I moved tiny copper fragments around under a magnifying glass with the aid of pin-thin tweezers—*red ones to the left, black ones to the right.* There was a game with turning pipes and dials and getting a flow of water from point A to point B, and a lovely sorting game involving parts that looked nearly identical but weren't.

I was so enamored with the sorting game that I jumbled the pieces up and replayed it three times. By the time I came to myself, Albertus, all gangly limbs and gray hair, was discussing the terms of my apprenticeship with my mother. He required nine years, a long term for an apprentice, but the post was a coveted one and there was a lot to learn. My mother gave him her hand, and my fate was sealed.

"This is the greatest opportunity of your life, Tinker," my mother said through her tears as she hugged me good-bye. "Be good. Be brave. I'm so proud of you, my brilliant boy. This will change your destiny."

I clung to her, sobbing out protests that were ignored. She forced me from her arms and hurried away. It was the first time my heart broke, but it wouldn't be the last.

2. Crimean Peninsula, 1854

He had green eyes.

Irises the color of Kolmården green marble with flecks of gray and gold and a black outer band.

Major Barker had been summoned to the hospital, and I went along. He'd been called from our work in the machinists' hangar, and that could only mean one thing: a potential for flesh and metal to mate in a bloody marriage.

CARESS

Tingles of excitement wanted to tug up the corners of my mouth, but I was adept at keeping my face blank. Even after a year in the army, surgery was still a savory puzzle to me—*repair, stitch, restore.* Flesh was simply a gorier form of clockworks at such times. But that was only if I managed not to think about the weapons-testing room.

Don't think about that.

Our outpost of Her Majesty's Service had taken over a small village south of Simferopol. The machinists' hangar was a giant collapsible tin box assembled on the outskirts of the village and heavily guarded round the clock. The hospital was in the old church. A nurse ushered us to the patient. He was lying on an exam table and the colored light of an Orthodox stained-glass window fell across him, dissecting him with yellow, blue, and purple.

His skin was white with shock but he was awake. When I saw the horror of his injuries, I wished to God he hadn't been.

"Dynamite blast, poor chap," said the doctor, Major Winslow. "The arms are the worst of it."

I stood two steps behind Major Barker, as was my lot, but I assessed the damage as if I were in charge, also my lot. *Forearms ended below the elbows, stumps coated in gore, edges raged and torn and partially cauterized.* Part of a radius bone jutted an inch from the torn muscle on his right. Tourniquets above the elbows stanched the bleeding, but they could have done nothing for the pain. His pants were stiff with blood.

And his eyes. My gaze travelled up his chest to the most beautiful eyes I'd ever seen. The soldier's face was handsome, even with the damage from the blast—a gash in his cheek that would leave a scar and a mosaic of soot and blood. Pain dug deep into his features, but what struck me the most was the defeated resignation in his eyes. It was an expression you might expect to see on a man's face seconds from death, as a carriage slides toward him on a slick road.

Major Barker looked over the stumps with a petulant moue. "Far too damaged," he pronounced, annoyed at having been disrupted from his work. "There's nothing to connect to. It can't be done."

Brigadier Warwick, the man in charge of the outpost, happened to be walking by. He stopped and approached us.

"Most unfortunate," he grumbled. He gave the soldier a smile that was both falsely sympathetic and told him to buck up. Warwick was a man of the times, not a terrible commander, but at that moment I disliked him intensely. "Well, put him under, for God's sake, and clean up those stumps."

"Wait," I said, stepping forward.

Three pairs of eyes gazing at me, four, five. Sweat skittered down my spine. I don't know what made me do it. Well, that's not true. His beauty stirred me, even in his bloodied state. But more than that, I could read his future clearly in his eyes. He would be sent home to England with two stumps and no way to fend for himself or make a living. Like so many before him, he would take his own life. It was already there in his eyes.

"Well? Speak up, Tinker," Major Barker said impatiently.

"I can salvage the connections," I said. "Permission to try, sir."

Major Barker glared at me angrily. I had contradicted him in front of the brigadier. That was unforgivable. But I knew my master well. I put an adoring regard on my face.

"Your marvelous golem, sir," I purred. "He'll need hands, and I have so little experience of them. Perhaps I could practice by making hands for this man."

"Capital idea!" Brigadier Warwick said. "What do you think, Major Barker? Won't hurt to give it a go, hey?"

Barker smiled tightly, but I knew he was still angry and that I would pay for it sooner or later. "I doubt my apprentice will be able to pull it off. The forearms are too damaged. But he does need the surgical practice. If"—Baker picked up the chart—"Captain Davies does not object to being operated on with so little chance of success."

Captain Davies. The tattered rags of his uniform came sharply into focus. *Officer. Cavalry.* He was still clinging to consciousness, his jaw shaking with the pain. He looked at Barker, then at me. I tried to reassure him with my eyes. *I can do it.*

He nodded once.

Barker turned to me. "I can't have you skimping on your regular work, Lieutenant. It's far too critical."

"I'll operate tonight. I'll be back on the job in the morning," I promised.

Barker's eyes narrowed, telling me he'd better not regret it. Then the brigadier started asking questions about the progress on the golem and the two of them strolled away.

The doctor prepared a needle of morphine and sighed. "I can't assist you in surgery, Tinker. I have a dozen other patients. If this were a simple amputation, it would take me ten minutes, but this…. I've no time for this."

"I'll make do," I said. I stepped closer to Captain Davies. His gaze never left mine as I gripped his upper arm, offering comfort, I suppose, and a distraction from the injection. *Right biceps muscle, diameter of the plunger one centimeter, needle point-three-oh centimeters. Effects in ten, nine, eight….*

"If you can't—" Davies whispered. He didn't get to finish before the drug glazed his eyes. Nevertheless, I knew what he wanted—a reprieve I would never have it in me to give.

Don't let me awaken.

"I hope you know what you're doing," the doctor muttered as those green eyes slid closed.

3.

Albertus made me a new heart, and he gave me an even more precious gift—knowledge. He taught me everything he knew. Hunger of the mind replaced hunger of the belly. There was always enough food in the genius's rambling London workshop. And enough food for my mind as well.

He taught me how to work with fibers as delicate as the hair on a lady's arm. He showed me the magic of tiny gears that ran in perpetual motion, feeding each other energy like an ouroboros. He built mechanisms as large as an elephant for the queen. Albertus's creations were unique. He gave them little flaws—a dandy's shoe with a cracked heel, a horse with a bump on its nose, a shepherdess's stocking that was falling down. Because reality was never perfect, he said, and it was the imperfections that made his creations feel real.

But I, I preferred tiny things, miniatures so complex not one more filament could be crammed into their perfection. I made frogs and spiders and glittering eggs that opened a dozen times to reveal smaller and smaller works of art. They sold to the highest bidder. Victoria herself carried one of my mechanical butterflies in her purse. And we made limbs too, when St. Bart's sent for us. Men often lost parts of themselves in the maw of the Industrial Revolution. *Snip snap.*

One day in the operating theater, Albertus suddenly stepped away from the patient with the halting gait of one of his automatons. His scalpel dropped to the floor. He fell and I reached for him, barely catching him before he hit the boards. He looked into my eyes for a second and then he was gone.

Unlike mine, his heart had given us no warning. He saved me and then died in my arms.

I was twenty and only a year away from my freedom. *Three hundred sixty-three days, twelve hours, ten minutes.* But Albertus, the greatest mind of the century, had forgotten to mention me in his will. My contract went to his widow, a woman neither Albertus nor I could abide. She sold me, for a great deal of money, to Major Barker. Barker had been after Albertus to work for the British Army for years. Albertus had refused; I could not.

Albertus placed his deepest secrets in me, and Major Barker bought them as if they were nothing more than a cheap whore.

4.

I operated on Captain Davies from five till four in the morning. *Eleven hours, twelve minutes.* Major Winslow sent in a nurse to assist me for a short while, but when she had to leave, I didn't get another. This was a war zone, and the battle that had brought in Captain Davies had brought in other wounded. The hospital staff had no time for the delicate work required.

As I worked into the night alone, I was gripped with doubt. Why had I said I could do this? What if I failed? The arms were terribly ravaged. I had to saw off and smooth the edges of the bones and shave the ragged flesh before I could begin to coax the delicate nerve fibers and tendons to the surface. I would need them to connect to the prosthetics. I had to control the bleeding and recirculate the blood. The patient's sedation with ether had to be constantly monitored and hot cloths applied regularly to keep the tissue pliable.

By midnight, I knew I would succeed. By four I was finished and dead on my feet.

I wrapped the prepared stumps and gave Davies more morphine. I wanted to stay with him, be there when he awoke. But Major Barker would expect me in the hangar in an hour to begin a day's work.

I bent over his bed. In my exhausted state, and after so long focusing on minutia, his face was blurred and soft in the glow of the lamps. He was a large man, at least six two and fifteen stone. His shoulders were broad and muscled. But in my altered state he looked angelic lying there. His hair was dark blond and clipped short. He wore a slim mustache. He looked young. His lips were full and soft, his jaw square and rough.

"Don't die," I told him. "I'll make you hands, marvelous hands. You'll see."

5.

For three days, Major Barker had me working on the golem around the clock. He refused every request I made to go the hospital to check on Captain Davies. Barker said the stumps should not be disturbed for a week so there was no point in checking them. The truth was, he resented any moment I was not slaving on *his* project. Barker had made big promises to the brigadier, and he knew no one else had the skill to accomplish the thing.

I often contemplated how to turn his need of me to my advantage. But Barker was hard and ruthless. And while I could see wires and rods in my head as clear as day, people remained a mystery to me. When I tried to insist on seeing my patient, Barker threatened to ban me from the hospital for good. I relented.

I'd never liked Barker, but in those few days, I learned to hate him. I felt a craving to check on Captain Davies, an obsession of the sort I developed around important projects. Having it thwarted was painful.

On the fourth day, Major Barker was summoned to the hospital by Brigadier Warwick himself, and he nodded at me tersely to go along. We found the brigadier standing at Captain Davies's bed. The patient's color had returned, a rosy glow, and he was sleeping peacefully. He looked much improved.

Deliberately, I stepped around Major Barker to check the captain's forehead for fever. There was none.

"Well?" the brigadier asked. "What's the prognosis? Can we use Captain Davies to prototype the golem's hands or not?"

Major Barker went a little red, having ignored the issue for days. "Unwrap his hands, Tinker," he ordered. "Show the brigadier how he's got on."

"Yes, sir." I unwrapped the bandages, anxious to see the stumps for myself.

As I reached the final layer, I took care, checking his face frequently for pain. But he didn't awaken. The nurse must have given him something strong. I exposed both stumps. The flesh around the connectors was red but healing nicely. The stitched seams were tight and pale. I touched the connectors one by one with a steel rod I'd brought for the purpose. Each time, the small tube on the end of the rod lit up. The connectors were live.

Major Barker's expression cleared and he smiled like the satisfied fox he was. "As you can see, it's going splendidly. The nerves and tendons are attached to those connectors. The mechanical hands will slot right onto them. And then they'll be screwed into these divots here and secured to the bones."

He went on to point out all my hard work as if it were his own marvelous doing. I was used to it. He always took credit for my skill. I only felt relief that Davies was living, that he was healing, and that the arms were excellent candidates for my prosthetics. I would be able to give him a future in which he was not helpless.

"But the golem won't have nerves, will it?" Brigadier Warwick asked.

"No, the golem will have wires and gears," Barker said. "And it will be powered by a small engine in the torso. The prosthetic hands will be run by the electrical pulse of Captain Davies's heart. It's a technology I myself invented."

Albertus had invented it, and I'd refined it, but I wasn't going to argue.

Barker continued. "But the basic function of the hands will be the same. They'll be exceptional weapons."

"Crushing, as I recall," the brigadier said. The golem was an important project and he knew the design well.

"Yes. The hands will be far stronger than human hands. They'll be able to crush a throat in seconds. And of course, the grip for climbing will be superb, and the force of a fist blow will shatter bone on contact."

I knew all this about the golem. It was, after all, laid out in my own blueprints. But now the words sank into me as if I'd never heard them before. I looked at Captain Davies asleep on the bed and felt a sharp pain of regret and guilt. Suddenly the hands did not seem so much a gift as a curse.

"I say!" The brigadier was impressed. "But the golem will be controlled with code words. Will we be able to control Davies the same way? Or will he have his own mind? I suppose he must. He's a man, after all."

Major Barker looked at me. He didn't know the answer, but he was warning me to say what he wanted to hear.

I swallowed. "He'll have his own mind, sir. Of course. But the hands could be engineered to override that on a code word. However, it might be best—"

"Marvelous!" Brigadier Warwick said. "Naturally, one would hardly expect to need such a thing, but do put it in, put it in. I'll want a list of the code words. I suppose they'll be a different word for each possible action, hey? 'Crush,' for example. Not that we'd call it that! It wouldn't do to have him killing someone accidently, would it? For example, if you said 'It's a crush in here.' No, that wouldn't do at all."

"The code words will be things unlikely ever to be spoken aloud," Major Barker assured him.

The brigadier seemed so cheerful at the prospect. And after all, that was what the HRH Machinist Corps was for, wasn't it? To invent new weapons, to take life. From the first time a caveman raised a bone and struck a rival over the head, it's been a race to create the biggest stick. We were the British Empire. It was our right to create deterrents. Our duty, even. That was what they'd told me.

I'd been so naïve when I first came under Major Barker's wings. He'd been nice to me then—fatherly, even—and I'd been grieving for Albertus. I bought into every platitude he'd uttered. "For queen and country." "To end the war and bring our boys home." I preened under his praise of my skills like a wallflower soaking up compliments from a handsome gentleman. I'd been putty in his hands. *Foolish Tinker. Foolish, queer Tinker.*

I knew Albertus had rejected Barker time and again, but I'd always assumed he was too busy making pretty marvels for royalty and couldn't be bothered. For a short time, I considered myself *better* than Albertus for using my skills in service of our fighting forces, of England, of *peace*. I took up the mental challenge to make killing things as if it were a delightful puzzle to be solved.

It wasn't until I saw my weapons tested on prisoners of war that I realized the obvious—why Albertus had rejected such work. *Blood, brain matter, bones, screams, pleas....* But it was too late. They put my designs into production. There were thousands of them out there. *My* devices.

I would never be forgiven—not by God, if there was such, not by the spirit of Albertus, not by my victims, and not by myself.

"When can a prototype be ready?" the brigadier asked. He and Major Barker strolled away together, chatting enthusiastically.

Dismissed, I stepped closer to Captain Davies's bed and looked down at him. He opened his eyes. There was a dull horror in those deep green pools and a grievous crease between his brows. He'd been awake, then, the entire time. He'd heard.

"I'm sorry," I whispered to him. I began to rewrap his stumps. *Over, under with the bandages, gentle on the connectors.*

"What's your name?" he asked me quietly.

He didn't sound like he hated me. I looked at his face. We were only a few feet apart, stooped as I was to bandage him. It felt troublingly intimate but I didn't look away.

"Lieutenant Gray," I said.

"Gray. Like your eyes." There was nothing in his voice but weariness, but the mere fact that he'd noticed the color of my eyes made me feel a wave of something—simple gratitude perhaps—at being seen for once. More than that—pleasure.

Gray like my heart, I thought, meaning the steel of it and also the fact that it was no longer pure. But black would have been a truer color. I said nothing.

"You're the one who'll be making the hands?"

I nodded. "Yes. I'm a machinist." I went back to bandaging his stumps. I wanted to say I was sorry again, but that was stupidity.

"Gray..." he murmured, and he fell asleep.

6.

Now that the brigadier was excited about the hands, Major Barker allowed me to spend as much time on them as I liked. Two days later, I brought the skeleton of them to Captain Davies to test the couplings. I found him awake and sitting up.

"The fittings will be painful," I told him regretfully, "but once the hands are finished, you won't have to remove them. I can give you some morphine now."

"No. No more morphine. Just do what you must."

I wanted to argue with him. But his face was determined, his resolve as solid as a barred door.

"All right, Captain. But I'll stop the moment you say."

I fitted the hands. *Gold connectors, pins to pin fittings, snap, secure.*

Even though the connectors themselves had no sensation, just shifting them caused waves of pain to shoot up the living fibers. But Davies never said a word. By the time I was done, he was pale and sweating, his jaw clenched so tight it would surely ache for hours.

"I'm sorry about the pain," I said. I seemed to do nothing but apologize to him, like a toy drummer that could only beat one note. I wet a cloth in a nearby basin and wiped his brow, waiting for the pain to fade. The mechanical hands lay on the bed like dead things attached below his elbows.

"What these hands will do…. I deserve to feel every bit of the pain of attaching them," he managed when he could finally speak. He sounded bitter.

I didn't know why he felt he owed me an explanation for his behavior, or why he would be so honest. I was no one. I didn't know how to respond. But I couldn't seem to stop wiping his brow and face. The nurses shaved the men when they could stand it, but it had been at least a day for him. The stubble on his jaw tugged at the cloth. I found it fascinating.

"Where are you from?" I asked, to change the subject.

"North Hampshire. My father was a small landholder. Fifty acres. We raised sheep and we had horses."

I smiled tentatively, but I was surprised. He had a sort of noble bearing I would not have expected from a sheep farmer, though, at fifty acres, his family were not paupers.

"We used to slaughter the sheep, you see. So I was a perfect candidate for the army." He attempted to make a joke of it, but there was no humor in his voice. I rewet the cloth and began to wipe down his upper arms.

"I always hated it," he said.

"Farming?" I met his eyes.

"Killing," he answered. I didn't know if he was talking about the sheep anymore.

"You made captain. You must be a good cavalryman."

"Effective at least," he said flatly.

I should have moved on with my work then, but he was still pale, though his trembling had lessened. I told myself I should give it a few more minutes for the pain to fade before I made him move the hands. I rewet the cloth.

I continued to wipe down his left arm, holding it gently at the elbow—and I became mesmerized at the sight and feel of his muscle and skin. I lost myself for a moment, then realized I'd become aroused. I was aroused by touching him, a patient, and I was touching him all wrong. The slow drag of the cloth against his skin could not be mistaken for clinical duty.

Shame and fear flooded me. I felt my face burn. I turned, put the cloth back in the basin, and breathed deeply, schooling myself. *Pulse 130, 120, 110.* When I had myself under control I turned, my face deliberately blank. He was watching me, but he looked thoughtful, not angry. I stuffed my hands into the pockets of my uniform jacket. Thankfully, it covered up my sins.

"Where are you from, Gray?" he asked.

"No one calls me Gray."

"What, then?"

"Tinker."

"Is that your Christian name?"

I smiled. "Yes. It's a family name. My mother's ancestors made clocks." I had never told anyone that. No one had ever asked.

"Tinker," he said as if testing the word. "And you must call me Colin."

I started to protest, but it would just sound like another apology. I shut my mouth. I could not seem to look away from him.

The way he studied my face, so openly, stole my breath. I'd never had anyone look at me like that. Albertus was usually distracted by his work, and when he did look at me it was either with a paternal fondness or annoyance, depending on what I'd done. Major Barker treated me like a tool he could manipulate as he liked. I was small and mostly I was ignored. No one saw me the way Captain Davies—*Colin*—was seeing me now, like a person, an interesting one, one worth studying and puzzling over. It made me shiver with alternating twinges of hot and cold. It made me want to excuse myself and escape, and at the same time it made me ache for more, for my allotment of human contact.

I told myself it was just his way. There was nothing in Colin's face that indicated more than curiosity, nothing to suggest his interest in me was carnal. But my body reacted to the weight of his gaze as if it was a physical touch. And oh, I craved that touch.

"You don't like being a solider," I said, forcing my eyes to look away from his.

"It's my job. It's what I signed up for," he said with no emotion.

"If you weren't a soldier, what would you be?" My eyes shifted back to him of their own accord.

He looked surprised at the question. "I…write music. In my head." He started to gesture toward his head and his right hand obeyed, fingers flowing. He stared at them for a moment, swallowed audibly, then carefully let the hand rest back on the bed.

"You're a composer?" I asked.

He shook his head. "Nothing so grand. Never been published. Never even heard my music played other than in my head. I've written reams of it, though. Foolish. Helps me cope, I suppose."

"Not foolish," I said. "Do you write it down?"

"Yes."

"I'd like to see it."

"Why?"

Green eyes. Very frank green eyes. Should I not have said that? *Be quiet, Tinker. Know your place. Hands, mechanics, work. Do your job.*

"Is the pain bearable now?" I asked hastily. "I need to test the hands."

"It's bearable."

I held out my palm, waist high. "Place your hand on mine, very gently."

His left hand moved and slowly raised to mine. It rested there.

"Excellent. Can you turn it over so that your palm faces the ceiling?"

He did.

"Now wiggle your fingers."

The tapered steel fingers moved up and down.

"Make a loose fist. Good."

We repeated the test with his right hand. I had him grasp a pencil.

"I'll be able to eat by myself? To write?" he asked.

"Of course."

He looked relieved. I wondered if he was thinking about writing his compositions. Or perhaps he had a girl back home whom he wrote to. Of course he must.

I tested each finger in turn. Though the hands worked, the pinkie was slow to move on the left and the thumb almost immobile on the right. I would have to make adjustments.

"There will be at least one more fitting," I told him as I removed the hands. "And then... we'll have to test the full range of features for the brigadier."

He looked down at his chest, his brow furrowing. He knew exactly what I meant.

"I'm sorry," I said again. It was such a weak thing to say. I had to stop saying it. But I could hear his voice in my head.

I always hated it. The killing.

He raised his eyes to meet mine. "Thank you, Tinker," he said, absolving me in a way I didn't deserve. He turned his back to me and pretended to go to sleep.

7.

When Albertus gave me a new heart, he gave me other things as well. A love of walking, which I had never been able to do as a child without getting winded. I roamed all over London when I had the chance. I particularly adored Highgate Wood and Queens Wood. My mind would slide over problems during such walks, as if the faster-pumping blood and fresher air were feeding my brain. I would return to the workshop eager to test new ideas.

The heart also gave me a less useful thing—crushing sexual desire. Perhaps I was not unlike any other fifteen-year-old boy, but it didn't seem that way. Once I was healthy, I was always randy. Even when my mind was deeply engaged in my work, there was a tingling little itch in my groin that begged for attention. And when I was not working, it became a need that was impossible to ignore.

At the slightest provocation, I would harden. My baggy trousers and long waistcoats were my greatest allies. It didn't take me long to discern that, while the barmaid's breasts did little for me, my prick would stiffen at the merest glimpse of broad shoulders in a fitted jacket, the muscled thighs of a man on horseback, or glossy black hair curved near a masculine jaw. I never spoke of these things to anyone, but I listened to others talk. I came to understand the condition I had and its relative rarity. It was a crime under English law.

I'd never been what you might call normal, so my irregularity in this regard did not distress me. I felt no shame. But it did convince me that my life would be one of work and invention, not love and family. I was unlikely to find many willing partners, nor was I prepared to take on the wife society would expect of me. I would be alone.

We often had great lords and ladies visit the London workshop. Lord Winthrope was fascinated with mechanisms and he came often. Sometimes his son, Rupert, would accompany him. While Lord Winthrope and Albertus discussed projects out in the shop front, Rupert would wander back to my workbench, a place well tucked away from patrons' eyes.

Rupert was a pompous ass, so I would work on, ignoring him as best I could. But he loved to tease me just to see the blush that stained my cheeks. One day he leaned over my back, placing his chin on my shoulder as I worked. I should have shaken him off, but the warmth of his chest pressed against me, his breath in my ear…. It felt good. I must have groaned or sighed, for he guessed my predicament. His hand stole over my thigh to my groin. He purred in my ear at what he found there.

"Ooh…you have a big tool for such a little lad, Tinker."

His tongue flicked my ear. My hands stopped moving but I kept my tools clenched in my fingers, my breathing harsh. He rubbed me through my trousers. I felt his answering hardness thrust against my rump and lower back as I sat on the stool.

I knew we could be caught at any moment, but I couldn't make him stop. It felt so delicious to have someone else's hand on me, to feel a stiff prick against my back. I floated in delight for an endless few minutes.

Stroke, once per second, twice per second, applied pressure thirty psi. Harder, oh God, harder. Please.

With a small whimper, I spent in my trousers. I felt him tense up and spasm too.

He left without another word and never came back with his father again. I was only a mechanic's apprentice, after all. I did not miss him.

It was the only sexual experience I'd ever had with another person. I knew where the johnny boys worked, and I always had a few bits in my pocket. I daydreamed about sneaking out to see them, just to feel another's hand, mouth, on me. But the threat of disease, and the fear of getting caught and shaming Albertus, kept me from acting on the fantasy.

I made do with my own clever hands and the boundless plains of my imagination.

8.

Major Barker was most particular about the killing features of the hands. I programmed them and tested them in the lab while he watched, running them through an engine that would eventually empower the golem. Either hand could crush a brick to dust in seconds. They responded to spoken command. Barker was pleased.

On the next fitting, I had no choice but to explain the features to Colin.

"Only think what you want the hands to do, and they will do it," I told him. "But you'll have to strongly will it. Don't worry about doing something accidently."

I placed a towel over his lap and gave him a brick. "Squeeze it as hard as you can."

He looked down at the hand.

Thought impulse sent to receptors, receptors filter out minor impulses, strong impulse drives the hands. Three thousand psi. There.

The brick disintegrated. Colin huffed something that was part laugh, part sob.

"You'll be able to climb anything," I assured him.

"And to punch hard enough to shatter bone," he said flatly. He *had* been listening that day when he'd pretended sleep.

"Yes. Maybe the hands will save your life one day."

"But I won't always control the hands, will I? The brigadier said…they'll respond to spoken commands too. From someone else."

There was a catch in his voice, and I knew the idea truly frightened him. I focused on the hands, adjusting a screw that didn't need adjusting. "Yes. But hardly anyone will know those commands."

He sighed as if defeated. "It's all right, Tinker. The army doesn't build hands like these without asking for their pound of flesh. I know I should be grateful. Without them…."

CARESS

He lay back on the pillow, and I cleared away the brick dust and towel. I cleaned the hand of tiny red particles. I liked holding the hand while he was wearing it. Just the simple act of attaching it to his connections, slotting it to the end of his arm, made it *alive* to me, made it *his hand* in a way that was completely illogical. By now, the skeleton was sheathed and there were enough feedback sensors in the fingers that I knew he could feel me as I stroked them clean. It gave me a strange thrill.

He didn't pull away. I could feel the gaze on my face as I worked. Maybe it was the intimacy, but he began to speak haltingly. "I was in the expeditionary force that landed at Eupatoria. I fought with the Light Brigade at Balaclava. Almost half our men were killed or wounded in that battle. But I wasn't. I mowed down everything in my path. Do you know why? Because I was terrified, you see. I killed so I wouldn't be killed, like a sick dog lashing out. And the Russians, by God, they were so young and inexperienced. It was like scything down tender grass. I still see their faces when I close my eyes. Since then, there've been too many battles and too many faces."

"I have killed too," I said before realizing I was going to say it.

He looked at me in surprise and I could see the question in his eyes. At twenty-two I was still small and ever would be. My hair had been cut short when I joined the army but as a machinist it was not tended to with much frequency. It lay against my nape and, unruly and thick, stuck up on the top of my head. My face was thin and pale, the face of a scholar. To put it bluntly, I probably looked as dangerous to him as a plate of peas.

"Weapons," I said with a tight smile. "I design weapons."

"Like what?" he asked, curious now.

"The dervish," I admitted. It was a device shaped like an orange. But when it was activated, slicing blades emerged and spun. They acted like wings, allowing the device to fly. A mercury core steered its course to the nearest warm body. Its navigational system was calibrated to move forward for a dozen yards, and from thence in a widening cone seeking a target. This would presumably ensure that the sender, and his fellow countrymen, would be safe. And yet I could not pretend the thing had not killed the innocent or even a horse or dog unlucky enough to get in its path. I had nightmares about it chasing me.

His eyes widened. "That was yours?"

Easton

I nodded. "And the stinger." The dart was a better design; it carried death a little less randomly. It had to be aimed at a specific target and engaged. Then it would fly to that target with the speed of an arrow. *Point-one milliliters of poison injected into the flesh, a killing dose.*

He was staring at me in shock. I felt a debilitating pain of the heart. He saw it now: I was a monster. I looked at the floor, blinking back the unfathomable threat of tears.

His left hand closed over mine and tugged me closer. If I'd been less embarrassed, I might have felt a creator's pride at the tenderness with which he could grasp my fingers.

"You're brilliant, then, Tinker," he said quietly. "A genius."

I gave a bitter laugh. "Only a trained mind, one in the service of the devil."

"No," he said firmly. "We need all the help you can give us out there. But—I do understand."

I looked up and saw regret and sympathy on his face. I swallowed a lump and nodded.

"Liberty and ease for those at home—it has a high price," he parroted.

Did he still believe those words? That the scrabble for bits of the Ottoman Empire really affected the lives of people back in England? If he could believe it, I was glad for him.

I suddenly realized how close we were. I was pressed against the side of the bed. My left hand rested in his mechanical fingers and my right, somehow, had moved onto his chest, which was covered only by a thin hospital johnny. We were staring deeply into each other's eyes. It was rather a shock to realize how we were arranged, as if I'd woken from a dream with no idea how I'd gotten there. I almost pulled away, but I stopped.

If this was being offered to me, why shouldn't I take it?

It was a moment of vulnerability, a moment of understanding, of humanity, a moment of something else too—lust, not to put too fine a point on it. He was strong, rugged, and handsome, the stuff of my erotic dreams. And what I saw in his eyes was no less longing than my own. I didn't understand how it could be there, not for me, for small, unimportant Tinker, but I drank it in greedily. Heat rushed through my body.

In my mind, I drew back, knowing this was dangerous ground. But my body didn't obey. My hand remained heavy on his chest, my fingers barely stroking. I was painfully aroused where I pressed against the bed, but thankfully, my white coat covered my folly. If only I could as easily hide what must be written all over my face.

"Tinker," he said, questioning.

I nodded, not trusting my voice.

"Could I ask you something terribly personal?"

I nodded again.

He blushed. "I—" He tried again. "I know the hands must be set to kill. I know this. But…."

"Yes?"

"Can you make them do other things as well?" He looked down where his hand held mine, frowning at it as if he didn't trust its current gentleness.

"Anything."

"Can you make the hands…caress?" His blush deepened and he couldn't meet my eyes. "No one will want a mechanical man, you see, to be touched by things like these." He held the hands up to look at them. I missed the weight of his hand on mine immediately.

"That's not true. Many men have prosthetics. And you're a handsome man."

He looked at me sharply but without much hope. "You're used to mechanisms. But for most people…. They'll frighten away any lover."

I noted that he did not say the word *woman*. I swallowed.

"And if the hands don't keep them away, the blood on them will," he said roughly. "I'm already a killer. But with these…. If I ever see England again, I'll be soaked in blood."

I couldn't argue with him. I knew what duty he and his hands were bound for. But my fingers rubbed his chest to offer comfort, as if they had a will of their own.

He closed his eyes as he choked out the request. "Allow me to be tender to myself at least. No one else will ever want to touch me."

I felt my face heat, understanding his meaning perfectly. *Ten pounds psi, twenty, scrotum, shaft, glans.* The ideas it sent rushing through my head overwhelmed me, intellect and body both.

He mistook my silence and pulled away, rolling onto his side to put his back to me. "My apologies. I didn't intend to ask. I shouldn't have. Please forget I ever said it. Please, Tinker."

He was distraught. I felt the strongest urge to lean down and kiss his hair. I was losing my mind. I did lean down, but only to whisper in his ear.

"I will teach the hands to caress, Colin," I vowed with all my heart.

He froze, then nodded.

And before I could do anything else irredeemably foolish, I removed the hands and took them away to be finished.

9.

So I taught the hands. During the days, I taught the hands to grip and climb and maim. At night, I taught them to caress.

I was fortunate that, although I was a mere Machinist, Second Class, I had privacy. As Major Barker's apprentice, I slept near his quarters in a room that was little more than a closet. But I had a cot with an iron frame as sturdy as a granite mountain and a lock on the door.

By now, I was an expert at touching myself. It was my only relief from the sexual demands my body made upon me, demands more incessant than even hunger and thirst. But though I knew how to pleasure myself, usually it was done furtively, expediently, and, to pardon the pun, mechanically. I'd never made a study of the thing.

Now I was motivated to use my art to its highest effect. I wanted to give Colin some beauty to cling through in the midst of the darkest night, in the terror and uncertainty of the front lines. And my only means of doing so were through my own body. How could I teach the hands unless I first taught myself?

Every night when I went to my cell, I would take the hands with me. I'd lock the door and remove my clothing. My own hands played upon my body, learning, feeling, and then I'd adjust the delicate gears and wires. I imagined I was touching Colin, or that Colin was touching me.

I composed odes for fingertips and palm, teasing touches of adoration, strokes upon his length, circles in tender places, ancient rhythms of cresting need and completion. *You are beautiful,* the hands said as they caressed. *You deserve to be loved.*

Of course, the hands would be wired to his will. He could override their training, tell them what to do with a mere thought. But when his will softened, when he stopped consciously guiding and gave in to sensation, the hands would revert to the blueprint I'd given them and perform upon his body the notes of the composition I had written.

The thought made me heady with desire. And as the mechanisms of the hands became ever more finely tuned, I tested them upon my own body, imagining that I was Colin, that the hands were giving him the sensations I was feeling, sensations *I* had created. They teased and tickled, handled the ball sac gently, rubbed the space behind, stroked with exquisite pressure, thumbs circling just under the glans. When I was certain they could wring no greater pleasure from my body, I considered them complete.

10.

My time with Colin was shorter than I'd ever dreamed. The war was not going well, and there was a push from the top for the golem army Major Barker had promised. They wanted the prototype hands in the field as soon as possible. So it was only a matter of weeks before we stood in a hangar with the brigadier and demonstrated the hands. There was a wall, which Colin easily scaled. Stacks of bricks were broken; steel rods were bent. The brigadier was thorough. He enjoyed seeing Colin use the hands on his own, and then he'd read from his list of commands and watch the hands take over, his eyes gleaming with satisfaction.

Colin steeled himself not to give anything away, but I knew him. I could see the fear in his eyes every time the hands moved with a will of their own.

Then they brought in the prisoner of war. He was an older Russian, afraid but holding his chin up proudly. I wished I could stop it or at least turn away. But if Colin had to bear it, so did I. I was concerned he would refuse, but the brigadier was too interested in his own power to even test Colin's will. He himself ordered the hands to crush the man's throat and they did, thoroughly and quickly, without even a spurt of blood.

One thousand psi crushes the windpipe and the arteries. Death is inevitable within five seconds, complete in thirty.

When it was done, I turned away, unable to bear the look on Colin's face.

I went to say good-bye to him and to give the hands one final adjustment. The hands were his now; he'd been wearing them for nearly a week. He was sitting on an exam table, dressed in a new uniform. His packed kit was next to him. We were in a room where they gave exams, which had the advantage, at least, of being private. My heart was hammering in my chest, an engine run amok. This was the last time I'd ever see him.

It was disturbing how much my mind had become wrapped up in him, how deeply he'd burrowed under my skin. Even when I worked in the hangar on the golem, he was never far from my thoughts. If I opened my chest plate, would I see the stain of him against the silver of my artificial heart? If I drew my blood, would I find tiny traces of him in it, like the filaments we used in the automaton oils to keep them fluid? Would each filament be engraved with his name by a minuscule pen? Foolish thoughts—and ghoulish as well. But I knew I would remember him always, like some pathetic spinster who remembers the one man she'd danced with once in her youth, the one man who'd looked at her kindly, who made her feel beautiful.

"Tinker!" Colin said as I entered the room. He looked relieved. "I didn't know if I'd be able to say good-bye to you."

I gave him a tight smile, not trusting my voice. I hoped my singularly stupid adoration was not on display all over my face. I took a tool from my pocket and placed his left hand, palm up, on my sternum. I opened the plate on the forearm.

I looked up into his eyes, which were watching me, and then used a small pick to make an adjustment.

Flip switch to disabled. Smash the switch with a hard tap so it can never be reset.

I closed the plate and repeated with the other hand. This time, I left the hand on my chest when I was done.

I spoke aloud the command I'd given the brigadier, the command to crush.

Colin recognized it. For a moment, his eyes flared with panic. But the hands did not move. He stared at me, wide-eyed. Slowly, the steel fingers on my chest turned and closed around the lapel of my jacket. He blinked his eyes, which were suddenly bright.

"These are *your* hands," I said quietly. "They'll do everything we tested, but only when you ask." I moved my fingers of flesh and blood up to squeeze his metal ones.

He breathed out a shaky sigh. "Thank you, Tinker. God bless you." His voice wavered.

"Mechanisms fail," I said with a tight smile. "Most unfortunate."

His gratitude, and the admiration on his face, flooded me with joy. At least I would have that. At least I would know he didn't hate me in the end. But there was nothing else for me to do, no reason for me to linger. I took one last look at him and turned to go. But his fingers firmed on my lapel, not allowing it.

I turned back to him. We were close. I was standing between his knees. His gaze on my face was intense and I could feel the heat rolling off him. I suddenly found it difficult to breathe, as if the need for oxygen had been replaced by a need for something else, and my body was struggling to make the adjustment.

"The hands…. The way they touch me…. You did that." He was blushing, but he stubbornly held my gaze.

I knew at once what he meant. He had tried it—the caress. I looked down, feeling my face burn. I placed my hands on his steel forearms as if studying them.

"When you need comfort," I said, "pretend the hands belong to someone who loves you, someone who accepts you as you are, someone who…who aches to please you."

I bit my lips, my gut twisting with anxiety. I'd meant for him to understand, yes, to understand that it was me. But I imagined it would happen once he was far away, where I couldn't see how he would feel about that knowledge.

"Is that someone you, Tinker?" he asked, his voice rough.

I was too afraid to answer.

He pulled his hands free and clasped my shoulders. "Look at me. Is that someone you?"

I looked into his eyes. "Yes."

He sighed and leaned slowly toward me, his eyes reading mine, giving me plenty of time to pull away. I didn't. No, I fell into him like a collapsing bridge, meeting him more than halfway. His mouth on mine was needy and commanding. He parted my lips with his tongue. I'd never been kissed before, didn't think I ever would be. It was heaven. Our tongues met and slid and teased and I was swept away on a wave of lust and need and natural instinct.

He moved his hands down to grasp my waist, then slid them around my back and pulled me close, never breaking the kiss.

Oh, the marvel of those tender hands, controlled not by me this time, but by him. I'd never been held in passion, and not at all since my mother's last clasp as she left me with Albertus. My body craved it like it was water and every cell was dying of thirst. A storm of feeling overwhelmed me. I pressed closer, between his legs, wanting to never leave his arms. I felt his prick stiffen as it pressed against my own. *I am desired! Me, Tinker Gray.* My heart thundered like a million bells tolling. This was too wonderful to believe—and too dangerous to sustain, for both of us.

We were not alone in the hospital and we both knew it. We could be shot for this. He withdrew from me reluctantly and I from him. I took a step back. We stared at each other.

"Tinker," he choked out. "Will you…if I make it…."

I could hear footsteps approaching. *Dear God, not yet.*

"Find me in London," I said hurriedly. "I'll wait for you."

"No, don't wait. I probably won't make it. Only…."

"*Live*," I said fiercely. "I'll wait."

After they took Colin away, a nurse gave me a parcel from him. I didn't open it until I got back to my quarters. Inside were five notebooks filled with handwritten music. I was no expert on musical compositions, but we'd made music boxes in Albertus's shop, so I knew how to program notes. I stole some bits from the hangar and made a simple music box. I programmed it to play one of Colin's pieces. It was a melancholy and haunting little tune.

A composer. He was truly a composer. Oh, the terrible irony of war. A composer and a maker of miniatures, made to dance to the song of death.

11. London, 1857

In the spring of '55, we got news that English citizens had protested the war by throwing snowballs in Trafalgar Square. That made me laugh so hysterically that Major Barker threatened to have me thrown in the stockade for madness. By February of '56, the war was over.

Barker tried to convince me to work for him, to keep my commission. But he didn't try very hard. The golem had been a failure.

CARESS

Pins misaligned by point-oh-two millimeters, engine cross-wired, runs briefly, then fails. Pretend frustration, pretend chagrin.

Barker hated me by the time I took my leave of him; he gave me nothing. I didn't care.

In London I had a safe-deposit box. Albertus had allowed me to make creations for myself in my spare time. *To start your own shop someday, Tinker,* he'd said. My miniatures took so little material, after all. He was a good master.

I rented a few rooms at the edge of Seven Dials and went to see some of Albertus's most faithful clients. The marvels bought me a year's rent and the material to make many more.

I was in business. I was alone.

I sought news of Captain Colin Davies, but the war department could tell me very little except that he was not on the lists of the dead. I made larks and gave them to dying children. I made inventory for my store. I worked until my eyes could focus no more and forced me to sleep.

In my dreams my devices lived on. Perhaps a dervish would be discovered in a barn in Russia tomorrow. Perhaps it would be activated and kill a young sheep farmer's son. How many did the army make? One thousand? Two thousand? Ten? I would never know.

I had only one reason to live, to prosper—a hope lodged deep in my mechanical heart.

It was a Wednesday and the skies were drenching London in rain when the door to my shop opened. I looked up from my tools. He was in a rain cape, hood up. My pulse started to race even though I couldn't see his face.

Adrenaline released 500ng/L. Heart pump accelerates in response. Pulse 90, 100, 120. Fingers drop tools, clutch counter.

He lowered the hood.

"Colin," I said.

He'd aged ten years. His hair was longer and there was heavy stubble on his face. He had dark circles under his eyes and he'd lost weight. He was the most beautiful thing I'd ever seen.

I was frozen in place but he came to me, his gaze searching mine.

"Is this all right? Do you still want to see me?" He looked anxious, as if I would tell him no, as if I hadn't been dragging through the months in agony for him to appear. The shop door wasn't locked, the blinds were not drawn, but I didn't care. I wrapped my arms around him and pulled him tight.

"I waited," I said.

His body was solid and hard and wet against me. He ran his hands up my back and into my hair. He kissed my forehead and then he was kissing my mouth, hot and hungry.

I wanted him so fiercely I thought I would die. I'd been denied for so long, a lifetime of want. I had to get him out of those wet clothes and into a warm bed, with me.

I pulled away from him long enough to cross the room and lock the door. I turned the sign in the window to *Closed*.

"I live in the back," I said, not hiding the need on my face. "There's a bed."

He shrugged out of his rain cape and held up his hands. "These first," he said, his voice strained. "Can you make them normal? Remove the killing strength? I want to touch you, but I…."

I understood. I swallowed down the ruthless passion raging through my veins and took up my tools. My hands trembled.

Grip strength down to seven hundred pounds. Blow force five hundred. Set the maximum duration to something human; blood and bone tire even if steel does not.

"It's done," I said, closing the panels.

"Can you be sure?"

I pointed to a mannequin, a ballerina with a long steel throat and an egg-shaped head. He looked at me, silently asking permission.

"Try it," I urged.

He walked up to the mannequin, raised his right hand to her throat, and frowned in concentration. His fingers closed around the silver tube. He squeezed, then smiled. He tried harder. He threw back his head and laughed. I grinned at the sound.

He took two long strides and caught me up, spinning me around.

"Oh, Tinker. What I owe you. What I owe you!" He trembled with emotion.

"Shhh. In the back." I began kissing his neck, and he carried me into the back room.

CARESS

As soon as the curtain closed, my lips were on his. We kissed until we were drunk with it. His breathing turned harsh and his caresses needy. The fire in my blood roared back hotter than before. He was still lifting me, my feet off the ground, but he finally put me down so he could undo my clothing. We fumbled with each other's collars and shirts. The air was cold against my skin as he bared my chest. I worried about him catching his death, wet as he was.

"Let me get the fire," I said. "You climb into bed."

I pulled away to light the tinder in the stove. I heard him undressing behind me, and a thick surge of lust threatened to make a quick end of things right then. The fire caught at last, despite my fumbling. Dreary daylight spilled in through the curtains over a small window. I felt terribly self-conscious as I dropped my trousers and smalls. I crossed my arms over my chest, held my breath, and turned. He was already in the bed, but he had the covers back, waiting for me, and I could see his bare chest, his arms, his muscular thighs, the thick, hard shaft of him, its foreskin fully retracted.

Scarred body, too thin, strongly aroused, male, beautiful.

I couldn't believe this moment had come, that I had a lover, that we had both survived the war, that Colin was really here. I went to him, slipped between the covers, and pulled them up to hide myself. I was so hard I throbbed like a metronome.

"I'm sorry I'm not more to look at," I said, even as my fingers, caring nothing for my modesty, stroked the heavy muscles of his chest.

"Tinker"—he laughed sadly—"you are sweet as an orchard peach. I thought so from the first moment I saw you."

I looked at him skeptically.

"Lovely and brilliant and brave. What you gave me. What you risked for me...." He took a deep, shaky breath.

"Hold me," I said, desperate. I could feel his naked skin next to mine, still cold from the rain. I pressed against him, needing more.

He took my lips with a groan and rolled on top of me. *God.* The weight of him pressing me down was the remedy to everything my body had ever craved. I put my arms around his ribs to cling all the tighter.

There was no more talking then, only his tongue stoking my mouth, his hands, the hands I had taught to caress, teasing my sides, my arms. His prick lay heavy against my hip.

Easton

His is two-point-five centimeters longer than mine, hard and hot with blood (a quarter pint, circulating), pulsing every third beat, bollocks tightening in preparation for release, male, my Colin, mine.

I had no finesse in me. I'd taught the hands to tease but at that moment I wanted him so violently I was incapable of subtlety. I slid my hands down to cup his arse, and I began to thrust against him. I was making embarrassing sounds in my throat, but it was like distant thunder for all I could control it or cared. He broke the kiss to pant my name and I latched on to his throat, his collarbone.

"Please," I begged over and over as I rutted against him. The indescribable pleasure in my prick and in every centimeter of my skin where he touched me made my eyes roll back in my head. "*Colin.*"

I don't know what I was begging for, only that it never stop, that he never leave me. He grunted on top of me, thrusting. I fell over the edge, convulsing as my release emptied out. I felt him jerk, his seed mingling with mine.

"Tinker," he said, burying his face in my neck. A pained sound, deep and terrible, escaped him.

He rolled off me and covered his face. I found a cloth and cleaned us both. I lay back down and held him as he trembled. "Shhh. It's over now."

He shook his head. "I killed so many. Soldiers all, but still…."

"Shhh." I rubbed his arm, wishing I could take away his pain. When his breathing slowed, I got up and pulled on my trousers. I went into the shop and picked up one of my favorite automatons. I took it into the back and sat on the bed.

Wait and see. Do not hope too much. He may still leave.

"Look," I said with false cheer.

He did, rubbing his eyes to see more clearly. On my palm was a piano four inches long. A tiny man in a top hat sat at the keyboard. I wound the key. A melody began to play as the tiny man moved his hands and pressed keys. The tune was bittersweet.

"Mine?" he asked, surprised.

I nodded. "Didn't you see the sign over the shop?"

He blushed. "Yes, but I didn't want to presume."

"*Gray and Davies, Musical Wonders.* I put your songs in my automatons. If you don't like it, I can remove them. But I thought…if you *liked* the business and wanted to stay…."

CARESS

He took my hands in his and squeezed. "You were with me in the night, Tinker, when I was alone in the cold and the dark. You were a caress on my cheek. It was only thinking that you might be here waiting for me, that we might be together in the end…."

"Me too," I whispered.

"But I never expected all this. I'm not worthy of you. Of your talent. Of your faith. But I'll try hard to be. I swear on my life."

In answer, I kissed him.

Two hearts broken. Two souls lost. The figures move together, holding each other up. An artificial heart, artificial hands, a love outside the lines. It is the imperfections that make something real.

Dance.

Because I am an idiot who still hasn't learned how stories and movies mislead us, showing us how things ought to end up, which is never how they do; and because stories are oracles whose prophecies we can't unravel until it is too late.

57 REASONS FOR THE SLATE QUARRY SUICIDES

Sam J. Miller

Because it would take the patience of a saint or Dalai Lama to smilingly turn the other cheek to those six savage boys day after day, to emerge unembittered from each new round of psychological and physical assaults; whereas I, Jared Shumsky, aged sixteen, have many things, like pimples and the bottom bunk bed in a trailer, and clothes that smell like cherry car air fresheners, but no particular strength or patience.

2. Because God, or the universe, or karma, or Charles Darwin, gave me a different strength, one that terrified me until I learned what it was, and how to control it, and how to use it as the instrument of my brutal and magnificent and long-postponed vengeance.

3. Because I loved Anchal, with the fierceness and devotion that only a gay boy can feel for the girl who has his back, who takes the *Cosmo* sex quiz with him, who listens to his pointless yammerings about his latest crush, who puts herself between him and his bullies so often that the bullies' wrath is ultimately re-routed onto her.

4. Because after the Albany Academy swim meet, while I was basking in the bliss of a shower that actually spouts hot water—a luxury our backwoods public school lacks—I was bodily seized by my six evil teammates, and dragged outside, and deposited there in the December cold, naked,

wet, spluttering, pounding on the door, screaming, imagining hypothermia, penile frostbite, until the door opened, and an utterly uninterested girl opened the door and let me in and said, "Jeez, calm down."

5. Because it's not so simple as evil bullies in need of punishment; because their bodies were too beautiful to hate and their eyes too lovely to simply gouge out; because every one of them was adorable in his own way, but they all had the musculature and arrogance of Olympic swimmers, which I lacked, being only five-six of quivery scrawn; because I loved swimming too much to quit the team—the silence of the water and how alone you were when you were in it, the caustic reek of chlorine and the twilight bus rides to strange schools and the sight of so much male skin; and because of those moments, on the ride home from Canajoharie or Schaghticoke or Albany, in the rattling, medicine-smelling short bus normally reserved for the mentally challenged, with the coach snoring and everyone else asleep or staring out the window watching the night roll by, when I was part of the team, when I was connected to people; when I belonged somewhere.

6. Because I had spent the past six months practicing; on animals at first, and after the first time I tried it on my cat she shrieked and never came near me again, but my dog was not so smart, and even though his eyes showed raw animal panic while I was working him he kept coming back every time I took my hand away and released him, and pretty soon working the animals was easy, the field of control forming in the instant my fingertips touched them, their brains like switches I could turn off and on at will, turning their bodies into mirrors for my own, but I still couldn't figure out a way to harm them.

7. Because once, while she slept, in my basement, engorged on candy and gossip and bad television, I tried my gift on Anchal, and it was much harder on a human, because she was so much bigger and her brain so much more complex and therefore more difficult to disable, and even though I tried to only do things that would not disturb her, her eyes fluttered open and then immediately narrowed in suspicion and fear, the wiser animal part of her brain recognizing me as a threat before the dumb easily-duped mammalian intellect intervened and said, *no, wait, this is your friend, he would never do anything to hurt you,* and she smiled

a blood-hungry smile and leaned forward and said, "How the hell did you do that?"

8. Because Mrs. Burgess assigned us Edgar Allan Poe's "Hop-Frog" for English class, which helped my vengeance take shape, and because none of the boys had read it.

9. Because Anchal did read it, and came to me, after school, eyes all laughing fire at the ideas the protagonist gave her—Hop-Frog, that squat, deformed little dwarf who murdered the cruel king and his six fat ministers in a dazzling spectacle of burned flesh and screaming death, and her excitement was infectious, and we worked on my gift for hours, until turning her into a puppet was as easy as believing she was one.

10. Because *Carrie* came on television that same night.

11. Because I am an idiot who still hasn't learned how stories and movies mislead us, showing us how things ought to end up, which is never how they do; and because stories are oracles whose prophecies we can't unravel until it is too late.

12. Because Anchal worked long and hard on the revenge scenario, sketching out all the ways my gift could be used to cause maximum devastation, all the ways we could transform our enemies into an ugly spectacle that would show the whole world what monsters they truly were.

13. Because I didn't listen when she said we would have to kill them, that they were *sick sons of bitches and would never stop being sick sons of bitches.* Because I still believed that they could be mine.

14. Because Anchal, equal parts Indian and Indian—Native American and Hindu—always smelled like wood smoke, lived with her Cherokee mom in a tiny house barely better than a cabin, and so I thought that she was invincible, heiress to noble, durable traditions far better than my own impoverished Caucasian ones, and that she could survive whatever the world might throw at her. And because she was beautiful; because she was smart and strong; because boys flocked to her; because she knew that if there was one sure thing we could depend upon, it was that teenaged boys were a lot more likely to make dumb decisions when lust was addling their brains.

15. Because Spencer, alone among my swim team mates, would smile at me for no reason, and speak to me sometimes when the others weren't around, and because some tiny actions gave me hope that he too was gay, and that we were each other's destinies.

16. Because Rex, on the other hand, an ogre of rare and excellent proportions, thick-headed but shrewd when it came to cruelty, served as the ringleader, and just as they had all obeyed him in his plan to pour Kool-Aid into Anchal's locker as punishment for stopping them from stomping my skull in, so I knew that *he* was the linchpin, the only one I would need to work, and that once I had him, the others would fall.

17. Because coach was sick that day, and our next meet wasn't for a week, so we had the day off from practice, an unheard-of gift of free time, and I knew that this was our shot, and we couldn't waste it, so I texted Anchal *We are* GO and then after school, while Rex was alone in the weight room, I stood outside in the hallway and called her cell, and said in a maybe-a-little-bit-too-loud voice, "Hey, so, I got a couple hours to kill, wanna meet me by the slate quarries in an hour, maybe bring some of your mama's vodka?" and she said, "Yes," and I said, "Great," and whistled while I walked away.

18. Because I hid myself in a darkened classroom where I could watch the weight room through the window in the door, and I saw how Rex called them all into a huddle when they arrived from their own classes, and they rubbed their hands or licked their lips or punched each other in the arm in glee, and then they left, as one, and I knew the bait had been taken.

19. Because they had their bicycles and I had mine, and after they left I let five minutes go by, and if I had stuck to that timeline everything would have gone exactly according to plan.

20. Because as I was about to unlock my bike I heard someone holler my name, and I swooned at the sound of it in Spencer's mouth, and I stopped, and saw him standing sweaty and tank-topped at the cafeteria window, smiling, nervous, looking exactly like he always did in the dreams where we finally told each other our separate, identical secrets, and said "Can I maybe talk to you for a minute?"

21. Because I have an easily-duped mammalian intellect of my own, and because if there's one thing you can depend upon, it's that teenage boys are a lot more likely to make dumb decisions when lust is addling their brains.

22. Because I went to him, and said, "Hey," and he said, "Hey," and we stood there like that for a second, and his pale skin had the same faint green-blue tint as mine from soaking in chlorine four hours a day for months, and his eyes were two tiny swimming pools, and somehow there wasn't a single pimple anywhere on him. And he said "That Edgar Allan Poe shit was pretty fucked up, wasn't it?" and I laughed and said that yes, it was, and my heart was loud in my throat and it had hijacked my brain and I could not disobey it, through several long minutes of small talk, even while I knew what it meant for Anchal.

23. Because he smiled and said, "Do you think I could, I don't know, come over some time?" and I grinned so hard it hurt, and said "Yeah, yes, sure, that'd be great," while my mind scrolled through a zoetrope of blurry images, heavy petting on the bean-bag chair in my basement, pale skin warming pale skin, us walking hand-in-hand through the hallowed horrible halls of Hudson High, me and Spencer against the world, my heinous monastic celibacy broken.

24. Because his phone buzzed, then, and he took it out and looked at it and then looked at me and said, "Yeah, uh, so, I should be going," and I saw at once that my plan had been seen through, my timeline tampered with, and I knew what even these six minutes of delay might mean for Anchal—and I left him in mid-sentence, and ran for my bike and ped-aled as hard as I could, heading for the slate quarries.

25. Because the long rocky road in to the quarry was littered with giant jutting slabs of slate, obscuring my view and slowing me down, so I didn't see her, or any of them, until I arrived at the top of the quarry and saw Anchal standing her ground, the five of them in a semicircle around her, but nothing between her and a drop to the jagged rocks and quarry lagoon below, and her face was bruised and bleeding but she was still on her feet and holding something in her hand, and she turned, and saw me, and saw Spencer coming close behind, and knew what I had done, how my weakness had hurt her, how only her own strength had saved her

from the horrific fate I abandoned her to, and she knew, in that moment, exactly what I was, and what I was was a sick son of a bitch just like the rest of them.

26. Because Rex had taken off his jacket, and his sweater, and his shirt, even though it was mid-December twilight, and he was freezing, and goosebumps armored his torso, and he turned and smiled when he saw me ride up, and said, "Hold on for a minute, boys, let me just take care of something first."

27. Because I tossed my bike to the ground and advanced on him, unafraid for once in my life, because guilt and shame over how weak I was had overpowered the fear of physical pain that usually held me back, and one of them laughed with surprise at my aggressiveness and said, "Damn, Rex, look out," and I yelled, "Get away from her, you pigs!" and Rex laughed and said, "Or what? You'll take us all on? All six of us?"—for Spencer had taken Rex's spot in the semicircle—and I said, "I'll kill you all," and I knew, hearing myself say it, that it was true, that Anchal was right, that there was no way *not* to kill them, that being a threat was who they were, and only death would make them cease to be one.

28. Because Rex said, "Come on then!" and I reached out for him, and he evaded me, and I reached again with the other arm and he leapt back, and I wasn't throwing fists because all I had to do was touch him, bare skin to bare skin, to possess him.

29. Because the terrible thought occurred to me, when Rex had successfully dodged several of my grabs, and threw his arm out at me, not in a fist but in the same extended-finger grip as mine, *What if I'm not the only one with this gift?*

30. Because our fight looked more like a ballet than a battle, ducking and leaping and flinging our arms out, and I was gaining ground, pushing him back toward the circle and the ledge, and his friends were laughing but in a nervous kind of way, and because I knew that he was thrown off balance by trying not to make eye contact with any of his fellow thugs, but that so was I, in my efforts to avoid looking into Anchal's eyes, for fear of what I'd find there.

31. Because Anchal's arm shot out then, and sprayed the little mace canister in Rex's eyes, and he stopped like someone pushed *pause*, and I struck his bare shoulder with one triumphant palm.

32. Because his scream of pain was cut short in that instant, and we stood like that, frozen, touching, for a solid thirty seconds, while I battled Rex for control of his body, and I saw how ill-advised this plan had been, because only the pain and confusion caused by Anchal's mace kept him from easily turning my gift back on me, and if any of his friends had touched me my control would have been broken and I'd surely have died that day.

33. Because none of them did touch me.

34. Because once I had Rex, the rest were easy.

35. Because I reached out my left arm and Rex reached out his in a precise mirror-motion, and touched it to the right arm of the boy standing beside him, and now when I reached out with my left arm *both* boys reached out with theirs, and touched the next boy, and so on, until all six boys, including Spencer, were linked hand to hand with me, and every move I made, they made.

36. Because my gift had established a field of control that no longer depended on mere touch, and when I took my hand away the boys were my vassals, my puppets, unable to move or speak on their own, free will gone, their hearts pumping at precisely the same rate as mine, their lungs taking in and casting out air in perfect rhythm with my breath.

37. Because I, on the other hand, felt nothing at all beyond the slight tension of the muscles that I always felt when I used my gift.

38. Because I raised my arms and they raised theirs; I jumped and so did they; I let loose a wolf call matched by six baying voices.

39. Because their eyes, I was surprised to learn, retained their autonomy, and the semicircle now showed me an impressive ocular display of hatred, fear, pain, anger.

40. Because Anchal stood up, and looked at me, and unlike my captive animals her eyes told me nothing, and she ran, silently, into the dark, and when I called her name those six boys said it too.

41. Because I let a long time pass, standing, listening, waiting for her to come back.

42. Because she didn't.

43. Because it is not a simple thing, to kill a man who mimics your every move.

44. Because Anchal chose the slate quarry for just that purpose.

45. Because I squatted, and they squatted, and I picked up a heavy rock, and their hands closed on nothingness, and I stood, and they stood, and I hoisted the rock over my head, and they raised their empty hands up just as high, and I threw the rock as hard as I could at Rex's head, and they made the same gesture.

46. Because Rex could neither flinch nor blink nor budge as the rock struck his face, nor even snap his head back to soften the impact by moving with the rock's inertia, and blood covered his face in seconds, and in the darkness we could smell the blood but not see the extent of the damage, and now every emotion other than terror was gone from those eyes.

47. Because I spoke, then—I shouted, and their screams formed around my words, a ghastly chorus of doomed men, echoing: "Once I dreamed of being one of you, of having your bodies, of moving so easily and fearlessly through the world, of belonging so effortlessly to a group of friends—but now that I can taste it for myself, now that I have your bodies, now that I am you, all of you, I see it for the horrid meaningless thing that it is."

48. Because the speech was not for them, and I'd spent a long time practicing it, and I was proud of it, but its intended audience was gone, fled, betrayed and hurt, by me.

49. Because suddenly my anger was gone, replaced by shame, and I had no more energy for our plan of a moment ago, of slowly but surely inducing them to bash each other to bits, to leave a grisly mess for forensic scientists to spend decades puzzling over.

50. Because the water at the bottom of the quarry was still an eerie blue with the light from the sky, even though the sun had already slipped past the horizon.

51. Because they were all standing so much closer than I was to the uneven lip of the quarry, and I reached out my arms and clasped my hands on air, so they were linked up in a human chain, and I ran and leapt and they went over the edge but I still had another three feet of solid ground ahead of me.

52. Because I stepped forward and looked down and there they were, far below, their backs to me, waist-deep in water and looking down into it, still holding hands, some of them unable to stand on broken legs, and there was blood in the water.

53. Because it was more from weariness than anything else when I lay down on the ground, head pressed to the dirt, and I knew even though I couldn't see them that they were all fully underwater, and I opened my mouth and breathed in that sweet cold December night air and then breathed it out, breathed it in and breathed it out, until the tension slackened in my muscles and I knew the field was broken, because they had drowned.

54. Because I got up off the ground knowing I had lost her forever, that she had seen straight through to the cold twisted heart of who I was. And in seeing who I was, she had shown me myself.

55. Because I had been too dumb to see how this power, this privilege I didn't want but had nonetheless, far from helping me to see, had blinded me to the truth of who we were.

56. Because in the movie, Carrie's punishment for killing her foes was to die, and mine was to live.

57. Because Anchal knew what I did not: that we are what we are, and we act it out without wanting to, and only death can break us of the habit of being the bodies we're born into.

I was always a sensitive child, finding
terror in the tiniest, most ridiculous
things, like the time I watched in
mystery and horror as my mother and
father cracked open long, bizarrely
shaped and spiked, pink crab legs
at the kitchen table, and, over
newspaper, sucked the insides out,
mouths garishly covered in melted
butter.

HAPPY BIRTHDAY, NUMBSKULL

Robert Smith

I grew up in aluminum houses all over Michigan. You can still see it in my face. You can see the rusted cars in the front yard, and my mother vacuuming the bottoms of above-ground swimming pools as if they were Olympic sized. If you look close enough you can see kids with lice and cousins with fetal alcohol poisoning kissin' and touchin' each other in the woods. You can see crack addiction and Canada, where tiny hand-written letters tied to helium balloons ended up.

I remember my mother telling me that a penny thrown from the Empire State Building could kill somebody. Maybe it was then I realized it didn't take much. I was always a sensitive child, finding terror in the tiniest, most ridiculous things, like the time I watched in mystery and horror as my mother and father cracked open long, bizarrely shaped and spiked, pink crab legs at the kitchen table, and, over newspaper, sucked the insides out, mouths garishly covered in melted butter. As they scoured over the messy and seemingly extraterrestrial pile, I was convinced my parents had been the victims of "body-snatchers," and it took the better part of my youngest years before I was ever convinced otherwise.

I can also remember being completely terrified as my father whittled the strange, coarse, alien-like rind off a pineapple, working in some weird nostalgic trance, reminiscing about the year he lived in Hawaii with his older brother. Again, I visualized some sort of Martian mind control, but for years, even without being under the psychic influence of a pineapple, he would talk about the time he went surfing in Hawaii and saw a shark swim past him. When retelling the story, my father would make the shape of a dorsal fin with his right hand and slowly move it through the air in the space between us, and I could imagine rows and rows of shark's teeth snapping at my feet below me, wherever I was. I was a highly imaginative and anxious kid. It didn't take much more than unfamiliar fruit or spindly shellfish to push me over the edge.

I used to get bloody noses in the middle of the night from sleeping next to the furnace to keep warm. Once, my father had to remove a blood clot from my nose, a cluster of cells and mucus rooted all the way to the back of my sinus, like wild plants clinging to clumps of dampened soil. When he pulled it out, I felt relief and a newfound empty space in my head I didn't realize until then I had, as if somebody scooped out my brains and left me a cleanly shucked, less cluttered skull. I remember my father laughing at my reaction to my new sense of self as I shook my head back and forth, amazed at the feeling of emptiness.

"I can't feel my brains," I said, rattling my head in bliss. My father began to laugh along with me for the first time I can ever recall. My father now being rendered in memory as a passive bystander, a mystery of a man, either at work or absent from work or just completely missing. When home, he was a loving father, yet somehow never managed to fully express it. He was always somewhere else, even when in the same house.

"I can't feel my brains!" I giddily exclaimed over and over again.

"You Numbskull," he playfully christened, and at that moment I didn't want to be known as anything else.

In the Midwestern winter mornings my mother would send me out to warm the car for my younger brother, Calvin, and the twins. She'd give me the keys and I'd sit in the driver's seat and secretly read one of her V.C. Andrews paperbacks while the windows were still frosted over, concealing me from the rest of the world. I wasn't allowed to read my mother's books. They were not for little boys, which made me covet them even more. I'd project myself right into the portraits of sinister looking families that were found behind the book's jacket, and inside I poured over the absurd stories of Gothic horror, family secrets and forbidden love, fantasizing about a life outside my own, which was that of an awkward eight-year-old boy who got crushes on other boys, was the oldest of four, and son to two very young parents who fought all the time about things he didn't quite understand.

It seemed like everybody was always talking about eating people back then, which only heightened my seemingly inexhaustible fears and anxieties as well as unanswered questions. Jeffrey Dahmer was in the news, *Silence of the Lambs* was on pay-per-view. For the first time, I was hearing phrases like "cannibalism," "necrophilia" and "homosexuality". Hearing those words lumped together was an obvious cause for even more confusion and concern for me as I struggled to figure things out about myself, by myself, and why I was made to feel wrong for the way I acted, which, for a lack of creativity on the part of my critics, was more or less like a girl, a *strangely terrified* girl. But for a few moments every morning I was alone in my own igloo, behind windows covered in snow and ice, with the steam coming from the old muffler growing into white, condensed clouds all around me, and I felt that was the only part of the day I was ever really safe. At least until the windows defrosted, and the crystallized corners slowly rolled back onto themselves, curling at the melting edges like a page from a book I wasn't supposed to be reading thrown onto a fire.

My family eventually moved into a perfectly square, three-bedroom home in Warren, Michigan, a small, poor county on the outskirts of Detroit. My father immediately built a giant deck from bleached lumber. It attached to the back of the house and was twice as big as its host. Four steps from the ground, the yard beneath forever cast into a shady place for hiding, for stray cats to give birth to their kittens, for soft balls and other small things to end up missing. He wrapped it up in a lattice of wood to keep anything larger than a small animal from getting underneath the floorboards.

A snake's jaw doesn't actually unhinge at the skull to swallow something larger than its mouth. It simply stretches…

The first summer in that house I celebrated my eleventh birthday. My mother wound streamers across the banister and tied clusters of balloons from the posts. My cousins threw water balloons at each other from over the rails. In the driveway another cousin picked out the raw center of his grilled hamburger with his chubby fingers and rolled the pink meat into little fleshy balls before popping them into his mouth, a clown face of red

Faygo stains outlining his grin while he watched two other sunburned and shirtless neighborhood kids perform a duel with Super Soakers in the driveway. They put their backs together, then walked away in measured steps, counting to ten before whipping around and blasting each other with the water guns.

My younger brother, Calvin, was in the above-ground pool pulling the tightly suctioned snorkel mask from his face, releasing it with a POP, tipping out the water that leaked in.

The twins wore bright orange floaties that held their delicate arms forever suspended on the surface of the water next to their ears, which barely bounced above the carefully chlorinated three feet of water. My family had dug out a slight, gradual slope in the yard beneath the surface of the pool lining, adding an additional inch and a half of depth at the very center. Here the twins couldn't reach the bottom even on the tips of their toes so they just kicked their legs back and forth with an excited sense of freedom and danger.

I was watching all this from the deck, hiding behind the girth of my Gramma Mae, my father's mother. Gramma Mae had poor blood and fluid circulation, and as a young adult the doctors made the mistake of simply removing the collapsed veins from her lower legs. Consequently she became dependent upon a wheelchair, and over the years she continued to gain weight and her legs swelled up and scabbed over in protest. She only got out of her chair to use the restroom and then later to go to bed. She wore large floral-print muumuus and taught me how to play rummy and gin rummy, and read to me from a children's Bible, illustrated and abbreviated, whenever I would come and visit. After Genesis we always became uninterested and put the book down.

She'd scrub her legs with pumice stone, and I would watch as she attended to her suffocating limbs, the exfoliated skin and scabs drifting around her, catching light in great-whittled swarms while she sang:

"Gonna dance with the dolly with the holes in her stocking's / Knees keep a'knockin' / Toes keep a'rockin' / Gonna dance with the dolly with the holes in her stocking's / Dance by the light of the Moooon!"

And I always felt safe with my Gramma Mae, preferring her company to kids my own age.

The neighbors next door were grilling out back as well. It was a group of brothers, all young adults sharing the house with their single, shut-in father. They were rebel boys that liked to hunt. On this day they had just returned from a trip upstate and brought back with them a deer loosely wrapped in a black tarp in the bed of their truck. I overheard my mother ask them to leave it where it was until after the party, before moving it to the garage, because she didn't want the kids to see it.

When it was time to open presents and sing "Happy Birthday" my mother tied a T-shirt around my head and sat me in front of a birthday cake in the shape of Garfield's head, lit by eleven dripping, pastel-colored candles. When she untied my blindfold, it seemed as if all of my cousins had encircled me, towered over me grinning with stained teeth and faces, savage war paint from artificially colored popsicles, sodas and ice cream cones. Their arms held behind their backs as if to protest their innocence.

"Come oooooon, make a wiiiiish!" my mother prompted, always quick to grow impatient with such a nervous son.

I sucked in and clenched my eyes like jumping from a large cliff and inched my face towards the miniature flames, anxiously aware of everybody watching me. I pushed the air from my chest and just as my breath passed my O-shaped lips I opened my eyes and saw my birthday guests had been concealing small aerosol cans behind their backs and were now pointing them at me. As I blew my wish into the candles, coils of Silly String spiraled towards me, combusting into little blowtorches of fire as the flammable confetti grazed over the birthday candles then licked my face just inches from the cake.

My mother, also caught unaware by the practical joke, and horrified by the unpredicted disaster, let out a quick yelp. The eyes of the other adults widened in awe, stunned and mesmerized by the simple beauty and hypnotic qualities of the fire. The fireball of gas quickly rolled over my face, and extinguished itself before anybody really knew what happened. Although not before scorching my eyebrows and eyelashes into minuscule black balls of crusty protein. Two beats after the last eyelash went up in a wisp of smoke, Herb the stoner neighbor from across the street heroically threw his mug of beer at me.

The neighbors next door, separated by a chain-link fence, but just as present as the rest of the guests, let out howls of approval at the fireworks display as the entire deck four steps above fell into a moment of silence. Two of the brothers gave each other high fives, and the third tuned the dial on the old pickup's radio, which was parked in front of their garage carrying the secret, bloating cargo. He cranked up the volume as the opening cords of Black Sabbath's "Children of the Grave" presented itself through the static, then made the sign of the devil with his left hand, saluting total righteousness. A breeze caught beneath the tarp in the bed of the truck and peeled it back, providing a creep show to instigate the already horrified party.

"Hell yeah, little dude!" The neighbor yelled and nodded from the open door of the truck towards me, signaling my very first memory of acceptance *ever*. I saw all this from behind the remains of my eyelashes, and noticed my cousins, neighbors and parents looking back at me with a new-found respect and fear as they waited to see what would happen next, as if I would be the one willing it to be. As if I could summon the elements, scorch the earth with fire, unveil scores of covered corpses by my command of the wind. Only my Gramma Mae looked on with an innocent delight and slight confusion.

While my heavy-metal neighbors rocked out to my total wickedness, the corners of my lips began to curl up into a wise grin, much to the fright of most of my family and guests. A stray cinder floated over to one of the balloons tied to the banister, and let out a loud **bang** as it landed.

This time everybody jumped in unified nervousness, except for me.

My wish had come true.

In my parent's bedroom my mother aggressively tried to conceal what could have possibly been considered to be the mark of the devil. Screams of children playing outside could be heard as she searched her makeup kit for the proper instrument. She tested eyeliner on her hand then steadily applied it to my bald eyebrows.

"Hopefully your hair will grow back by the time you start school. You need to make some friends. Stop being such a little girl all the time. Scared of your own shadow," she said as she labored, checking the results.

She sketched the last effect onto my brow then whirled me around to face the mirror of her vanity.

"Shit! That won't work, will it?" On my face were two thickly drawn eyebrows at arches that gave me an exaggerated, comical expression of worry. My mother rummaged around again, pulled out a long floral scarf from a dresser drawer and a pair of large sunglasses and affixed them both to my head.

"It's time you start acting like a man. Okay?"

As my mother contemplated her creation, unaware of any irony, there was a knock at her door. She looked into my face for some recognition, but was visibly disappointed as she walked over and opened the door, revealing my birthday guests and their parents, grouped together like Christmas Carolers. They stood awkwardly on the threshold, the kids obviously having been prompted by the adults to apologize and say goodbye, the twins in front of the chorus, still wearing their bright orange floaties.

"Sorry thank you for having us happy birthday goodbye I'm sorry about that thank you goodbye happy birthday!"

My mother stood holding the door open for the guests. She had cemented a fake smile on her face as if to suggest everything was okay, until she turned away from them and faced me with a look of threat.

"Say goodbye, young man."

Theatrically, as if mustering the strength from my deathbed, I drew a breath and managed a mutter as I raised my chin, and clutched the scarf close to my face. My mother was horrified, my guests begged their parents to take them home, and the twins laughed hysterically.

"Thank you…and…good-bye."

I tell him I found sword fighting to be a violent pursuit, and I have abhorred violence since my terrifying birth.

Right There in Kansas City

Casey Hannan

My friend enters my apartment, takes off his shirt, and accuses me of being a brown recluse spider. He senses my desire to devour him in the dark of my living room. He'll shake out his clothes from now on to make sure I'm not lurking inside.

"It's a hot den of iniquity in here," he says.

I call it a nest. I don't believe in air conditioning. I've torn the stuffing from the couch cushions and made a bed in the corner. The light fixtures don't have bulbs. I smile to survey it, which is a mistake because of my teeth.

My friend has it in his head I have fangs. My canines are long. All parts of me are long. My face has been the real joke. I went as a happy crescent moon for Halloween for many years. That was during my social phase. My medicine phase.

Now I never go outside. I buy cereal on the Internet. I have a full-length mirror I pretend is a window into the neighbor's place.

"Do something," I say to my reflection in the mirror.

"Do me," my friend says.

He's part blind from where his pet tarantula flicked irritating hairs into his eyes. They are grey and opaque as raw almond milk. He can discern shapes and make do with the fuzzed aura of a new outfit, but he never knows if his hair is saying what he wants it to say.

"I want to silence my hair," he says. "Get it shorn completely. Will you do that for me?"

I say I consider shearing hair an erotic act, and I won't have any involvement in it.

"You used to be so horny and homosexual," he says.

I tell him I found sword fighting to be a violent pursuit, and I have abhorred violence since my terrifying birth. I'm only now starting to grow into my mangled parts. My head could be the bullet God used to kill the dinosaurs. All the better for my friend. He favors unique shapes. He tries to kiss me, and I recoil out of habit, not disgust.

"You don't deserve my gay rights," he says.

We move to the front door frame of my apartment. My friend steps outside. He puts his shirt back on.

"Let's go get wasted," he says.

He has dressed to lure me. His shorts are small as they come. A scant nod to decorum in that they cover his penis but not his thighs. I'm good to stand back and admire in the shadows.

My friend pulls my arms.

I push my friend. He bends back at the knees. He's been standing with his legs crossed, posing as a tall vase. As he falls, the skin of his legs separates on clean and invisible perforations. The sound is a thumb sliding into an envelope and tearing.

My friend's calf skin sinks down to his ankles. The colors of undergore are the same as a slice of pizza without cheese. I don't cross the threshold. I've memorized the number to Domino's. It's the only place I can think to call. I don't even pull out my phone.

My friend screams. I scream. I hear the neighbor's door open, and I hear the neighbor scream.

I close my door and press my eye to the peephole. I flatten my body into the pretend wood. I wish to merge with the industrial fiber. I wish it on my friend's exposed kneecaps.

The neighbor calls 911 and uses gator clips to secure my friend's skin for the short term. My friend is experiencing shock. I was once shocked to learn he loved me.

"If you ever tease me," he said, "about my love for you, I'll kill myself with the worst tool. Something with glitter suspended in its clear plastic handle."

The skeleton out there won't say anything like that again. He'll have only two words for me.

"Fuck you," he'll say from his recovery bed.

"Fuck you, fuck you, fuck you," he'll repeat until all he can do is slowly mouth the letter F.

Sometime later, when my friend is back in one piece and all is forgiven, he calls to say that the spontaneous appearance of cuts on his arms, legs, and trunk was not, as he once believed, the work of ghosts haunting his duplex.

"It's a skin condition," he says, adding that he doesn't believe in ghosts anymore.

He asks if I still cling to macabre fantasies. I close my eyes, and there they are—his two pale legs rolled down like socks.

I say it's hard to cling to anything but.

I take a deep breath. The release of
saying something true though warms
as if I were buried in Gus's arms
on a winter's night and we were the
only people in the world. No wonder
all the cool kids suspend themselves
between truth and lie.

THE WATER THAT FALLS ON YOU FROM NOWHERE

John Chu

The water that falls on you from nowhere when you lie is perfectly ordinary, but perfectly pure. True fact. I tested it myself when the water started falling a few weeks ago. Everyone on Earth did. Everyone with any sense of lab safety anyway. Never assume any liquid is just water. When you say "I always document my experiments as I go along," enough water falls to test, but not so much that you have to mop up the lab. Which lie doesn't matter. The liquid tests as distilled water every time.

Uttering "this sentence is false" or some other paradox leaves you with such a sense of angst, so filled with the sense of an impending doom, that most people don't last five seconds before blurting something unequivocal. So, of course, holding out for as long as possible has become the latest craze among drunk frat boys and hard men who insist on root canals without an anesthetic. Psychologists are finding the longer you wait, the more unequivocal you need to be to ever find solace.

Gus is up to a minute now and I wish he'd blurt something unequivocal. He's neither drunk, nor a frat boy. His shirt, soaked with sweat, clings to a body that has spent twenty-seven too many hours a week at the gym. His knees lock stiff, his jeans stretched across his tensed thighs. His face shrinks as if he were watching someone smash kittens with a hammer. It's a stupid game. Maybe in a few more weeks the fad will pass.

I don't know why he asked me to watch him go through with it this time, and I don't know why I'm actually doing it. Watching him suffer is like being smashed to death with a hammer myself. At least Gus is asking for it. I know I'm supposed to be rooting for him to hold on for as long as possible, but I just want him to stop. He's hurting so much and I can't stand to watch anymore.

"I love you, Matt." Gus's smile is radiant. He tackles me on the couch and smothers me in a kiss, and at first, I kiss him back.

Not only does no water fall on him, but all the sweat evaporates from his body. His shirt is warm and dry. A light, spring breeze from nowhere covers us. He smells of flowers and ozone. This makes me uneasier than if he'd been treated to a torrent. That, at least, I'd understand. I'd be sad, but I'd understand.

He's unbuttoned and unzipped my jeans when my mind snaps back to the here and now. It's not that his body doesn't have more in common with Greek statues than actual humans. It's not that he can't explicate Socrates at lengths that leave my jaw unhinged. It's that not only did "I love you, Matt" pull him out of his angst, but it actually removed water.

Fundamental laws of physics do that. Profound theorems of mathematics do that. "I love you, Matt" doesn't count as a powerful statement that holds true for all time and space. Except when Gus says it, apparently.

"Wait." I let go of him. My hands reach down to slide to a sit.

Gus stops instantly. He's skittered back before my hands have even found the couch cushions. His head tilts up at me. This is the man who seconds ago risked going insane in order to feel soul-rending pain for fun. How can he suddenly look so vulnerable?

Oh, if there's anything Gus can do, it's put up a brave front. He does that stony-faced thing where his mouth is set in a grim, straight line better than anyone I know. But behind his hard, blue eyes, I can see the fear that's not there even when some paradox rips him apart.

Best to take the pain now. I'm half-convinced nothing can actually hurt him, even when he's afraid it might. It'd only hurt him more later.

"That's some display you just did there, Gus." I'm stalling. Stop that. "I don't love you, not as much as you obviously love me."

The water that falls on you from nowhere is freezing cold. I slip on the couch, but it just follows me. When it's this much water, it numbs you to the bone. I want to scream, "What the fuck?" but if I even breathed, I'd drown. Gus tries to shield me, blocking my body with his, but not even he's fast enough. I try to push him out of the downpour. However, he's a mixed martial artist and I'm not. We share everything after the initial shock. The torrent lasts for seconds. We're both soaked and he's laughing so hard that he's fallen off the couch, doubled over on the wet floor, flopping like a fish.

I feel like I should be insulted, but his laughter is joyous. It's like the peal of giant bells, low booms that vibrate through you and make everything in the room rattle. I can't tell if those are tears on his face, or just the water from nowhere.

My body shakes so hard, I can't stand. The cushions squeak around me, keeping me bathed in ice cold water. Gus stands up. He's not even shivering. He picks me up, wraps me in his arms, then kisses me gently on the forehead.

"I'm sorry, Gus. I just ruined your couch." The floor is covered in rubber weight-lifting mats. I'll mop that up once I can move again.

This just sends him into another fit of laughter, more controlled this time. His hands are gentle around my waist. Without them, I'm pretty sure I'd crash onto the floor.

"You've just told me that you love me in I think the only way you can, and you're worried about the couch?"

Coming from anyone else, that sentence would make me feel too stupid to live. Still, he has a point. I fumble but can't find any words to answer.

"It'll dry off," Gus says. "Besides, you bought the couch for me."

Biotech engineers make more money than personal trainers, even the world's most overqualified ones. Who knew? Rather than actually moving in together, I've been slowly furnishing his apartment. Gus has patiently assumed that once the apartment no longer looks like a cross between a library and weight room, I'll move in. He's long offered to move in with me, but I don't want him to. My efficiency isn't worthy of him. It's just a body locker.

"I should clean up the mess I made." I pull away and Gus catches me before I fall. He literally sweeps me off my feet.

"Stop fretting. It's okay."

We get out of our wet clothes in the bathroom and huddle together under blankets in bed. It isn't until he starts shivering that I realize he's just as cold as I am. The mixed martial artist has just been more heroic, or stupid, about it.

"You know." Gus's voice is surprisingly steady given how his teeth chatter. "Now that we know how we feel about each other, how about we solemnize the relationship? Make it official."

My brow furrows so tightly, it hurts. He's serious. As lightly he tossed it off, he meant it.

"You risked permanent insanity just to ask me to marry you?" Honestly, there are less life-threatening ways.

"No, that was just training." He's not joking. "I can't imagine life without you. You can't imagine life without me. Say yes?"

The air stays resolutely dry. He could have made it all one big question to avoid letting whatever makes the water fall have a say.

"My family…" I have no idea how to broach this. It's totally possible for him to love me and still never want to see me again.

"They know about me, right?" I swear the man reads minds.

"Yes?" It's not a lie, but it's not the truth either. The air gets distinctly humid. My arm hairs stand on end, as if thunder were about to strike. I'm still shivering from my last lie. My mind is in tatters, torn between the cruel truth that will make him lose all respect for me and the blatant lie that will plunge me into fatal hypothermia. The pang that gnaws at my heart grows and spreads. It wrings me, twisting and squeezing the life out of me. I jerk my face into what I want to be a smile.

"Matt, this isn't a root canal. Don't stretch it out. Whatever you have to say, it's okay."

I take a deep breath. The release of saying something true though warms as if I were buried in Gus's arms on a winter's night and we were the only people in the world. No wonder all the cool kids suspend themselves between truth and lie. However, rehearsing this speech for months in my head has not helped one bit. The words rush out so quickly, I'm not even sure what I'm saying.

"Mandarin doesn't have gender-specific third-person pronouns. Well, the written language does, but it's a relatively recent invention and they all sound the same and no one really uses the female and neuter variants anyway. And it's not like there aren't words for 'boyfriend' or 'girlfriend' but I always refer to you as '愛人.' It means 'sweetheart,' 'lover,' 'spouse.'

And never using your name isn't all that unusual. Names are for friends and acquaintances. Members of your family you refer to by title—"

When Gus interrupts me, the only thought in my mind is "Did I just tell him that I call him my spouse to my parents?"

"Wait. Slow down." Gus's intellect trains on me like a sharpshooter. "The way you talk about me to your family, we might as well be married?"

"Yes." My stomach is in my throat. The world bobbles around me and I'm stumbling at a cliff's edge.

"But they don't know my name, or that I'm male."

"Yes." His bullet strikes my heart and I've just crashed on the rocky shore.

"Hmm." He wears his "I'm going to fix this" face, but then it hardens into that grim, stony thing that breaks my heart. He nudges himself against me, then holds me as if only I can fit in that gap between his arms and chest. "We can't marry until you're ready to come out to your family. I'll wait as long as you want."

His skin transforms from cold and clammy to warm and dry. He uses declarative sentences. The truth of each one is obvious. No weasel words or qualifiers. Instead of being soaked in water though, Gus is soaked in disappointment. Normally, his smile glows and I melt in its heat. Right now, he's wearing a cheap copy. He's about as likely to admit that I've hurt him as he is to use anesthesia.

This isn't like him. I expected an argument. I mean, I should have come out to my family a decade ago. If they don't suspect anything, it's because I'm still years younger than Dad was when he married Mom. Instead, we behave as if I hadn't just said no to him, albeit tacitly.

Gus chatters on about Procopius's Wars of Justinian. He's just finished volume four, in the original Greek. I talk about stem cells and gene splicing. It's as if tonight were any other night I'm over, and we're just catching each other up on how our day went. His hands and his tone slowly ask if I'm interested even though he always interests me. I'm still cold and he covers me with his now warm body. The thoughtful smile, the affectionate way he holds me, nuzzles and kisses my neck, they try so hard to let me know that everything is fine between us, that he desires me as much as I desire him. He's not aggressive. We'll go as slowly as I want.

"Let's visit my family this Christmas. The two of us." My voice is louder than I'd expected. "Not the 'Christ is born' Christmas, but the 'get together with family and give presents to the nieces' Christmas. We stopped when my sister and I outgrew the whole Christmas present thing, but when she had kids, we started again. With the water falling now, I wanted to skip this year for my own sanity but—"

"Stop." He's on his side, his arm around me. He's not as happy as I want him to be. "Are you sure? I can wait years if that's what you want."

"I should have done this a long time ago. I don't think I'll ever be any more ready." If Gus realizes that I'm outing myself to my family for him, he'll probably refuse to go out of sheer principle. I'm not sure I can do it with him, but I know I can't do it without him.

Gus senses that all I want is to be held so that's all he does. The condoms stay in the drawer. He drifts off to sleep, and I lie next to him listening to the calm rhythm of his breath. I'm the only son. All I can think about is my parents' "you're responsible for carrying on the family name because when your sister marries she will become part of her husband's family" speech. It freaked me out even before I'd come out to myself.

The family gathers in the atrium of my sister's mansion as we stomp the Christmas Eve storm off our boots. The high vaulted ceiling has room for the sweeping staircase and the Christmas tree, big enough to dwarf Gus, that sits in the handrail's curve. Ornaments. Tinsel. Holly. Ivy. A copy of Michelangelo's God giving Adam life tacked taut on the atrium ceiling. We've entered Victorian Christmas Land. No half measures here.

The disappointment when the family sees that my friend is a man is palpable. It's like the adults were all my nieces' age and someone told them there was no Santa Claus. Mom asks me if we've eaten. According to the textbooks, it's a polite greeting, but she always means it literally. If I tell her I'm not hungry, she'll say, "不餓還需要吃啊." (Even if you're not hungry, you still need to eat.) That must be true since that never causes the water to fall. Fortunately, rather than being forced to eat dinner again, this time I have Gus to derail the conversation.

I introduce him to my parents, my sister, Michele, her husband, Kevin, their kids, Tiffany and Amber, and, to my surprise, Kevin's parents. As I negotiate the simultaneous translation, a horrible thought hits me. Everyone in the room speaks at least two languages, but there isn't one language everyone speaks. Besides English, Gus speaks only dead languages. Kevin's parents speak Cantonese and Mandarin, but not English. My parents haven't needed English since they retired, not that theirs was good before. I've trapped Gus in a mansion where he can't speak to half the people. Repeatedly slamming my head against the handrail now would send the wrong message, so I don't.

The instant Gus crouches down and starts talking to the nieces, they stop being scared of him and start playing with him. All physically imposing people seem to be able to win over little kids in mere seconds. They head off to the living room. I start to join them when my sister marches me into her home office.

"How dare you?" She slams the door behind her and I remind myself that I'm bigger than her now and it'd be harder for her to beat me up. "Are you trying to kill Mom and Dad?"

Well, that was easier than I'd expected. She knows and I didn't even have to tell her. Also, I've broken my record. It usually takes an entire day before I make her angry. At this rate, I could be kicked out of the house and in a motel room by sunrise. I reserve one for every trip. She gets all offended if I don't stay with her at first.

"No." Ideally, Mom and Dad accept it. That can happen. "I want everyone to meet the man I'm going to marry."

The future's not fixed, but right now, Gus and I are headed toward marriage, so the air stays dry. She slaps me. My cheek stings. I'd slap her back but I need to out myself to our parents before she throws me out of the house.

"Mom and Dad always let you get away with being selfish, don't they? I don't do whatever I want." She's blocking the door. "Doesn't it matter to you that you're embarrassing Mom and Dad in front of 婆婆 and 公公?"

Phrasing things in the form of a question. That and weasel words work as insurance against the water that falls from nowhere. They just make it extremely obvious that you're hedging against the truth.

"Like I knew your husband's parents were even coming." Not that I'm embarrassing Mom and Dad. Well, not this time anyway.

"Your job, 何德培"—my full name in Chinese including family name, just in case it isn't clear she's furious at me—"is to give our parents a grandson."

We both already know this. She just enjoys showing me the dry air.

"I don't think I can do that by myself." I wish I hadn't said that.

She slaps me again. My cheek hadn't stopped stinging from last time.

"Do you love Mom and Dad? Dump that slab of beef. Find a Chinese woman to marry. Put your penis in her vagina and make Mom and Dad a grandson. Make them happy."

She turns to leave but not two steps stomp by before she whips around. Coming out to Mom and Dad, she hasn't ordered me not to do it yet.

"And you're not coming out to Mom and Dad." With that command, she leaves.

No water. She must mean it. She'll never leave me alone with Mom or Dad.

I close my eyes and remind myself why I'm doing this. Right. Gus. He refuses to stop insisting it's okay if I don't come out to them. He'll understand if I don't. That just makes me want to do what he really wants, but won't say out loud. Coming out would have hurt less a decade ago and it'll hurt less now than a decade from now. Unless I just keep quiet and wait for my entire family to die off. Now there's a cheery thought.

Christmas day. When I wake, Gus is most of the way through his forms, his movements silent and precise. I make an exaggerated show of sneaking out of the bedroom. His face cracks the tiniest smile when I look back at him from the door.

My sister pointedly ushered us to different rooms last night. I return to the den where I was supposed to sleep to get ready to join Dad for his daily early morning walk. It's awful. We'll plod in circles at some local mall while I try to get him to talk about himself and he answers in single syllables. At least this time, I'll actually have something to talk to him about. I guess I've had something to talk to him about for years. This time, though, I'm going to do it.

When I get downstairs, my sister insists on joining us. First time in…. Actually, she's never done the morning-walk thing with Dad before.

"Great, sis." I start back up the stairs. "You go with Dad to the mall this time. See you two later."

I ignore her sputterings. If she wants Dad to keep thinking that she's their Good Child, she won't dare to do anything to me right now, and she'll go with Dad on the mall walk. I'll pay for this later, of course, but by the time she comes back, Mom will have woken up and I will have had a chat with her.

Or at least that was Plan B. The morning-walk ritual is supposed to be that, after the walk, he goes to have his sausage biscuit, luxuriates over a cup of coffee, two if you count the free refill. Only then do we come home. However, they're home too early. Mom's still asleep. My sister has apparently forced Dad to skip the fast-food-breakfast part of his morning ritual.

When I hear the garage door, I lean over the sweeping staircase's handrail. Dad's grumbling. My sister's chirping bright words about how the kitchen has something just as good. She glares at me as she rushes Dad past. Like it's my fault he's angry at her.

The rest of the day is like an extremely tedious game of basketball. My sister plays a tight defense, but legal. No contact while there are witnesses. Since I'm trying to get time alone with my parents, one of them is always a witness.

She's even helping Mom make tonight's feast. I'm kneading the dough for Mom's steamed, stuffed buns when my sister inserts herself into the process. After years of preparing meals for large gatherings together, Mom and I have a system. At some point, she stopped insisting that my wife would cook for me someday and started teaching me to cook. Either she got sick of me nagging her, or she realized I kneaded dough more quickly than she did. Anyway, with some luck, dinner won't be too much later than if my sister had just left us alone.

Gus is doing his best imitation of an apartment mate who had nowhere else to go for Christmas. I wish he'd stop that. He spends time with my nieces, my brother-in-law, even my parents, but he only skirts the kitchen. I get that he doesn't want to out me for me, but I like his conversation too. It's stupid to be in the same house as him and still miss him so much. After my first few whacks at the duck with the cleaver, Mom takes the heavy knife away from me, then tells me to go rehydrate mushrooms.

It doesn't take a solid day of cooking to make dinner, but my sister conveniently has questions about how to make the filling for the stuffed buns and how much sesame oil for the scallion pancakes. She leaves the kitchen occasionally, but never long enough for me to work up the nerve to tell Mom. Whenever I leave the kitchen, it isn't two minutes before she finds me, claiming she needs my help. I manage to say, "Yes, I think you're a terrible cook too," in front of her husband and her parents-in-law in our respective languages in common before she drags me back to the kitchen. Water doesn't fall when I say that. I have to take my pleasure where I can.

When the nieces pull Mom away to play with their Erector Set, she decides that my sister and I can finish dinner without her. My sister complains that she needs Mom's help. I agree wholeheartedly, but it's not enough. The two of us are stuck with each other.

"You do know why Gus doesn't come into the kitchen, don't you?" Despite her casual tone, we both know this is not idle chatter.

"Does it matter?" I'm slicing pickled radishes. "You're going to tell me anyway."

"Do you really think you can keep him?" She drops spinach into a skillet pooled with oil. The water coating the spinach hits the oil and splatters back at her. "He's spent more time with Kevin today than with you."

I force myself to slice slowly. Cutting my fingers off is a distraction I don't need right now. My heart pounds in my ears. I'm not sure who I'm more angry at, my sister or my lover.

"I have no idea what you mean, sis." We immigrated here when she was a teenager and I was a little kid. There's a good chance she'll miss the sarcasm. The water gets it though and I stay dry.

"Kevin's a good-looking guy, maybe..." The line would have more impact if she didn't look scared of the spinach sautéing before her. She jabs the spatula as if it were a fencing foil.

Kevin's not my type. I'm pretty sure he's not Gus's, but I guess I don't know. It's not like he didn't date lots of men before me. It's not as if they don't all throw themselves at him. My mind spins for seconds before I realize she hasn't actually accused Gus of anything. Kevin is stolidly straight, and if Gus has tried anything with Kevin, not that he would, she'd throw Gus and me out of the house, not taunt me with the possibility that Gus might be unfaithful.

"Maybe what?" Usually, I don't have this much trouble arranging sliced radishes in a pretty pattern. Right now, they're just a bunch of ugly yellow discs.

"You understand what I'm saying. I shouldn't have to spell it out. You don't trust your own sister?"

When I was eight, she convinced me that she was psychic, then fore-told exactly how horrible my life would be if I didn't do exactly as she said. It's embarrassing how many years she got away with it. If the water had been falling back then, she'd have flooded the house.

"Only your family loves you enough to tell you this." Listening to her is like being pelted by rocks. "What can he possibly see in you? Dump him and marry a nice Chinese woman instead. Stay with him and he'll cheat on you or dump you."

Three words into her last sentence, I know what she'll say. I leap to pull her pan away as I shut off the burner. The water that falls from nowhere drenches her and the burner where the pan was. Had the water hit the pan, the steam and splattered oil would have burned her.

"Go get warm." I plate the spinach onto a dish on the counter. "I'll mop up the water."

"People change, but maybe he'll still love you, even as you shut him out like you have me, Mom, and Dad." Her arms wrap around her body and her words come out between chatters. "We still do, but I wonder why we bother. You'll break Mom and Dad's hearts if you never pass their name and blood on. Are you really willing to abandon your family for that man?"

She stomps off before I can answer. Hiding so much of myself from my family, in retrospect, that totally counts as shutting them out. There was only so much of my life I could share with them. Once the water began falling I couldn't even lie to them. But I hid because I wanted to keep them, not abandon them.

Dinner is going well, too well. My sister is a gracious hostess, too gra-cious to complain when Gus and I sit next to each other. Instead, her eyes question my every action. Why is my right hand below the table? Why am I spooning tofu onto Gus's plate? What am I saying when I whisper into his ear?

Gus eats as if he has pig's ear and cow's tripe every Christmas. When we get home, the next time it's my turn to cook, he's getting pig's blood soup for dinner. I've wasted years afraid he'd hate my favorite foods.

My nieces love him. They stop dueling each other with chopsticks when he asks them to. To half the adults at the table, he may as well be speaking classical Greek, but they laugh at his jokes and listen with rapt attention as he talks about the time it thunderstormed as he and his brother were climbing the steep eastern face of Mount Whitney. My mom resuscitates stories of her childhood in 台南. Even my sister is sick of those stories. Gus, however, asks about raising chickens and about the grandmother I barely remember. Okay, I'm translating like mad, but the point is they enjoy Gus's company and Gus enjoys theirs. In the rapid-fire exchange of words, my parents surprise me by asking about my research in biotech. I almost forget the impending doom hanging over me like an uttered paradox.

"你已經三十多歲了," my sister's father-in-law says as I'm clearing the table after dinner. "你甚麼時候會給你的父母生孫子?"

No family meal is complete without the marriage question. Actually, it's always some variant of "You're over thirty. Where's the grandson?" Marriage is just the necessary precondition.

I think I'm smiling blandly, but Gus's eyes reach mine and I realize he sees the marriage question on my face. It's hard to believe the man doesn't read minds. My sister's glare is this pressure that squeezes my chest.

Telling everyone I haven't met the right woman might humidify air, but it won't cause the water to fall. It's true so I won't even feel any angst. Gus will understand and, for once, my sister will be happy with me. She and I can't be in the same room for ten minutes but we've always wanted the best for each other. But she doesn't need to tell me what that is anymore.

"我找到了我的對象. Gus." I've come this far; I might as well go all the way. "他上月向我求婚."

Providing a grandson can't be that important in the grand scheme of things. Kevin's parents still love him. Maybe mine will still love me. And they seem to like Gus as my friend. Now that they know he's proposed, maybe they'll also love him as their son-in-law.

My sister's fury explodes and overwhelms every other reaction in the room. Her words are clearly in English, but the only ones that make any sense are "Get out, and don't ever come back." Kevin's trying to calm her down. Gus weaves around the family toward me. However, I'm upstairs in the bedroom before I realize I've moved.

Gus is extremely tidy. It's easy to repack his luggage. I never unpacked so I don't have to repack. He's such a generous soul. For all I know, he may still think we're not leaving. I shouldn't have left him downstairs. Maybe the nieces can translate for him.

"Matt, you're leaving out of spite." The doorjamb neatly frames Gus. "Okay, your sister had a bad reaction, but poe poe and gohng gohng don't seem to be taking it badly."

I blink and shake my head. It takes me a few seconds to realize that he's talking about my parents.

"Did you just call my parents 婆婆 and 公公?"

"Yeah, poe poe and gohng gohng." He looks confused. "I tried to call them Mr. and Mrs. Ho this afternoon, but they both corrected me before I got past hello. Am I pronouncing it wrong?"

"We can work on that, but that's not my point." I shut his suitcase. "'婆婆' means husband's mother and '公公' means husband's father."

That he can call them that without water falling on him…

"They'd already figured us out." Gus steps into the room to make space for Mom, trying to burrow past him. "Hi, poe poe."

"Lonely boy." My mom looks at Gus, but points at me. "He always lonely boy."

I really wish she'd just let me translate for her. In Chinese, she's effortlessly witty and erudite. That's the person I want Gus to know, not the inchoate stranger I knew until I'd spent a decade trying to get my Chinese up to snuff.

Gus takes her hands and doesn't speak too loud or down to her. Metaphorically, that is. Literally, he's about a foot taller than Mom.

"Not if I can help it, poo-oh poo-oh." He's trying too hard to imitate the way I said it and now he's over-pronouncing. "I'll make sure he's never lonely again."

Mom turns to me. At first, I think she wants a translation, but she must have understood because she doesn't give me a chance to speak. "你是研究生物科技的. 孫子能給我嗎? 有你們兩個的基因的?" Okay, this isn't an example of her being witty or erudite. My mom is also very practical and direct.

I hear my heart pound. Gus is looking at me for a translation. We don't have a relationship if I filter what he hears.

"She said: You're a biotech researcher. Can you give me a grandson? One with genes from both of you?" Gus must have really impressed her. "What were you two talking about this afternoon?"

"Not that." He looks as surprised as I feel. We've never discussed kids. He turns back to her. "We need to talk about it."

Chu

And I need to win a Nobel Prize if she's dead set on a grandson with both our genes. Parents.

The clincher is that she leaves, trusting Gus to talk me back from the edge. Normally, she tells me that once Michele calms down, she'll want me to stay. Michele's only angry at me because she loves me. But now, it's Gus's job to keep me civil. Mom's probably so happy about this, she doesn't care that Gus is a guy. Gus isn't any better at keeping me from the edge than Mom though.

The motel is a five-minute drive from my sister's house, but it feels like another planet. For one thing, we've gone from Victorian Christmas Land to Operating Surgery Land. It still smells like pine, but the flat, medicinal one. For another, when I drop my suitcase and curl into a ball on the bed, it's as if I've held one of Gus's bizarre isometric exercises for weeks and I've finally let go. Just like the end of any other trip home except this time I'm still tethered to the world. Gus stands at the door. Snowflakes glisten off his hair and hooded sweatshirt.

"They're your only blood relatives in the country." Gus flicks on the light and clicks the door shut. When I turn away, his weight dents the bed. My body falls toward his. "Matt, don't freeze me out too."

Gus's words pummel me no matter how softly he tosses them. My own words scrape my throat. I taste salt and metal when I swallow. Lying, then letting the water wash my throat and fill my lungs tempts me as much as pretending Gus isn't sitting on the bed. Every trip, I decide that I'll sort things out later. Then I go home and pretend the trip never happened. That won't work this time. Gus is, if nothing else, a witness and a reminder.

"Fine." I sit up and stare at the carpet. "Once, I gave Mom flowers for Mother's Day and Michele humiliated me because flowers wilt and how dare I send Mom something that would die. Michele accused me of ruining her birthday because one year I sent her a card with blue birds on it. Like I knew her parakeet had drowned itself in her toilet. One Christmas Eve, Michele asked me to shave for Christmas day. I didn't really have any stubble so I forgot. She couldn't understand why I would refuse to do something to make her happy, especially something so simple, so she ambushed me with a razor. I wish she had better aim. Shaving cream stings your eyes. For weeks people wondered why I had scars around my neck and on my face. Is that enough, or do you want more? Why should I have to keep putting up with her?"

I am so tired. My body won't stop shaking. Air won't stay in my lungs. Melted snow pools around my boots. I wish Gus weren't looming over me. I wish he were in his apartment, or visiting his own family.

Gus sits, mouth agape, for a moment, but if he expected water to fall on me, he's done a terrific job of not showing it. His arm straps across my shoulders and pulls me to him. He presses a finger under my chin and guides my head until I face him.

Part of me wants to bolt, get into the rental car and find somewhere else to stay for the night. The rest of me knows that'll hurt Gus and he'll be too much the hero to admit it. Like screwing up all of my relationships at the same time is a good idea.

"You shouldn't have to put up with her." Gus unzips my jacket, then peels it off me. "But are you going to write your parents off too? Say we have a kid, and I'm not saying we should or shouldn't, don't you want the kid to know their grandparents?"

"So I'm right and she wins anyway?"

I rub my face. Telling me I'm right is a change. Once, Mom told me everything Michele does to me, she does because she loves me and wants the best for me. Why couldn't she just hate me instead, I asked. That talk didn't go well.

"What you mean by winning?" Gus shrugs. He hangs my jacket on the coatrack next to the door. "You broke today. It happens. Maybe some time away from her is a good thing. Tomorrow, we'll go back and we'll try it again, okay? If you want, I'll stick to you the whole day."

I take a deep breath. It feels like the first time my lungs have expanded in hours. The pine and wet leather assault my nose. "Sure."

I take off my boots. Melted snow has soaked through to my socks. My feet are cold and clammy. Gus is still standing at the door.

"I'll be back in a few hours." Gus holds a hand up to interrupt me when I ask him to stay. "You don't want me around and frankly, right now, you're too wigged out to be good company. I know you're not angry at me, but it'll be better in the long run if I leave now while we're still on speaking terms."

I'd protest but that would just make his point. Gus turns out the lights before he leaves. The comforter is wet from melted snow. It sticks to my skin when I fall into bed. I curl up into a ball and roll the comforter over me. Buried, I finally start to relax.

This time, I have left the world but it still doesn't feel right. The mattress ought to be sunk deeper. My arms should be around the hulk of a man who can't ever admit hurt or pain. I should be immersed in the warmth of his body as he is in mine.

"I love you, Gus." Now, I just have to figure out how to say it while he's in the room.

Snow evaporates off the comforter. I'm warm and dry. I wriggle my head out. Flowers and ozone replace the smell of pine. A spring breeze grazes me. I stare at the door in the dark, wishing it would open.

The men slipped the claws of their bars under the lid. It creaked and began to lift. They twisted away and swore again. I smelled rot, sweet and sharp.

SEVEN LOVERS AND THE SEA
Damon Shaw

1. CHRYSOPHILE

Do not struggle. You will not break free. A sailor knows how to tie knots. And nobody can hear you so far from shore. Do not strain your voice.

You will need it.

We will be…companionable. We will talk like friends. I will tell you of my life. And you will tell me of yours. Afterwards, perhaps, I will let you live…

I was never a good man. The fracture in me, the weakness, was gold. I loved it, as all men love their addictions, deeply, faithfully, and utterly in secret.

The old man on Varna Quay promised me a coin, heavy and yellow and warm in my palm. Enough to take me back home to Saint Petersburg and to eat well for a year should I be foolish enough to squander it so. I should have known not to trust him, this nobleman in filthy clothes. As he took my arm, I felt a chill all the way to my neck. I tried to pull away, but he held me like iron, leading me to the boxes piled on the quay. With his walking cane he scratched an X on the side of a crate.

"This is the one," he said. "It must not be opened, not by crew nor customs. Do you understand?" He withdrew a purse. I caught the smell of him then, musty, like rotten wool, and had to fight to keep the distaste from my face.

The gold coin he offered winked with a promise of more to come. I gave him a nod and slipped it to lie heavy against my thigh. I did not think of warning the captain we carried some unknown contraband. No, I worried how to give baksheesh to the customs officer in Constantinople when all I had was my one, fat coin. I could not break it like a biscuit. "I need more money," I said. "For bribes."

The rich man grew without moving. Taller than the mainmast, he seemed. He turned on me and his eyes flashed a dark red, like old blood. I tensed to run, but his hand whipped forth and held my chin. He lifted my head until I could not but look at him.

"You have a strength in you," he said. "Open the crate after the last customs inspection and not before. You will find your reward."

I could not pull away. I nodded and felt his fingernails break the skin on my neck. A warm thread ran down inside my shirt. At this, he threw me back. I fell to the cobbles and banged my head.

White light flashed as my teeth closed, sharp on my tongue. When my sight cleared and pain permitted, I looked up. Amongst whirling stars, I saw my own blood glint on his fingertip. He put the finger in his mouth and he swelled up, like the wind in a mainsail. He tore into jagged, black pieces and disappeared.

My heart crashed in my ribs. An echoing spike of pain pierced my temple. I blinked and swore. The blow to my head must have brought on visions. I crawled to where he had stood. There, I found silver coins scattered on the cobbles, like stars.

I filled my pockets. With every chink of coin on coin, my courage returned. The man surely had slipped between the crates of cargo. The night was dark. He had thrown me down—here I burned with anger at his arrogance—and while I was stunned, he ran. The lid of the marked crate stood an inch loose on its nails. I slammed it shut with the heel of my palm, and turned to look up at the warehouses and the far-off lantern of a tavern. I saw no one.

Only a skin of mist over the empty quay and a rat that fled even as I gazed upon it.

No matter, I decided. I was young and rich and full of life, and tomorrow we sailed. Ahh, gold, how its steady light blinded me to the monster in full sight.

2. ANDROPHILE

You die and find yourself at a doorway. No angel awaits to judge you, only a mirror set above a door handle. Stare at your face. Judge yourself. Will you open the door to paradise and let yourself enter? Are you, in your own heart of hearts, good…or evil?

All ships have their goat. Their fool. The man you blame when a halyard is coiled the wrong way. The man upon whom you cannot bear to look after a month at sea, for his filth and inadequacy remind you of your own.

I saw at once the new man, Olgaren, would be our fool. He was inexperienced and clumsy, and worse, he smiled without cease. He got the worst work that day, under the hoist, to guide the crates into the hold. Obviously, I had to go too, to hide the box with the mark.

The crew laughed at me for volunteering. Petrofsky said I was after Olgaren's arse already. Almost we fought for my reputation, but the mate held both our arms.

"Got a month at sea, boys," he said. "Save your passion for the sails." He winked at me.

I would not back down until Petrofsky swore it was not true.

When he swore, we shook hands and I climbed down to the hold, content. I did not want Olgaren.

Or perhaps I did. I did not know. His aspect was not fair to me.

He was short, though well muscled, and very pale. He always wore that half smile. You will pardon my frankness, but the men I loved did not smile. They were dark, and taller than I, and I never knew their names.

Olgaren's hair shone white in the gloom of the hold. He had in his eyes the look of a dog you kick, to stop the guilt it makes you feel, but I could not cease to notice how his strength shifted under his clothes as he pulled the swinging boxes across the deck. We lowered them together and fell into step. Away from the crew, he relaxed. His smile faded.

He raised one eyebrow when I caught the marked crate and slid it to the back myself. I did not hide it completely. I had to be able to open it after customs in the Dardanelles. To divert his attention, I said, "Stand up for yourself early on. Petrofsky likes to play with weaklings."

Standing in the light from the hatch, awaiting the next crate, he said, so quietly I had to strain to hear, "*The greatest rebellion is absolute submission...*"

I did not understand his words, but I saw him in that moment.

He had circles under his eyes and bruises under his collar. I did not think he would last long at sea.

We loaded the cargo and did not speak further. The wooden crates chilled my fingers and made me clumsy. I was happy to climb up into the sunshine to find the *Demeter* tugging at her halter, eager to take to the sea. At noon the captain blew his whistle. We cast off, and let her have her rein.

3. PHOTOPHILE

We have taken your ship. I, Amramoff, am first mate now.

Olgaren here is captain. He renamed your ship the Pochemuchka - the Asker of Questions. He aims to judge every cabin boy and captain from here to the Americas. I believe, with a crew of those such as us, he can do it. You, too, could be a part of this scourge. You could be one of us. If you convince him of your worth...

For five days the wind was favourable. We saw only blue skies, while off to starboard, the Bulgarian, then the Turkish coast slipped in and out of view. The sails took up little of our time, so we trimmed and tarred and made the *Demeter* a thing of clean lines and sharp edges. This can bring joy to a crew. The first days of a voyage are always full of promise. But though the sun shone, a cold crept from belowdecks. Our bunks grew damp. Tinder would not kindle in the galley until we laid it on deck to dry. In the hold, our breath hung in plumes before our faces.

Olgaren had nightmares.

He woke us three times a night, but would not tell us what he dreamed. Two hours before dawn on the third night, he woke us again. Petrofsky boxed his ears until his head hit a beam and he dropped to the deck. When he hit the boards, I saw he smiled. I remembered his words. *Absolute submission....* His smile was his shield. Even unconscious, he did not let it drop.

Perhaps he was stronger than I thought.

On the fifth morning, we entered the Bosporus and soon came into the city of a thousand names; Stamboul, Constantinople, Konstantiniye, Islambol, Istanbul…. Her yellow-walled city and seven hills shaded upward into the dusty air, in a hazy stench of spices and cured fish. The crew was divided into two. The larboard watch—myself, Olgaren and Petrofsky—were assigned to stay aboard while the starboard took three hours ashore. This was fortunate for me, as I thus did not have to scheme to ensure I met the customs officers as they made their inspection. More fortunately still, the Turkish officer was lax. He did not open any of the crates in the hold and I did not have to hand over the silver coins from Varna Quay to distract him. When he had left the ship, we played at dice on deck, and though the captain returned and saw us, he let us play on. Olgaren lost his coin and stretched out, clearly loving the sunlight. I took two more silver pieces from Petrofsky and felt myself a rich man indeed.

That night I needed sleep early, as I had the three-bells watch, long before dawn. But I had hardly dozed when a cry woke me, so full of terror it had me on my feet before my eyes opened. Even in my anger, I feared for Olgaren's safety. I leaned and shook him awake, but the men had had enough. They wanted to tie him upright to the fo'c'sle steps. Petrofsky wound rope around his wrists, and throughout Olgaren blinked and smiled as though his dreams were full of light.

I could not see a man so treated like a dog. "He can sleep in the hold," I said, untying his wrists. "I'll ask the second mate. I'm relieving him on watch."

"We'll still hear him screaming," Petrofsky said.

"And so will the captain," I said. "So none of us need be seen to complain."

The men nodded. Petrofsky clapped me on the shoulder and grinned.

"I won't scream any more," said Olgaren. "Don't make me sleep in the hold. It is too dark."

"Come on." I took his arm as three bells sounded. "My watch. Sleep well, shipmates."

But Olgaren would not stay in the hold. He did not beg again, but would not sleep in the shadow of the crates. He followed me on deck with a face like an abandoned dog and I cursed his company. The second mate, too, swore on seeing him, and sent him to sleep in the galley, which, to my relief, he did with no complaint. Alone, I watched the shore until the moon disappeared. I heard only the creak of the masts, and the whine of mosquitoes. Something splashed in the water nearby. Once a seabird called, low and sweet.

Then Olgaren screamed. The sound echoed back from the whitewashed buildings on the shore, a wild howl that raised the hairs on my arms. The once warm breeze chilled my neck. I should have left him alone for the captain to hear, but the cries went on and on and I could not bear to hear such pain. I pushed open the galley door and ducked into the gloom.

Olgaren thrashed on the deck between two sacks of grain. I knelt and took his shoulders, at which his eyes flew open. He clutched at me with desperate fingers.

"Save me," he gasped. "Protect me from the dark."

I could not look away from the terror in his eyes. "I am here," I answered, without thinking. "I will protect you. Everything is well. I am here."

Awareness was long in returning to his gaze. "Amramoff," he said. His voice surprised us both. It left behind a silence, in which I became aware of his grip on my biceps, and the closeness of his mouth to mine. From the fo'c'sle, the bell sounded five. Below us, the water lurched in shadow. Olgaren's eyes were wide and silver-blue. They closed as our lips touched.

We only kissed that night. I stumbled back on deck, confused, and terrified I had been caught, but nothing stirred above. Only the night bird, half a mile away on shore, cut the silence before dawn with its hollow cry.

4. AUTOPHILE

Did you think your cargo human? Did you think of them at all, chained in the hold? Why are they here? What were their crimes? Olgaren and I will not judge them on the legality of their actions. No—many break laws to feed those they love.

Here, today, we try to find a deeper judgment, not of laws, but of worth…

The next morning, I woke full of fear this would mean too much to Olgaren. He would reveal our kiss to the crew by favouring me. But neither did he seek to catch my eye while breaking our fast nor when we reefed the main sails to steer a course through the Marmara Sea. The sun shone hot but the breeze was fresh. As we were making such slow speed, at noon the first mate let our watch fish overboard with lines and feathers.

Petrofsky and I caught several fat mackerel while Olgaren tangled his line and lost his hook overboard. Finally, we set him to gutting. Three worries beset me as the hours slid past. The first: How was I to ensure I was kept behind this afternoon so the customs in Çanakkale did not open the marked crate? The second: What did the kiss with Olgaren mean to him? It meant nothing to me, of course, but I feared he might desire some terrible, clinging romance.

My third worry overshadowed all: How in all the hells could Olgaren gut the fish without slicing such clumsy fingers on the sharp knife? I could not bear to watch and had to turn away.

I should have known he had no experience with fish. He cut them into chunks, leaving the scales on, then tried to clean the pieces one by one. The fish were only fit for soup or the gulls.

Petrofsky picked up a handful and threw them overboard.

"A morning's work wasted!" he shouted. "Why not ask if you knew not how?"

Olgaren blinked up at him, the knife loose in his palm. Fish scales glittered in his eyebrows. "I thought it would be easy," he answered.

"The fish are biting," I said. "We have time to catch more."

But Petrofsky had an audience, and the men were bored. "It is easy, if you do not slice them up first." He threw another handful of fish. It bounced off Olgaren's chest. "What will we eat tonight?"

"They would make a soup," I said. Why was I trying to protect the man? I wanted to hit him myself.

"Make him eat them," someone shouted from the rigging.

Petrofsky bared his teeth like a shark. He reached out a thumb, red with blood. "Clean it," he said.

Olgaren reached with his shirt, but Petrofsky waved it away.

"Lick it clean," he said.

A seagull cackled above us. Nobody looked up. Olgaren narrowed his eyes. His smile did not fade.

"As you will," he said. He opened his mouth.

I looked away as Petrofsky leaned forward. I heard the crew laughing.

"Now eat the fish," said Petrofsky.

"As you will," I heard Olgaren reply.

I turned back to see Petrofsky's hand now clean up to the palm.

Olgaren knelt before him. He smiled, raised a chunk of grey, translucent flesh to his lips and began to chew.

Petrofsky nodded. "Is it good?"

"No," said Olgaren. He coughed. I thought he might choke on a stray bone, but he forced a swallow. His smile returned.

Petrofsky grew annoyed. He grabbed for more fish and tried to stuff it down Olgaren's shirt, while the crew whooped and jeered.

Olgaren shook and flopped in Petrofsky's grasp, but did not retaliate or try to prevent it. When Petrofsky stepped back, flushed and breathing hard, Olgaren settled back onto his knees, the same ghost of a smile haunting his lips. The jeers of the crew faded. *The greatest rebellion is absolute submission.* Petrofsky swiped at the deck for the gutting knife and at that moment, I saw the captain emerge from the hold behind him. As Petrofsky rose, I threw myself upon him.

He yelled as my weight hit, and we fell. His head thumped off the deck and I saw his surprise turn instantly to rage. Luckily the knife had tumbled aside or he would have stabbed me, I am sure. Instead he twisted and threw me free. His fist flashed. My temple exploded with stars. I managed to land three punches of my own, before firm hands tore us apart.

"What, boys?" The captain spat on the boards between us. His eyes flashed. "Who began this?"

I shook off the hands that gripped me. "He had a knife," I said, staring at the deck.

"I was not going to cut him," Petrofsky said. "I was going to show Olgaren how to gut fish."

The captain frowned and looked to the men for more answers, but, of course, nobody had seen anything. We were punished by cancellation of shore leave for the larboard watch. Despite the blood trickling from my brow, satisfaction made it hard to hide my smile.

Petrofsky glowered at me. "Are you mad? You know I would not cut him."

I shrugged, touched my brow, and winced.

In the smaller port of Çanakkale, the starboard watch ran to change into shore clothes, while I pretended to sulk. At the dock, the captain went off first, followed by the laughing, shouting crew. Olgaren dreamed on deck, supposedly splicing line, while Petrofsky glowered at me as he mended sails.

"You will go down in the hold," he said. "Not I."

When I only nodded in response, he spat. Twenty minutes later, I heard the boots of the customs officer and his two men on the gangplank. I led them down to the hold, keeping my hand against my thigh to stop the clink of coins. The officer shrank from touching the handrail. I noted his polished leather boots, his perfectly creased uniform, his neat moustache and smooth skin, and I relaxed. A man who loves himself always needs extra coin. Our hold stank. Worse than other boats. We had all noticed the streaks of mould on the timbers that returned, hours after being scrubbed away. I hoped the officer would stay back when he turned pale behind his moustache and held a white cloth to his nose. But though his men cursed, he led them down the hold, pointing out crates. He opened one in five, keeping an eye on me as he chose. I tried to hide my tension when he neared the marked crate, but his eyes glittered in the gloom. He actually showed his teeth at me as he pointed at the box I was charged to hide. I stepped close and pushed past, leaving a pile of silver on a crate at his hip without the clink of coin on coin. When I turned back, the silver had gone and he watched me with a half-smile.

His men neared the crate and lifted their tools to slip the top. Still he did not stop them. I raised my eyebrows and shook my head only the smallest amount, but his mouth twisted into a sneer. Hearing the sound of metal on wood, I took out the rest of my silver, snapping it into a neat pile with my thumb. I laid it on a crate before him, and again looked away while the money disappeared.

The men slipped the claws of their bars under the lid. It creaked and began to lift. They twisted away and swore again. I smelled rot, sweet and sharp.

"Stop," the officer said his Russian was crisp. "This ship stinks too much to bear. Leave it." He turned and stumbled away.

For no reason I understood, dread, not relief, settled in my chest as they left the hold. I stood by the crate, wishing to run after them into the light. Something glinted in the blackness under the lid. My gold. Should I claim it now? I could leave the ship today, rich enough to buy a boat of my own. I reached into the chill of the crate, stretched my fingertips into the darkness—

"What game are you playing?"

I jumped back in shock. Petrofsky stepped from the shadows behind the stairs. "What's in the box?"

"Nothing. Customs didn't close it behind them, is all." I hammered the lid closed with the heel of my hand, and made to leave the hold.

Petrofsky gripped my arm as I tried to push past him into the light. "I saw you pay the Turk. Baksheesh, eh?"

I pulled free, but he followed me up on deck.

"Where'd you get the coin?"

I turned to face him, my heart knocking so loudly I feared he must hear it. "Captain's business. Speak to him."

Petrofsky grunted, but I kept my eyes cold and still. "When did the captain ever deal with you?" he said.

It was true. The captain never spoke to the men unless it was to punish. But for that reason I knew Petrofsky would not ask. I stared at him until he turned away. The first mate set us to store provisions in the galley. The ship seemed only half alive with her crew ashore. Petrofsky watched me under half-lowered lids, so I could not sneak back and claim my gold. Halfway up the mast, Olgaren lifted his blond head to the sun, his eyes closed. What dreams played out behind his eyelids? What terrors haunted his sleep at night? Why, if I was so rich, did I care?

5. HEMOPHILE

Listen to the cries! Your cargo freeing itself. Did you treat them well? There were two dead in your hold before you even left Albion's waters. No, no, of course that is not your fault.

The law is bound to hand them over to you in fit condition to voyage and if it fails in that respect, you are not to blame...

I could not return to the crate that day. Shore leave had not calmed the rest of the crew. They seemed nervous and constantly scanned the deck for some unnamed threat, leaving me no chance to slip away. Three days passed, and my imagination filled the crate with treasure, enough to buy a ship, a palace, an entire town. The urge to possess my gold grew with every strike of the bell until I could resist no longer.

That night, with the wind dropped, we anchored in the Grecian Archipelago. The crew slept. I had the midnight watch, and knew this to be my best opportunity. As soon as I was alone, I pushed open the galley door. Olgaren slept, his neck bare in a splash of light from the porthole. I sought not to think about kissing him, failed, and whistled him awake.

"Take my watch for ten minutes," I said.

Olgaren stood, blinking. I felt a wave of heat from his body and smelled the sleepy, dark scent of him as he pushed past me into the open air. He looked out over the rail. A wide, bright moon cast cloud shadows on the sea. Dark slivers of land to larboard. A low easterly offered no challenge to a novice watchman.

"Only ten minutes," I said. The faintest scent of rot wafted up from the nearby entrance to the cargo hold.

Olgaren inhaled. He shivered. The moon reflected in his eyes.

"Do not go down there," he said.

"I was not—" I began.

"*Please.* A beast waits below. I dream of him."

I scoffed, but Olgaren did not look away. "How will you protect me if you are his?" he said.

I shook my head. "Protect you?"

"As you did with Petrofsky and the knife." His hand strayed to my sleeve. A moment.

"Take the watch," I said, a sudden anger making me brusque.

"As you will," he replied. "I will not beg you."

I turned away. "Whistle if you hear anyone."

"As you will."

I spat over the rail but the sour taste did not leave my mouth.

Then the clean desire for gold overwhelmed the fog of anger and confusion. I took the steps down into the hold with relief, despite the stench.

I had half a tallow candle in my pocket, but now that the gloom surrounded me I did not dare light it, as only thin planks separated the far end of the hold from the crew's quarters, and I fancied I could hear the murmuring of conversation from where I stood. The hold darkened as a cloud covered the moon. The hairs rose on my arms. I fought not to shiver.

I remembered Olgaren's words: *A beast waits below.* He was a superstitious fool, but even so fear feathered the back of my neck.

I moved silently, despite my thundering heart, counting crates until I reached the box that held my gold. It was damp and chill beneath my fingers. Should I risk my flint to check the marking?

I did not dare. Instead I waited until the moon returned and the hold brightened about me. This was the correct crate.

I felt some of my fear fade. It was a work of moments to find the loosened board and force it upwards again. The sweet, high scent of rot surrounded me and my gorge rose. What could this crate contain? Almost I turned away, but the thought of my gold held me still. A faint red glow brightened in the darkness of the crate, as of a pipe's ember seen far away. My heart lurched. Rubies? Treasure to be sure. I leaned forward. Another light kindled beside the first. They brightened.

Eyes, I thought. Eyes! Before I could fall away in terror, a hand burst from the crate and gripped my throat. Stinking soil filled my mouth and eyes but I could not choke. I clawed at the arm that held me. Knotted muscles flexed, taut as iron, under filthy, black cloth. As I fought to breathe, the moon slid behind a cloud.

The hold went black. Boards creaked, then lifted free, and a cold air licked my face. The eyes approached. They did not blink. Fire boiled through cracks in the iris, tinting the entire eye crimson, lit from within.

A deeper darkness sparkled black in my vision as I began to lose consciousness. Then the moonlight returned. If I had the breath to scream, I would have split the main mast with my terror. The old man from Varna Quay grinned at me and his mouth was laced with fangs. Flesh hung loose on his bones. He looked older, dead already, but a mad vitality burned in those red eyes.

"Good prey," he said in a voice dry as a broken board. "You came." He loosed his hand from my throat.

I took a roaring breath to scream for help. The old man, the monster, lunged at me, his mouth wide, and his teeth pierced my neck in a spike of pain. And then…

…everything changed.

When a man is taken by another, the pain of the assault turns to richest pleasure in an instant. My fear turned to shocked excitement, my agony to a sensual burn. My limbs weakened further. I would have fallen but for the kiss at my neck that pinned me upright. Waves of gooseflesh rippled across the small of my back, up my thighs, down my arms. The monster called my blood to him like a lover and I felt it flow from me, felt his body swell against mine. When he drew back, his teeth scraped against some tendon deep in my throat. The pain brought clarity and I saw him anew.

Years had fallen from his form; he looked younger than when he had stood on Varna Quay. Tall and dark, with high cheekbones and full lips. "Sweet," he said. He frowned. "You do not struggle. Do you…want this?"

At the distaste I read on his face, any last remnant of fear turned to anger. "No." My voice, though, wavered and I struggled still to breathe. "I want my gold."

He hissed, and I thought he would kill me until I realised he was laughing.

"Ahh, single-minded men." He pulled me close. "Not a one will survive this voyage. You will not disembark alive. But…" He licked his lips. "You may do so…*vampir*."

I gulped. The word had no meaning to me, and, in my confusion, only the steady glint of gold stayed true. "And rich."

"Gold will not interest you after you drink of my blood," he said. "You will have other wants."

I wanted both to run for help and to have him bite me again. But under both those desires, that from a younger age burned brightest. I wanted that soft, heavy metal in my palm. I lifted my open hand.

He let me go. I slumped against the crate in which he stood.

Now was my chance to flee, but my legs trembled just to hold me upright. Reaching into the soil at his waist, he lifted out not gold, but a double handful of dark loam.

"Take this," he said. "Leave a trail from here to the deck and thence to the captain's cabin."

Filled with disappointment, I frowned. "Why?"

He hissed. "I should kill you now."

I folded my arms and did not take the soil. I do not think I was truly sane.

The monster sighed, though he seemed amused. "A ship is of the sea," he said. "I am of the land."

I shook my head.

"I cannot walk the naked boards. A ship is of the sea," he repeated. "I need land beneath my feet. My native land, where my body lay…in death."

In the silence, a voice in my head screamed at me to run, but his eyes held me fixed. "Spread the soil. Free me to walk the ship and I will give you what you desire. Take it." The last of the humour left his voice and I trembled to obey.

I took the soil. Our hands did not touch.

"You will keep my presence a secret." His eyes glowed brighter. "Send a man down to me unknowing, tomorrow night, and I shall be pleased."

I lifted my chin. "I…will try."

"Good." He turned from me and sank back down into the blackness of the crate, leaving me gasping and alone.

I pressed the planks of the lid down flat and took my handful of soil, leaving a thin trail along the hold and up the side of the steps to the deck as the monster had instructed. The cool, sweet, night air shocked me into one last moment of clarity. Olgaren stood at the wheel. I held the soil in my cupped hands, and could not look away from him. He shook his head. I saw sorrow in his eyes.

More, I saw myself. Self-disgust rippled in my gut. I had brought the monster aboard. I was his slave.

I staggered to the rail. Perhaps I would have thrown myself over, but I slipped and the soil fell from my hands and pattered into the sea. I wiped my hands on my trousers. I feared they would never feel clean again.

"Amramoff, are you—"

I turned to Olgaren and fell into his arms. I trembled like a child. He held me until I calmed.

"Shh," he whispered. "All will be well."

But how could it? I already burned to return and collect more soil to finish my task. Worse, tomorrow night I had to send a man down to the hold. With the calm in Olgaren's arms rose a stupor, filling my mind like fog. I cannot remember waking the next man on watch, nor returning to my bunk….

6. ANTHROPOPHILE

You left Portsmouth, what? Four days ago. Already prisoners have fresh whip cuts. Already I smell them on your loins. You have used them, more than one, and more than once. I fear you are losing my good opinion. Pray that your story redeems you…

SEVEN LOVERS AND THE SEA

And now I lose the straight line through my tale. I remember little and only in brief snatches. The monster's kiss had loosened my mind. I spoke and worked as hard as the next man, but was asleep. Only near Olgaren did voices rise to shriek warnings within me, so I avoided him as we threaded the Hellenic Isles and made our way westward…

Midnight. Rain patters on deck, though the wind is light. I shake drops from my hair and make my way to where Petrofsky shelters at the prow under a stretch of sailcloth.

"Nothing to report?" I ask.

"All well." He turns to leave for his bunk.

"Wait." Under the lantern's glow, I show him the warm glint of my golden coin. "There's more. Down below. Enough to share."

His eyes gleam.

Dawn. The *Demeter* rings to the sound of booted feet and calls of alarm, but Petrofsky cannot be found. Olgaren grips my arm, so tight he leaves bruises, but I will not meet his eye. I shake him free and my terrors subside until he requests to speak to the captain….

Dawn again. The sea is rising. Slabs of turquoise water shatter across our bows. We search the ship again, this time for stowaways. In the hold, I see black soil rubbed between the planks. I do not think I did it myself. The ship is declared clean and something inside me breaks. I laugh and laugh and cannot stop.

Noon. Dark as night. A storm has blossomed above the *Demeter*. The ship lists hard to starboard. The captain screams orders while ropes crack and waves sweep the deck. I climb rigging and untie knots and tie them anew and sleep and climb again for an eternity. Lightning illuminates stark moments—

Flash! Black mud slicks the deck. Ropes and rungs are caked and treacherous. The first mate is screaming, but I cannot hear his words. More men have disappeared. It was not me. It was not me—

Flash! From the top of the main mast, I see sunlight on the horizon. A strip of blue sky and calm sea. Thunder shakes the mast and I reef the topsail. When I look up, the strip of blue is there, unchanging, five miles ahead. Always five miles ahead.

The storm races with us. We cannot leave its shadow—

Flash! Teeth strike and sink deep. I moan in pleasure as the monster drinks of me. He croons and whispers.

Shaw

"I love you all," he says. "You are so sweet." But he does not give me of himself to drink. "Send them down to me first," he says.

I nod and forget to ask about my gold as he draws me close again—

More men have disappeared. I have not slept for three nights. I weep and shake as Olgaren pins me against the galley wall. He stands braced against the heaving deck. He has found his sea legs.

He is poised and intent and will not let me free.

"Wake up, Amramoff." He bites my ear. "Come back to me."

I shake my head and find his lips on mine. His stubble grates my cheek. Our tongues meet. Clarity slaps me like a wave and I cry out at what I have become. "The things I have done, Olgaren!"

"It was not your will," he says. "You are a good man." His mouth silences mine, but breaks away too soon. "I could not trust you otherwise. You will protect me." Spray plasters his hair to his head. His face shines blue-white in the lightning's stuttered flare. I see his exhaustion and his fear. I see his faith. It crushes me. Who am I to protect him? I cannot even care for myself. Worse, I am the cause of his suffering, and of this voyage into nightmare.

"Olgaren, I cannot—"

He turns within my grasp and pulls my arms closer around him. I feel the hot length of his body through his wet clothes. The back of his neck smells of nutmeg from the galley. I trap the scent against his skin with my lips, to save it from the lashing rain. I do not lower my arms as I feel him reach around and undo the buckle of my belt.

I take him there, in the heart of the storm, while the *Demeter* heaves under our feet. The men I like are taller than I, and dark.

They take their joy from me and I find my own. But here, against the galley wall, I find I am solid, older, a man of weight and purpose. A man I do not know. I am responsible for Olgaren's pleasure and for his pain. I will not take without giving. I will not hurt him or see him hurt. We move together while the wind shrieks about us, and though the watch might see, I do not care.

7. NYCTOPHILE

If you join us, you will open your eyes, and a liquid fire will burn in your veins. It will thread your flesh. Every nerve will sing, and as suddenly—quieten. In the silence you will hear, not your heart, never that, but the heartbeat

128

*of the sea. You will know her, will be of her, and her touch upon your skin
will tell you of faraway shores and deep currents. The blue depths will call as
much as hot, red blood. Poised between both, you will see the balance. The
fine line we walk....*

I had the wheel. This was rare, but the last steersman had disappeared
the day before. I had not sent him below. The monster was free. I had
not seen the captain in days. We no longer anchored at night, but fled
where the wind took us. I held us clear of the coast as the sun set, my
arms numb with exhaustion. Was that black shore Portugal, France, even
Belgium? I am ashamed to say I did not know.

Venus shone above the darkening horizon. North. We flew north. The
sea, still high, was slow in calming, though the storm had broken hours
before. Curls of spray swept the deck. From the wheel, I saw two sil-
houettes take shape at the prow. They leaned together, pulled apart and
closed again. Upwind, I could not hear their words.

I lost concentration on the sea and the *Demeter* struck a wave with a
shudder. The figures staggered. I saw them clearly then.

"No!"

The monster ignored my cry. In his grip, Olgaren struggled, then
slumped, perhaps unconscious. The beast lifted his limp form to its
mouth.

My heart thrashed in terror, but I could not move. The monster's
hold on me was as strong as ever. To disobey him was unthinkable. But
Olgaren needed me. I had promised to protect him. I could not stand by
and let him die. Other crewmen remained. Let the beast take them.

I almost left the wheel, but they were forty paces away, the beast
already drinking from Olgaren's neck. Instead, I heaved the wheel to
larboard, feeling the deck surge and lift as the prow swung out. Then
we slid from the crest and fell lengthways into the deep valley between
waves. A wall of water slammed the hull and broke in a sweep of rushing
foam across the deck. The two figures fell, and I lost them in the gloom.
Searching the racing shadows, I swung the wheel back as fast as I could
to help the *Demeter* lift her prow. Water streamed from the deck as she
heaved herself clear, and at last I saw him, wrapped around the mainmast,
unmoving. I strapped the wheel in place, ignoring the shouts from the
fo'c'sle, and ran.

Even after the storm, the deck was treacherous. Mud oozed from the joins between every plank. I skidded to a halt at Olgaren's body. He was cold and white, his eyes rolled back, his teeth chattering. Blood, his own or the beast's, smeared his jaw and darkened his lips. As I leant to touch the pulsing wound at his throat, a shadow slipped from the prow and slid along the deck towards us.

I stooped and swung Olgaren over my shoulder. He seemed light as a child. Where could I run? Where would be safe?

Upwards, I thought. At the top, there would be a stretch of rigging free of soil where the beast could not tread. I clutched Olgaren to me and began to climb the mainmast, lunging one-handed, upwards from rung to rung. I climbed until my limbs weakened, until I feared I must fall. When I looked down, the monster hung, scant feet below me. His eyes burned red.

"Drop him," he said. I heard him clearly, though the wind shrieked in the rigging all about. He grinned. "It is time for your reward."

I gripped Olgaren tighter and forced myself upwards, while the monster's voice followed me into the swinging, empty sky.

"You want me," he said. "I shall be your master. You will have no uncertainty, no doubt. Your station will be absolute. You need never struggle to define yourself again. Leave him. Come to me."

Behind his eyes, the red glow grew bright. It drew me downwards, more than the weight of Olgaren on my shoulder.

Even up this high, the ropes were black and slick. I pulled us upwards, dreading to feel the monster's jaw clamp on my heel.

The deck swung past under me as the *Demeter* heaved herself up onto the next wave. For one small moment, if we had fallen, we would have landed on the wet boards. Around that instant, the dark of the sea crashed in foam-streaked chaos.

I reached the boom. There was no higher to climb. I could edge out along the horizontal beam, but to what end? It, too, was smeared in mud. Olgaren twisted and slipped a hand's breadth from my shoulder. I tightened my grip and when I looked down, the monster was flying towards me, his arms outstretched, his hands crooked into claws.

My body seized. Every muscle locked. My heart clapped once, louder than lightning—and the beast struck. He caught the boom with one hand, causing the entire mast to shudder. The boom swung out and back, whipping the monster's cloak out behind him. He hung below, grinning at me, then in an impossible movement, pulled himself up one-handed, to stand on the narrow, wooden beam. He reached out a claw.

Olgaren screamed. He writhed and fell. I lunged for him. My shoulders almost tore from their sockets as I caught his shirt. The sea swept beneath me, then the brief flash of the deck, then the sea again.

"Drop him," the beast said. "In England, you shall be my hand and I your will." He stood, hardly swaying on the beam, so high above the deck. He was young and strong and dark, having drunk from many men. *He was taller than I, and I did not know his name.*

Yearning built in my chest to be free. To be free of choice, and of duty. This beast could wrap me in his cloak and I would not feel the cold. I would not feel anything at all. *Absolute submission....*

Olgaren moaned. My arms cramped with a distant pain. The beast waited, as again the deck swept beneath me. I would not feel.... *The greatest rebellion—*

No, I realised. There would be no rebellion under the beast.

Olgaren was mistaken. Absolute submission was the minimum the monster required.

I let go of the mast. For an instant, we hung, high above the waves. The smile whipped off the face of the beast. He fell away upward as the wind built to a roar about us, foam flashed, and we plunged into the black water.

The shock woke Olgaren, who kicked and struggled free of my arms almost immediately. A slap of salt water filled my mouth.

When I had finished choking, the *Demeter* was nothing more than a receding shadow against the silver-streaked horizon. High above the deck, two glowing red eyes faded with distance. Not once did the beast look away before the wind bore the *Demeter* out of sight, but with her passing a heaviness left me. My limbs grew bright with motion in the chill water. I scoured the surrounding waves. At last I spotted Olgaren clutching a length of dark wood, and swam his way.

More under the water than above, the sodden spar tipped as I grasped it. Olgaren gasped. His lips trembled. As I watched, his grip on the wood relaxed and he slipped under the surface. Once again I lunged and found his shirt. I pulled him against me and tried to hold his head above the waves. But the spar rolled, and Olgaren could not help, and my new-found strength ebbed fast.

The gold coin banged against my thigh with every stroke of my legs. Its weight seemed to pull me down. With numb fingers I held it above the water. My payment.

I threw it high and far and did not hear the splash.

All night I fought the sea. When at last dawn silvered the eastern horizon, I blinked myself from a dream, to find I had let Olgaren slip. He hung in my arms, below the surface of the water, his eyes closed, unbreathing.

I howled, pulled at him, tried to force the water from his lungs, but he had left me. I had refused the security of the beast. I had hefted responsibility onto my shoulders, only to fail before a single night had passed. I wept at Olgaren's cold features hanging in another realm, inches from my own, and at last, I resolved to join him. The sky lightened above me. I took my last look at Olgaren's face and found his eyes wide open, gazing at me from under the water. His grip in mine strengthened as he pulled himself from the sea. Water streamed down his skin. His eyes glowed, not red, but deepest green. He had drunk from the beast.

He smiled when he saw me, a feral stretching of his face that chilled me more than the freezing water. The emerald glow in his eyes shone bright. "Amramoff!" He reached a hand and cupped my cheek. Only then did he recognise his state. He turned his palm to his face and his smile faded. A wave slapped sea-water into his mouth. He let it drain, uncaring. "I submitted too far," he said. "I drank from him. Will I ever see the sun again?"

I could not but recoil, at which his eyes cleared and the glow faded. "I will not take you," he said. "I will not…do evil."

A wave lifted us. Over his shoulder I saw a strip of shoreline, black against the brightening horizon.

"Swim, Olgaren," I said. "Take me to shore."

In this state, he was stronger than I. His legs churned the sea into foam behind us. I slept, and woke to find him weeping. He had dragged me almost free of the tide, but now huddled behind, attempting to push me further up the shore.

"It hurts me, Amramoff," he said when he saw me awake. "I cannot leave the sea."

I grasped his hand and fought to pull him further, but he writhed in my grip. His hand darkened and shrivelled in mine. He howled. I had no choice but to let him go and watch as he pulled himself back into the surging waves. Separated by only ten paces, we watched each other.

"What am I?" he asked.

At that moment, the sun lifted a golden edge above the horizon. Before I could answer him, Olgaren sank beneath the water. He floated under the surface, his arms crossed over his chest. I could only find one answer to give his unbreathing form. *You are dead, Olgaren. You are of the night. And of the sea.*

I pulled him to a tidal pool. Once assured the receding sea would neither sweep him away nor leave him high and dry, I dragged myself up the beach and collapsed. My last thought was this: of course he could never leave the sea. Just as the monster aboard the *Demeter* needed its own unholy soil under its feet, Olgaren needed the water that had witnessed the passing of his life. The open sea was his grave and tomb, his consecrated realm…

The sun warmed my bones. I awoke with fine sand pressed against my cheek, to find the day passed, the sun not far above the horizon. A desperate thirst dried my mouth and cracked my lips. I must drink soon, or die. I stood and stretched my limbs.

The tide had returned. Olgaren floated near the shore. I had sworn to protect him. How could I do so now? Did my word still hold? Should I aid him in finding blood? The thought repelled me, all the more for having sent Petrofsky down to the beast myself. As the sun lowered and reddened, and seagulls arced overhead, I fought my conscience. I should leave him, and head inland in the hope of finding water. But if I broke my promise to protect Olgaren, who would I be? What was left of my soul? On that nameless beach of white sand and black rocks, I struggled until my mind at last fell silent. Beneath it I heard the steady voice of my heart.

Stay, it said. *He smells of nutmeg….*

I had no plan in mind when the sun slipped away and Olgaren awoke. His face had thinned and he hissed at me, waist deep in the water, before consciousness blinked back behind his slitted eyelids.

"You did not leave me." A wave broke across his back, but he did not fall. "I am hungry, Amramoff."

I nodded.

"I do not know how to be this thing."

I could think of no answer to the anguish in his voice. "I must find water," I said. "Let us walk."

Olgaren drifted beside me as I stumbled along the shore. The reflection of his eyes glinted green in the rock pools. No streams broke the shoreline. No lights twinkled inland. When we rounded a headland and I saw a five-mile stretch of white sand in the moonlight, I fell to my knees.

"I can go no further." My voice caught and cracked.

"I shall go ahead—"

"No, Olgaren." I swallowed, but my throat was made of sand.

"How will you bring me water? You cannot leave the sea. I am done. You must drink of me, now."

"No! I would never—"

"I have failed," I said. I felt the weight of it in my bones. "I could not save you. Drink of me and you may survive."

"This is not survival," he cried. "This is not life!"

I crawled towards the waves. Closer, I saw the hollows under his cheekbones, the skin drawn tight over the tendons in his neck.

I rolled into the sea, gasping as the chill water soaked my clothes yet again. Olgaren stepped deeper, shaking his head. I fought to keep my chin above the water against the pull of my clothes, spending the last of my strength to reach him. I gripped his cold hands and tipped my head to one side. "Drink."

He lunged in a blur of movement. His hand suddenly gripped my throat. He pulled me close. "There is enough evil in this world," he said. "I will not add more."

And in that instant, I knew what we had to do. "Olgaren."

"Do not ask me again." He dropped his grip and turned to swim away but I grasped his arm.

"Olgaren, I know how we can survive. I see how to make peace with what we are." I took his face in my hands while he kept us both afloat. A wild laughter bubbled in my throat. "It only requires that I die. By your kiss."

He shook his head, but I pulled him closer. "Shh. I am ready. This life is over. Listen, let me explain...."

Silence fell after I had spoken. Olgaren's eyes widened.

Emerald light boiled from his pupils. He licked his lips over teeth that lengthened as I watched. He pulled me closer, and his lips brushed my own, then swept past. Twin spears of pain sank into my neck. His legs twined about my thighs and we sank below the waves. A burning heat grew in my throat. I felt his tongue probing the skin. He drank from me. Waves of hot and chill pleasure rippled from his bite along every nerve in my body. My head grew light. I opened my mouth to tell him to stop, and salt water poured down my throat. I struggled then, and tore his teeth from my neck in frenzy.

Strong arms pulled me to the surface. They held me until I ceased to cough and turned me to face an Olgaren renewed. Red flushed his cheeks. His lips were full and dark. He had stolen my strength and I could not break his skin when he held me to his neck.

"Here," he said, and sliced himself with a fingernail grown long and sharp.

His blood tasted of salt, of fire, of whiskey and moonlight. It left me thrilled and sensual in the embrace of the waves. But I did not change. First, I had to die.

"Now," I whispered. "You know what you have to do. Do not tarry."

He pulled me close, while dark tears fell from his eyes. Our lips touched and again we sank beneath the water. I would like to say I did not struggle, but mortal life is determined and will not give up easily. I fought him while my weakened lungs ached for air and my thinned blood thundered in my temples. He did not let me free but watched with infinite sadness in his eyes as the last of my life fled. My vision darkened. I was for one moment a child, warm, wrapped in my mother's arms, then something left me with a snap—and all fear ceased. I opened my mouth and let the sea enter freely. It washed through me, chill and clear. I opened my eyes. I was reborn.

8. THE SEA

The shadowed water glowed blue and full of promise. Something slid over my naked eyes, and the seabed came into clear focus.

Moonlight-dappled kelp shone a rich purple. Fish glittered like gems. I pulled the blood-dark sea into my lungs and felt myself part of her. Whale song shook my bones. Icebergs calved in echoing rolls of thunder, half a world away. I heard children scream with laughter, heard men drowning, felt entire villages afloat on rafts of flowers. The vast sea contained all, and I loved her and all her loves.

I grinned and felt my teeth grow sharp behind my lips. My muscles burned. My heart had stopped but I had never felt so alive. I turned slowly. Olgaren hung before me. His eyes glowed with worry, with fear, with love. We kissed. His cool lips sent shudders of ecstasy down my spine. His yellow hair lifted about our kiss in a halo, and the halo was gold.

We sought the currents of the sea and sang to them and they took us to the wallowing belly of a ship, bound for Australia. Her hold ached with the moans of chained convicts. I feared we could not mount aboard, but a ship is of the sea, not of the land, and our feet stood firm upon her deck. Surely within this boat, of all vessels on the sea, would rest someone evil enough for us to kill?

We have not killed yet.

We are both hollow with hunger.

And this brings me to you. I have told how I came to be here. You know I am not a good man. Now it is your time to speak. Three fates await you. You may convince us of your worth, and we may set you ashore, free to begin your life anew. We may judge you not worth the soul that animates you, and we shall drink your blood to the death. Or perhaps we shall see a kindred spirit in you. Perhaps we shall offer you our blood in return and allow you to join our crew. The result will be a world slightly better than before. We will not be a force for evil.

I am filled with anticipation. Any one of the three endings will satisfy me. Olgaren will decide which is yours. Watch his face as you tell your story. If he smiles, even once, we will take you. I need not say how much I hope to see his smile again.

Be sure to tell the truth. We can smell a lie.

You may begin....

Estelle mentions that I gift-wrapped a scalpel for my lover.

IN THE BROKENNESS
OF SUMMERTIME

R.W. Clinger

The self-induced cuts—narrow, razor-sharp lines that proved infidelity, red-purple zigzags against his wrinkled and scarred wrists—would heal Cannon; that is what he often told me. Cutting was significant in his life, a means of his survival, and cutting produced by a tilted marriage was natural medicine, a means of Cannon learning to forgive himself for betraying our Valentine love/lust—something.

The bandages were a logic he used to prevent his insanity. Delicate wrist-armor that he sported almost all the time, never irregularly, keeping the visual atrocity of his sexual desire for another man concealed. And then he covered the bandages with fanciful, almost queer, accessories—a navy-blue scarf, a leather band purchased near the Vista del Rio in Barcelona, a red-white-and-blue bandana—which maybe caused him to believe they had healing powers for both of our hearts, but mostly his.

When his wounds—valley-like gashes at the bottom of both thumbs—were exposed, we were exposed. The lacerations were in view for all to see. Self-incisions because of man-with-man tenderness exposed. Raw tissue of our life together (seventeen years of marriage in Apartment J-1 on Padilla Street, next to the Allegheny River in Pittsburgh) unveiled, the bruised flesh of hardship and indecipherable pain between two men in love. Brokenness was discovered. Those cuts dissected our single unit into two cells: one of faithfulness and the other of radical sin.

Clinger

Cannon bled.

I was delighted to watch him bleed.

Shrink Time.

Estelle listens. It's her job to listen to me once a week, sometimes even twice a week. $150.00 a session. Says that I love Cannon with all my heart. Says we balance each other out. Says it's refreshing for me to call the man a jagged little fuck. Because I hurt. Because Armageddon swooped me up in its hulking arms and gave me a bad ass squeeze. Because Cannon Marshall Dixon could not keep his seven-inch crank inside his running shorts.

And I say to Estelle that it will never be the same between us. Things will always be and feel different. Our gay marriage/companionship/faggot union, or whatever Uncle Sam wants to label it, or not label it, no matter what, the ideal will always be sour. A skim of poison will reside on its surface for years to come, decades.

Estelle says to take a breath. Calm down. I can overcome this challenge.

I reply with something like: Some days I want his cock to fall off. Does that make any sense to you? Is that in your psychology textbooks? Will it ever make any sense to me?

Estelle hits me with a bomb. Psychiatrists can be filthy terrorists in their own little sick ways; any sane patient knows this. She tells me to say his name three times. Do it. Say it three times.

I do. Very fast.

Kyle. Kyle. Kyle.

And I begin to feel better, exposing more of my woe-me pain.

"I should leave, Cannon. You can have the apartment for yourself."

"Where will you go?"

"My brother's. He has an attic room I can use."

"You need to stay here and we can work this out," Cannon said.

"I'm not sure if I can do that yet. Maybe I need some time alone. I have to heal."

"We can heal together, under the same roof."

"It doesn't work that way. I wished it could, but it won't. We can't even think that will begin to justify my sanity."

In the Brokenness of Summertime

It happened last summer—what an absurd cliché. The truth, though. The denial of it all. The acceptance on my part that may never happen at all. July. So hot and humid.

Sticky in Pittsburgh, even the bridges were sweating. When pretty boys like Kyle/Kyle/Kyle took off their shirts and exposed their strawberry-colored nipples and blond treasure trails, among other sinful body parts that men in their late forties became quite fond of. Married queer men who desired nothing less than to extend their slippery-naughty tongues and taste those pretty boys. And taste the sweet and refined blend of Kyle Kansas sugar: a steel-plated chest, beam-like shoulders, and comma-shaped navel. Both those men and boys shared grins-a-plenty, but for all the wrong reasons. Relentless sin in the city.

It happened along one of the city's rivers. In the brokenness of summertime, all the rivers looked the same, even to the urbanites. The two men were running together, staying fit.

I didn't know they were horny for each other. Who would have known in my position? I didn't reek of jealousy. But maybe I should have reeked.

They took a sabbatical from their run. And then they crept into the bushes and found themselves against a birch tree, among the honeysuckle and next to a holly bush. A *quickie* was shared, because that's what Cannon labeled the sexual event with Kyle/Kyle/Kyle. They were men who were unseen and unheard in Estarre Park, and communicated by tongue and touch, among other tools.

The details were explicit, which I cared not to know. XXX stuff that I couldn't deem audible. Two bodies meshed together in the steeping-heat of a July evening. Exercising while exercising.

I shouldn't have been writing, creating, toying with words, sentences, and paragraphs. I should have paid more attention to Cannon, and certainly to the other man. I could have become jealous. I shouldn't have trusted either of them. My clarity was smudged, something I will never forgive myself for. I was a fool being foolish, of course, and maybe part of me deserved that pain.

They broke apart, unhinged from each other's sexual skin. They went to Kyle's place to shower. They showered together, or I told myself that they did. Silence followed that period of space between men who have nothing to say to each other, and men who have too much to say to each other without saying anything at all. A sense of awkwardness was discovered between them. The park-party in their lives had come to an end. Slippage occurred.

Cannon came home; he didn't have to. He could have driven to his sister's in Fox Chapel. He could have spent the night at his uncle's Tudor in Brookline. He could have stayed at the Holiday Inn. But he came home. And he was quiet. Things could break inside the apartment and we were able to hear them break. A wedged soul within a man's torso began to creak. Something was wrong with Cannon. Something had happened. He couldn't hide from me. That wasn't possible.

Then he started to cut himself.

Shrink Time.

Estelle asks if I purchase items so Cannon can hurt himself with.

Yes. I won't lie. There's no reason to lie. I've bought a number of tools for his labor of love: Ginsu knives, an ice pick, a few different types of saws, and pocket knives. I am perfectly fine with the man's indulgence and longing that he has to mangle his own skin. It's the little price he has to pay for screwing a guy behind my back.

Estelle mentions that I gift-wrapped a scalpel for my lover.

I don't deny this. Why would I deny this? I tell her it was the perfect little pink present for him. I even added a bow and streamers to it. It was lovely and proved my pain regarding his sexual park-affair. I say to Estelle that I cannot hurt him. This is something he has to accomplish on his own. She gives me a look that says this is fucked up, a tragedy in the making. If I wasn't paying her she would probably think I was to blame for Cannon's affair.

She's silent for a few seconds, perhaps hashes out my situation between her temples and calls my action a projection.

I tell her to explain it to me in layman terms. She defines the condition as Jungian psychology.

She directly stares at me and says that I'm blaming others for my own actions.

I tell her I wasn't the one sucking cock in a park with someone outside my marriage. She doesn't like my tone.

I don't give a fuck what she likes and tell her that she really isn't helping me. I still buy cutting devices for Cannon to use on his wrists. She hasn't convinced me otherwise.

IN THE BROKENNESS OF SUMMERTIME

Estelle takes notes, listening to me ramble a list of all the tools I have gifted to my husband since the event in Estarre Park. Estelle stops me. She instructs me to say Kyle/Kyle/Kyle.

I do, without emotion. And now I decide that I am not healed and maybe I don't need her at all. Survival of the fittest comes to mind. Can I pull this off by myself? Maybe I should give it a try.

"I can taste his cock in your mouth, Cannon. Do you know that?"

"You're being a drama queen. That's absurd."

"I really can. His urine and semen. His saliva and blood. It's all in there."

"You're crazy."

"Crazy in love," I said.

"Call it what you want."

"And to think I'm the demon here, Cannon. To think I was the one who fucked around behind your back. To think I put our relationship in a topsy-turvy spin. Really.... Really?"

Kyle was Cannon's student the semester before their shared intimacy. Cannon taught at Pitt: Romanticism, World Literature II, The Critical Approach, A Semester of J. C. Oates, Origins of the English Language. Kyle flirted with my partner. His glinting, hazel-blue eyes must have melted Cannon. The eyes are like that, aren't they? So convincing, spell-concocting, and spoiling. They met for coffee once or twice; a fine line between professor and student was crossed at the Brew Emporium on Beechwood Boulevard. Did the two men—one who looked like a daddy and one who looked like his son—touch fingertips together across a four-person table near the back of the coffee shop? Were winks shared? Did they use the restroom together, pissing side by side and checking out each other's junk?

Nothing ever stops when you want it to; life doesn't function this way. Cannon continued to "see" the student. One short date after the next transpired: evening runs, coffee breaks, and meetings at Turn the Page Books. I was sure they kissed during those brief encounters, mixing lips and mannish body parts. Their conversations were challenging and most interesting; boredom was undiscovered territory.

Their "seeing" progressed into the naked, summertime rendezvous in Estarre Park. Actions I could not fathom, secrets compiled by the two men, filthiness that caused my mind to go numb, semi-paralyzed, and vomit to rise in the narrow passageway of my throat. Their "seeing" was the victorious dilapidation of my heart.

The cutting started after Cannon confessed his infidelity.

I only hoped he would cut out his tongue, saving me from his blunt honesty.

Shrink Time.

Estelle reminds me that I hunted Kyle/Kyle/Kyle down like an animal, hungry to—she looks at her notes on her lap to quote me—eat the home wrecker up and spit him out. She tells me that I followed Kyle for a week and studied his sex-fun with my husband. She says, You wanted to hurt him.

No, I say, I wanted to kill him. A good choking needed to be accomplished, and I was the man to get the job done. He had death coming.

Estelle asks who?

And I scream the guy's name three times at the top of my lungs. After my outburst, she reminds me that I didn't kill Kyle. In fact, you didn't even put a finger on him. I say it was Cannon who prevented me from murdering the once-student. Cannon started cutting himself, which saved me from being incarcerated. What can I say? Cannon had all my attention. No, let me correct that. His cutting had all of my attention, which prompted me to buy things/tools/devices/gadgets/instruments that he could hurt himself with—items I wanted him to own and use on his flesh, mind you. Hell, if I knew he would have used a chainsaw on himself, I would have picked one up at Home Depot or Lowe's. Because deep down inside I wanted that jagged little fuck to cut all of his appendages off, one by one, starting with his dick, of course.

Estelle confirms that I left Kyle alone in hopes that Cannon would mutilate himself.

I reply that this is the truth, and the truth hurts, doesn't it?

Estelle doesn't argue with me, although I expect her to.

"You can't see him anymore," I said.

"I didn't say I would."

"You have to promise me to be faithful."

"You don't trust me."

"How can I trust you?" I asked. "You've broken me…us. I see a shrink because of you."

"You don't love me."

"I never said that. You're putting words in my mouth, Cannon."

"We can separate tonight. We'll sleep in different rooms. For once…it will feel right for you. Don't disagree with me, please."

Cannon ended the affair with the other man. I remember the date as if it happened yesterday: December 12, 2011. A date I would never forget, for as long as we were together. He told me to my face that it was over, that he had no interest in Kyle Kansas any longer. He said he loved me, and would always love me, through good and bad. At first, I didn't believe him. Lies upon lies had been built behind my back. Trust between us was untouchable. A fool would have believed him; I had outgrown that position with much skill and ardor. He said his relationship with his former student was severed, completely dissolved. Kyle's telephone number was removed from Cannon's cell phone. No longer was he a friend with Cannon on Facebook. They didn't tweet each other. Even his e-mail address was deleted from our shared computer and laptop. To think that a delete button could erase the young man from our lives. That happened, though. So easily. So quickly. And I was left bemused because of it.

Cannon was still cutting himself, though. Almost daily. I found the bloody tools in the bathroom. Droplets of rose-red blood on a pair of gardening shears. Droplets of crimson-colored blood on a paring knife. Droplets of deep red blood on a pair of vintage nail clippers. He simply left his tools of manipulation behind. Maybe for me to find on purpose. Maybe not. I don't think I'll ever learn the answer to that mystery.

The bandages and accessories still decorated his wrists. He seemed depressed, lost in a world of his own. He was quiet and reserved, which told me that: *Maybe he still loves Kyle. Maybe they are meant to be together. Maybe I'm in the way of things.* I didn't ignore him, although maybe I should have. Things need to be ignored sometimes. Maybe what he was going through was normal. Loss happened. Pain was discovered. I digested that without feeling, and watched him closely.

Clinger

Six months passed and he was still in a state of depression. He didn't see a therapist, although I had often wanted him to. Cannon kept teaching at Pitt, going to his classes, coming home, and simply dozed away his free time. The man became a vegetable on his own terms: self-blemished, expunged from life, and unremittingly hopeless. Of course I tried to cheer him up. In February, around Valentine's Day, we rented a cabin in the woods for three days; it was freezing and I kept him warm with my bare skin. In April, we drove to Baltimore for a weekend of fun in Little Italy with two other gay couples. In May, we enjoyed Gay Days in downtown Pittsburgh.

The next horrendous episode of our lives happened in June, didn't it, because it was summertime, and he wanted it to happen in June as a symbol of sorts, an underlying perception, encompassing the brokenness of our lives, a sweet summertime evening with purple-red clouds in the sky, a sticky wind, and hungry mosquitoes, the time of day when the city's buildings finally have a shape to them because the sun is perfectly positioned in the sky, hovering.

In June we drove to West Virginia, spent the day gambling, won over two thousand dollars on a quarter machine, and ate at the buffet. That atrocious incident happened almost two hours after we were nestled back home. Smoke-covered from my time in the casino, I showered. What was Cannon doing? I didn't know. He was probably dozing in the spare bedroom, checking his e-mail, or reading a mystery. Maybe I should have known his whereabouts, and then the incident wouldn't have happened. You leave your eyes off the prize for just a second and…it falls away. You lose it. One snap outside the walls of reality and it's fucking gone. Or almost gone. Trust me, I know.

Following my shower, having nothing more than a Martha Stewart towel wrapped around my middle, I looked for him in the apartment: the kitchen, the living room, our bedroom, the spare bedroom. He wasn't anywhere to be found. Did I start to panic? Did something settle underneath my skin that caused me to feel disturbed, lost, confused, and selfless for the first time in my life? Where did Cannon go? What was he up to? Why hadn't he told me he was leaving?

(Kyle/Kyle/Kyle)

The Commander was parked out front, sitting on the street—a mere thirty feet from the apartment building's front door. Maybe Cannon was doing something under its engine. Checking its oil. Writing down its mileage. Looking for its owner's manual. I wasn't sure but wanted to find out. I buzzed through the apartment and looked onto Padilla Street. The car was there, and so was Cannon, slumped over its steering wheel. His neck was arched forward and his forehead was pressed against the black wheel. I called out to him but he didn't answer. I called out a second time, but nothing happened.

The remaining moments of that endeavor were a blur for me for the longest time: slipping into a pair of Rufskin shorts; bolting down the stairs and over the front sidewalk; panting heavily; heart wildly beating within the fold of my chest; pain skiing from one temple to the other temple; yanking the Commander's driver door open; finding Cannon passed out inside the vehicle; the accessories missing from his wrists; both narrow wrists sliced open with the scalpel I gave him as a gift; blood pooling into the Commander's foot well; the scalpel sitting on the passenger seat; the bittersweet stench of thick blood coagulating; the sight of his pallid-white-almost-yellow skin and…

That was his gift to me, I knew. The honesty of his affair, the bridge that would heal our dilapidated relationship. The growth of our togetherness. Simple love found by the attempted act of scalpel-suicide. A magnum deed that would only bring the two of us closer together. He had finally pleased me. I was happy to see him that way. I was thrilled and in love with him again.

All was forgiven, honestly.

Shrink Time.

Estelle says Cannon wasn't dead, although he should have been. He didn't kill himself. You called 911 and the paramedics arrived in time.

I say I didn't plan it that way. He deserved to die. We pay for our sins, don't you think? She chooses not to answer me.

Pause. Quiet for the first time since we met. Insanity.

She finally says you saved Cannon's life. You could have left him die, but didn't. You know that. You will always know that. It was the power you had over him. The control. He could have died and you prevented that from happening. It was your means of survival, your devotion to heal because of his affair with Kyle.

I stop listening to her.

Clinger

She says my name.

I look at her.

Estelle says it's okay to admit that you love him. Your hardship is over. Both of you have survived this. Even the tools are gone. You gave them all away. Anything he could use to cut himself. Everything like that is gone. If you didn't love Cannon you would have kept them. You know this. You can't lie to yourself. This is reality. Kyle is gone. And she tells me to say this three times.

Kyle is gone/Kyle is gone/Kyle is gone.

And I feel better, alive, and a part of Cannon again.

"Are you asleep, Cannon?"

"I was."

"Do you want to sleep?"

"Not anymore. What did you have in mind?"

"Sex, of course," I said.

"The rough and tough stuff?"

"I think I'd like that."

"You're demented," he said.

"And you love that about me."

Even now, decades after the events, I cannot describe his actions without bringing myself to tears and raising aching memories across my skin.

LACUNA

Matthew Cheney

I heard this story from an acquaintance of mine a few years ago, and he claimed to have heard it from his grandfather, who heard it from the daughter of the man whose story it was. I have filled in gaps with my own best guesses for how certain events might have happened; as an amateur historian of 19th-century New York City, I was able to draw on a significant amount of information accumulated over a lifetime of study. Nonetheless, I am painfully aware of how unlikely it is that everything happened as I tell it here.

I tried many times to write this story in as straightforward and objective a manner as possible, but repeatedly failed. There are too many lacunae. Therefore, I am taking the liberty of writing this story from the point of view of the person who is its main character. I have never written fiction before—its conventions are anathema to me—but I hope readers will forgive any awkwardness, for I do believe this is the only way I could accurately preserve what is, I hope you'll agree, a most remarkable history.

A Tale of the City

Let me call myself, for the present, Adam Wilson. My true name is not well known outside certain circles, but within those circles it is known too well, and the knowledge associated with it is more hearsay and fantasy than truth. Perhaps after my death, the truth of my life can be aligned with the truth of my name, but I do not believe such an event is possible while I am alive.

As a young man, I was passionate and indiscreet. I had been raised on a farm in northern New York, and had no knowledge of the world until I had nearly reached the age of maturity. My parents were taciturn country people, God-fearing and serious, the descendants of Puritans who escaped England and helped found the colonies that became our Republic. Ours was a singularly unimaginative race of people, but stubborn and loyal. My childhood was not what I would dare deem a happy one, yet neither was it painful or oppressive; instead, it was a childhood of rules and routines, most of them determined by the sun and moon, the weather, and the little church at the center of the town three miles south of our farm, the church we traveled to for every Sabbath, holiday, festivity, and funeral.

As I advanced in years, I became aware of desires within myself to learn more about a world beyond the narrow realm of my upbringing. Ours was not a family given to frequent newspaper reading, but I had read enough to know that the life I lived was not the only possible life. I dreamed of cobblestone streets, tall buildings, and crowds of people. Now I know mine was a common dream, but when I was the dreamer, I thought my dream must be unique in the force of its import and portent. My fate was, I was certain, a great one.

With only the hope of my naïve yearnings to sustain me, I borrowed a few dollars from my parents and rode in the carts of merchants taking their wares toward Manhattan. I don't remember how many days it took to wind a serpentine way to the isle of my dreams. My memory of that time is obscured by all that befell me, for within a day of arriving I had been most violently shown the enormity of the chasm between my imagined city and the one to which I had brought myself. Desperate and hungry, I found what work I could, but I knew no-one and could rely on only the barest charity. Huddled by night in shadowy corners, trembling from cold and starvation and fear, I gave thought to returning home, of settling down to the simple life that seemed to have been predestined for me, but the very idea filled me with a nausea of defeat, for I would have rather thrown myself into the river's muddy torrent than retrace my journey. An evil luck brought me into acquaintance with a certain group of young men who showed me a way to profit from certain men's dark desires, and soon I did not have to hide myself on the streets, for I could afford a small room in a ramshackle building among the most disreputable of the city's inhabitants. It was here I lived and here I sold the only good that I possessed: myself.

After I had worked for a time in this most shameful of all employments, one of the men I provided services to asked me if I would like an opportunity to work in pleasanter surroundings, for a better class of customers and certainly more income than I might otherwise make in my debased and impoverished conditions. I was wary at first, having, after bitter experience, become something of a cynic, but this was a man who had been particularly kind to me, his tendency always toward gentleness, and I knew from his attire and mode of traveling that he was a man of means. Habit kept me obmutescent at first, but he persisted every time he saw me in saying how suited I was to the work, given my fair and feminine features, and I believed he was sincere when he said it pained him to see me in such low circumstances as then composed my life. Therefore, one Sunday morning late in the spring of 184—, after we dined together in my room, I accepted his offer and he provided me with an address at which I was to present myself two weeks hence.

During the time between that Sunday and the later night, I imagined countless and baroque possibilities for what this place might be. It was an address near Thompson Street, an area I knew well enough, though I did not frequent it, my haunts being more to the east, and in the fortnight between receiving the address and going to my appointment there, I carefully avoided the vicinity, for I have always been a superstitious man, and I feared some ill might punish my curiosity. The closer the moment came to present myself at the address, the longer the time stretched out and the more excited grew my imagination. I slept fitfully, my dreams alternately haunted by visions of great pleasure and nightmares of grotesque, delirious pain. Entire lifetimes seemed to pour themselves into the last hours before I set out from my gloomy little room.

Eventually, the waiting time dissipated and I found myself walking almost without awareness from street to street at dusk on the appointed day, the scrap of paper on which the address was written clasped in my hand, for though the address itself had long ago lodged in my memory, I conceived the paper on which it was scrawled to be a fetish, a charm against forces I could neither predict nor apprehend.

Cheney

I arrived at the address as twilight gathered darkly and more darkly through the city streets. Though I had prepared myself to expect nearly anything, I was not expecting the address to lead to a few small, crude steps descending to a weathered grey door. Not knowing what else to do, I knocked.

This is one of the things I most dislike about fiction: the need to set a scene. Certainly, when writing a historical narrative there is context that has to be established, but it's not the same—here what we have is brazen lying. I know nothing about what the exterior of this building looked like. I don't even know that it was on or near Thompson Street. It was somewhere on the island of Manhattan, I do know that, but to be more realistic, I probably should have put it at one of the more remote areas—maybe up north in the 12th ward somewhere. I chose the location I did because once you move too far out of the city as it was in the 1840s, you get away from the sorts of buildings that could house the events that are central to the story. Honestly, I expect it all actually happened in Brooklyn, but the person who told me the story specifically said it took place in Manhattan, and so I am sticking to that.

My mood is bleak today, and it's affecting my writing. Adam came over to pick up some of his stuff, and inevitably we had to have a Conversation (I yearn for the days when our conversations were lower-cased). It ended when he asked me how I was doing and I told him it was none of his fucking business. I regretted it immediately, but regret is a useless emotion. He walked out. Just walked. Didn't storm out, didn't slam the door, didn't break windows or anything like that. Walked out. Again. Without a word.

Words. That's part of my problem: I'm trying to capture at least some of the diction of this character, and spending hours with the OED, looking up the histories of one word after another to make sure it's historically accurate, or to find others that are more appropriate. It took me all afternoon to write one paragraph. It's stilting the voice. I can't go on like that. I just need to write and not worry about the historical veracity of the vocabulary and syntax.

I'll never forget Adam unless I write this. The nights when we drank cheap wine and played word games, the delirious night when we fell into each other's arms screaming our various pronunciations of "Ulalume" and "Angoulême," and the one glorious night when silence was enough. I loved his blue eyes, his wild blond hair, his crooked tooth. ("My own little Aryan," I called him.) We told each other stories of our pasts, and his were always full of adventure and excitement—because they were never true, and I knew it, and I loved him for it, and he told me I should loosen up and let go of myself and let my imagination play. I never could, and never dared try, and I hated him for it.

He accused me of being a slave to the facts, and later on, in the nightmare days, I accused him of writing potboilers. The worst nights were when he did more drinking than writing. "Great writers have written stories like mine," he said after half a bottle of Jack one night. I laughed at him and said, "Keep telling yourself that. Crappy writers always think they're great. And drunken assholes figure if they drink like Poe, maybe they'll write like him." He took a swig from the bottle and then spat it in my face. I can hardly blame him. I knew the nerve I was hitting. Still, I was angry. "You're a fucking hack," I said, "and your stories are pathetic and disgusting. They wouldn't scare a child." At the time, I thought it was the beginning of the end, but really, it was the middle. The truth is, I'd never liked his stories, even when we first started dating.

Anyway…

The door opened, no more slowly or quickly than any other door might, and a small man wearing the most ordinary clothes imaginable stood there in front of me. I showed him the slip of paper I had brought with me, but he didn't look at it. Somehow, he knew I belonged here. He gestured to his side—his right, my left—and I followed his gesture through a nondescript room and perfectly ordinary, if narrow, hallway, to another, and unmemorable, door. I knocked, but there was no answer, and so I turned the knob and opened the door, revealing a set of carpeted stairs leading down. I descended. The air grew musty and cold, the stairway became grey and then dark, and I felt my feet hit stone. I looked down, thinking I had reached some sort of bottom, but in the greyness I could make out more steps, now made of stone. Granite. Descending.

Eventually, light slipped through the darkness from candles set on shelves at the bottom of the stairs. I know now that the stairs were not miles long, but that is the impression they gave during that descent. Certainly, the caverns they led to were deep, and the edifice as a whole a marvel of architecture and engineering, but there was nothing supernatural about the place, at least in its design.

What the stairs led to was a series of small rooms with rock walls. Within moments of my arrival, a dark-skinned young man dressed as a servant brought me to one of the other rooms, a place filled with piles of women's clothing. In the dim light, the clothing looked expensive and impressive, but soon the young man held some pieces out to me and instructed me on how to wear them, and touching the fabric I saw that it was tattered, torn, and stained. I should say here that I had not worn women's clothing before, nor had much cause to examine it closely—a fact that had purely been a matter of chance, given how many of my compatriots were instructed at one time or another to unsex themselves for their men—and so I was awkward and required much assistance from the young man. His touch was gentle and soothing, as if he expected me to be frightened or disgusted, but given the circumstances of my hiring and the strangeness of the setting, I felt little surprise at the necessary attire. "What is your name?" I asked him. His smile was unforced and uncertain, as if it was the strangest query he'd encountered in many days.

"You don't need to know me," he said, averting his eyes.

I shifted my gaze to grasp his again, then took his hand in mine. "Necessity is the least interesting force in the universe," I said, parroting an aphorism once uttered by a priest who insisted on philosophizing whilst I pleasured him.

"My name is Charles," he said. "But please forget me. They'll call you to the stage in a moment, and you need to be ready."

"Will we meet again, Charles?"

I pulled him closer to me, but released his hand when I saw tears in his eyes.

Hands gripped my shoulders, spun me around, pushed me forward into light. Whiteness enveloped me, blinded me. I stumbled forward, knocking my foot against an obstacle. I heard chattering voices, the rumblings of impatient conversation. My eyes adjusted slowly, bringing shapes and colors into focus, and then I saw where I stood: a living room with a long couch, three chairs, and a low table. No—as my eyes accustomed to the light, I saw beyond it, beyond what I had taken to be walls and windows—beyond the whirlwind of lamps, mirrors, crystals, and smoke that obscured the view—I saw faces stacked in a small and narrow amphitheatre: the leering, lusting faces of men.

Breathless, my knees trembling with infirmity, I staggered to the couch and fell upon it. At that moment, a figure appeared from somewhere behind me. A man in a swallow-tailed black coat—his visage concealed by a black silk mask, his hands protected by white gloves—moved forward and presented himself to the audience. The men applauded vigorously.

I sat up on the couch and whispered, "Who are you?"

The masked figure rushed to me, his hand struck my face, and I fell back onto the couch. My cheek burned, my forehead ached, blood crossed my tongue. Ringing filled my ears, but then I heard the audience through the noise: their laughter, their rallying cries. His hands pulled me up, turned me to face him. The fabric of his mask was wet at the mouth and nose; his breathing made the silk pulse like a sail in a storm. Again his hand hit my face, and then the other hand, and then again, again—and all the while, the audience applauded, their claps in sympathy with each slap across my skin.

My abraded cheeks bled, my nose and lips bled, blood filled my mouth, I coughed. His hands grasped my throat and pushed me back onto the couch. Men whistled and stomped their feet. He tore the dress at the shoulder, snapping its seams. He wrenched it down. I pushed at him feebly, my arms and muscles moving by instinct, but he was stronger than I and easily held me back against the couch. His fists hit my stomach, my kidneys, then the bones of my ribs, knocking sense and breath from me. I keeled forward, and again he pushed me back, slapped my face, grabbed my hair. My eyes saw swirls of colors more than shapes, but soon I discerned that he stood over me and was pulling back his mask. I expected any face except the one I should have known would be there: The face of the man who had so gently implored me to come to this place. His eyes, which I had once, briefly, thought displayed a kind of love for me, now burned with contempt.

My recognition fired his fury. He rained more punishment upon me, and then, as I lay on the couch, my body throbbing, my eyes blurred with tears, he lowered his face to my chest, and the familiar tenderness there found its parody in his nuzzling kisses. The audience grew silent, their attention rapt, and yet soon there were stirrings—they became restless.

My tormenter paused. He now prepared the *pièce de résistance* of his performance. Holding me under the arms, he pulled me up to stand. The dress I wore sagged around my hips. He wrapped his right arm around my neck and with his left arm pulled—slowly but fiercely—the dress and all my underclothing down toward my knees. He could not hold my neck and further undress me, and so he pushed me forward—I braced myself with my arms, but fell hard on the floor, cracking a bone—and then felt myself hoisted backward as he ripped the shredding dress and all the rest from me until I was entirely naked in the hot fire of the lights and the hateful glare of all the men.

He retrieved his mask from where it had fallen beside the couch. He covered his face with it, sat on the couch, and removed his shoes. His feet bare, he walked toward me, then slowly, gently, took off each piece of clothing until only his mask remained. I glanced at him, not letting my gaze linger, for the pains coursing through my body demanded most attention for themselves. A quick look was enough for me, though, for I knew his strong, supple body well, and the sight of it above me now filled me with terror—the engorgement of his desire offered no thrill for me—rather, he seemed entirely grotesque, a demon, a force of unimaginable agony.

Even now, decades after the events, I cannot describe his actions without bringing myself to tears and raising aching memories across my skin.

I do not have the words to describe his final abuses, nor do I want to remember all he did to me or to remember the wild joys of the crowd.

I don't remember writing the scene I just wrote. I would never write such an absurd phrase as "the engorgement of his desire". It's disgusting and ridiculous. Those are not words I would choose. I should erase them now, I should get rid of this whole thing. And yet I know I won't. I've written those words there—"I should erase them now, I should get rid of this whole thing"—to let myself off the hook. I had no intention of erasing any of this. I've enjoyed writing it. I've gotten out of myself, away from the shitstorm with Adam. I don't believe a word of what I wrote above about responsibility. That's not true, either, though. I believe in the idea of it. But it has no visceral meaning for me. Because I really am writing this for myself. Really. It's an escape, a bit of fun. Meaningless. Really. I don't need you to read this. I don't need you.

(The memories rest as jagged shards, sharp and ready to freshen wounds.)

The light burns and stings its smoke into my eyes. My body moves, pulled over the wooden stage, splinters pricking my knees and legs. Darkness, then soft candlelight. Fingers trawl my skin. Cold water washes me.

Charles won't meet my gaze. I realize why he had tears in his eyes. He knew. There are many words I would like to say to him, but my tongue is thick and my mouth dry. He dresses me carefully in the clothes I arrived in. Shadows shift in the room and take hold of me and drag me up the stairs and outside into early morning air, and I am carried around corners and dropped in an alley onto soggy newspapers and chicken bones and scattering rats. They toss coins at me.

I do not move. Movement is pain. I barely breathe.

(The subsequent memories are more dreamlike, less present, and they do not wound.)

The sun rose somewhere above me and distant voices fell and echoed through the air. A rat bit my leg. I coughed and yearned for water or, better, gin. I swept the coins from my chest and hid them away in my pants. My employer had been correct that this was more lucrative work for me—these were good coins, more than I would earn in a month usually—but the cost was too much.

I leaned against a brick wall and inched my way toward the street. Somewhere in this Herculean effort, I met my savior. He was a thin man, disheveled, and his attire making it seem that he, too, might have been dropped in an alley, but he sported no wounds to his bones and skin, just sunken, bloodshot eyes and an unsteady step.

I do not remember what conversation we had. I drifted from awareness to a kind of half-sleep where I was awake but uncomprehending. Somehow I told him the address of my room, and somehow he took me there. My first thought was fear: did he intend to add to my abuses? He seemed afraid to touch me, though, and so I did not long fear him. My second thought was embarrassment: at the squalor of my tiny room, at the weakness of myself. I had little reason for such feelings, though, for soon he had lain himself down on the floor and fallen asleep.

I woke in the night when he opened the door.

"Who are you?" I called, fearing I would never see him again, never see him when I was healthy enough to thank him for his tremendous kindness.

"A man who needs to piss," he said, and walked out. He returned some time later.

"I have a chamber pot," I said.

"I know," he said. "But you didn't have this." He held up a small bottle of whiskey.

"I have gin."

"I saw your gin. Indeed, I smelled it." He sat on the one chair in the room, a small wooden chair I had built myself from scraps I'd found near the docks. He opened his bottle of whiskey. "What you call gin is a fast road to blindness. I might consider using it to remove stains from my clothing, but I am afraid it would remove the cloth along with the stains."

"I wanted to thank you," I said, "for—"

"No need for thanks. My motives were entirely mercenary, and you still should receive the attention of doctors, especially given what looks to me like a broken bone in your arm. I have not called a doctor, however. I must leave that for you to do yourself. You were a useful excuse for me at a difficult moment. I needed to disappear from the vision of certain people for a few hours while they sought me out for debts I most surely do not owe them, and since you are a stranger to me, and we have no previous connection, it is unlikely anyone will think to look for me here. I trust you are sufficiently healthy to avoid immediate death, however, as I have no skill as a nurse. Also, I expect I will become insensibly inebriated within the next hour. I have been an advocate of temperance recently, and I intend to return to advocating temperance in the future, but in the present I desire nothing so much as the soft obliteration bestowed by this bottle." He drank deeply from it.

"I am still grateful to you. There is no telling what could have become of me."

After many more minutes and many more drinks, the man said, "How did you end up in this state, if you'll pardon my curiosity."

"I hardly know, myself. A poet might say I fell into a vortex of vice and infamy."

"A villainous vortex of vice. Or, perhaps, a villainous veritable vortex of vice. No, a vortex of villainy, a veritable vice of…" He sighed and swayed a bit on the chair. He emptied the bottle into his mouth, then carefully slid from the chair to the floor, his care undermined by his drunkenness, causing him to end up on hands and knees with little comprehension of how he got there. Eventually, he rolled onto his side and stared at me.

"Are you a thief?" he muttered.

"What?"

"You live in a thief's establishment."

"No, there are no thieves here. We are people of business."

He chuckled. "And what business is your business?"

I looked into his hazed and glassy eyes. "You won't remember anything I say in the morning."

He coughed fiercely, but somehow avoided vomiting.

"Men pay me money," I said. "And for that money, I pleasure them. I kiss them. I undress them. They kiss me and undress me. We pretend at love. Their tastes are, shall we say, Hellenistic. Some of them are strong men whose pleasure comes from dominating a weaker man. Some of them are weak men who fancy themselves women at heart. If they pay enough, I can give them any pleasure they desire."

"Do you enjoy…" he began, his words fading into gibberish.

"Sometimes, yes, I enjoy it," I said. "A shallow enjoyment, briefly real. I learned early to survive by trying to fall in love with them all. They pay better when I am convincing. They return. My best men seek my body's spirit, and they pay me for it, so I must…deliver it unto them."

He chuckled again, weakly, as he slipped away from consciousness.

In the morning, his body was so consumed with nausea and pain that the doctor I summoned to attend to my wounds spent as much time with him as with me. A few of my friends and regular customers paid a visit during the day, and while most of them assumed the man sprawled on the floor was an especially satiated customer, one of my favorite men, a lovely brute with mischievous eyes and a lady's lips, who worked among newspapermen, said he had seen my visitor around his own haunts and knew him to be disreputable and irresponsible, often a danger to himself but generally harmless otherwise, though he was said to have an acid tongue.

By evening, he had recovered sufficiently to depart, offering to return with provisions should I need them, but by that time my friends and colleagues had determined a schedule by which they fulfilled my needs in shifts, for though we may be lowly in our employment and circumstances, lowliness inspires fierce comradeship: my fate was one all my peers could envision for themselves, and though I knew of none whose experiences were as decorated with grotesque mystery as mine, few had escaped bruises, broken bones, and alley trash-heaps during their careers.

And so my savior departed, and I thanked him, and he seemed to remember nothing of our conversation, and I set my sails toward healing and forgetting.

I sent my customers away with apologies—the doctor had informed me that my body needed significant rest and tenderness, and my broken arm was going to be a problem for months. A few men offered me a penny or two for food and medicine, though most simply gave me a wary smile or hasty kiss before closing the door behind themselves. Many would never look at me with the same lust in their eyes as before, and most would pay someone else for their pleasures.

As the months passed and my body healed, if ever the terrible night left my mind, my dreams brought it back in monstrous nightmares. Shadow creatures tore all the skin from my face and chest and arms and legs— massive hands pulverized my bones—wild, full, liquid eyes flashed with red light across all my visions—and endless applause echoed through the maelström.

Many months later, as I undressed in darkness for a customer who sprawled naked across my bed, a shaft of moonlight illuminated my face more fully than he had seen it before, and he gasped and covered himself with the sheets. I knew then what I had first suspected when I saw him: This was Charles, the attendant to my nightmares. His face had grown more sallow, his body more angular, but this was he.

I jumped atop him and held him to the bed. (In the moonlight, we perhaps resembled a strange etching of midnight wrestlers.) My muscles flexed with fury, and I wanted nothing so much as to tear him apart with my hands, not because he had himself abused me—he had been nothing but gentle and sympathetic—but because here, for the first time since that ghastly night, I held in my hands some physical representation of the misery that still terrorized my mind.

Leaning down close, I spat his name into his ear, enunciating it as a vicious noise, an accusation and condemnation, a curse. I held him firm, but gave him everything he had paid me for, and more than that—for though I always made sure to keep him pressed to the bed to prevent his escape, my every caress was soft, careful, loving. Malnourishment and maltreatment had faded his previous beauty, but its shadow remained, and it was the shadow I sought, the shadow I held in my imagination. This was a greater torture to him than any I could have inflicted with fists or whips or the manifold tools of so many Inquisitions. Once I recovered from my terrible night, I took to keeping my room quite dark, for certain scars and bruises never left my skin, and only a minority of customers are excited by damaged goods, so Charles had not been able to discern my features and had not known whom he was buying—his intent was as innocent as any such attempt could be.

After, as he lay nearly comatose from exhaustion and shame, I retrieved some rope from a corner of the room and bound him with it. He fought listlessly against me. I hauled him to the floor and dragged him up against the wall. And then I waited.

Though first he resisted and pleaded ignorance, then wept over the consequences his words would bring himself and his family, by mid-day, he had told me everything I hoped to know. He did not know names, or at least not useful ones (the names he knew were descriptive: "The Sailor," "The Old Swede," "The Painter," "Doctors D and F") but he knew times, locations, and passwords. Though he wailed that he was certain things had changed since he had been unceremoniously relieved of his duties (for reasons he knew not), I thanked him and removed the ropes that bound him. I had brought a bucket of water into the room, and I cleaned him with it, and as I did so his tears subsided and his weeping gave way to stoic impassivity. I dried him with a small towel, then dressed him as if he were an invalid. I kissed him, but he did not respond. In the years since that moment, I have imagined many words that must have passed through his mind, but the truth is that he did not speak—he lifted his head high and walked away, a new force of will, or a newly willed force, propelling him from the room.

He had given me the address at which the malevolent club would meet, for they moved their meetings according to a strict plan, and he said it was always the third Thursday of the month, and that the revels began precisely at eleven minutes past eleven in the evening. That gave me one month to prepare, for Charles had visited me on the night of the third Thursday.

I spent the month perfecting my scheme and collecting the various items I would need to effect it. This required much cleverness and a certain amount of daring, for I had not nearly enough money to purchase all the items, particularly the clothing, and so I had to insinuate myself into places where such things could be acquired. My greatest luck came when a friend of a friend introduced me to an expensive card game in a building near Gramercy Place, and my experience with far less trusting competitors in far more complicated games allowed me to leave not only with what was, for me at that time, a small fortune in cash, but with what I had really come for: a fine hat, cape, and walking stick. (The other players were so amused by my encouraging them to wager their clothing that they insisted I return again in the future, as indeed I did many times, making the associations that would, in fact, send me toward the far more reputable sort of life I lead today.)

Thus it was that I was able to dress myself as a man of considerable means, and to secrete on my person two pistols obtained for me by a faithful customer who was also an officer in the Navy, and who provided me with, in addition to the pistols, ammunition and numerous small sacks of gunpowder.

I began writing this as a way to, I thought—or I told myself—exorcise Adam. But that's not it.

Words are magic. That's what he said to me when we started dating. I loved his words, and I told him so, and he smiled and he said, "Well, words are magic." It's only when you're first in love with somebody that such banal and empty ideas seem profound. I should know better, but those first, rushing, blinding moments of love make everything seem profound, unique, consequential. I should know better. I've got a master's degree, I've studied philosophy and literature and art and history—and yes, my daily life is not glamorous, I work as a shipping and receiving manager at a warehouse, yes, I know I am not, as he said, living up to my potential (whatever that is!), but you don't think I'm as aware of that as anybody else? I've spent a lifetime being told how much potential I have, how brilliant and talented I am, what a fine mind I have. At the warehouse they call me "Professor" and "Einstein," but that's nothing compared to what people say to me when I get into a conversation with them about, for instance, the building of the Croton Water Aqueduct or the history of the Tombs and then they ask me if I've written a book or if I work at a university and I mumble and I shuffle my feet and I cough nervously and eventually, if they're persistent, I tell them, "Actually, I work at a warehouse." You should see their faces. You have seen their faces. And I've seen your face when you've seen their faces. It's not just that you think I haven't lived up to my potential, no—you're ashamed of me. At your book parties, at your conventions and conferences. You were always happy to be around anybody other than me. Remember the party where, after at least a couple of bottles of wine, you grabbed me and groped me and people gathered around, laughing nervously, and you yelled to them all, "Look, friends, at my Hop-frog!" I should have grabbed a torch and hurled it at you and set you all aflame.

Words are magic.

No they aren't. I keep writing this, thinking of you, wondering what you would make of it, wondering if it would, somehow, be enough. Enough what? Enough magic.

Words are not magic. Words are echoes, shadows, ashes.

We tell stories because what else is there to do? This is a story. I am telling it. Summoning voices to keep me company through the night.

The entertainment that month occurred in a palatial private residence far north, at 52nd Street and Fifth Avenue. My card winnings easily paid for a fine carriage to carry me to the location, and though I had feared the password system Charles taught me would have been changed, it was not, for I was admitted without a second glance from the masked and muscled men who guarded the inside of the door. From there, a very small man—a dwarf, really—dressed in an expensive (and miniature) butler's uniform led me through a corridor and up two flights of stairs to a kind of recital hall. It was a circular room, very lofty, and received the light of the moon only through a single window at top. A few dozen chairs stood in rows in front of a small stage, at the center of which had been placed a settee, and above which hung an immense chandelier dripping wax from its countless candles. Most of the seats in the audience were filled by well-attired men, and none of us looked at each other or spoke.

Within minutes, the man in the world whom I most loathed, the man who had first enticed me to attend one of these performances and then scarred and humiliated me so brutally, so publicly—this man now stood on the stage, directly in front of the settee, his face unmasked. His words echo through my ears as if I heard them mere minutes ago:

"Hello, my friends. Tonight's revelry is a singular one for us. It has been arranged to honor one of our most devoted members, a man who has been a friend to these festivities for longer than most, and who has provided us all with much continued pleasure through the imaginative chronicling of the emotional forces that are unleashed here every month. His is our true voice, his words the metaphors of our reality, his dreams the ones we share. He has, alas, fallen on hard times, as can happen to any man, and to lighten the burden of his days, I asked him what spectacle he would most like to see, and so tonight's pantomime is one that we should consider authored by our dear friend."

With that, the man gestured to a figure sitting in the front row, a figure who stood and acknowledged us—and it was at that moment that I nearly gave myself away, for I could barely stifle a gasp of shock and revulsion on seeing the face of my savior, the man who had rescued me after I had been subjected to such evil, the man who guided me home and stayed with me on the first night of my recovery.

I hardly had time to absorb the fact of his face before most of the lights in the room were extinguished, save for the chandelier above the stage, and a young girl stumbled forward, golden braids bouncing over her face. She looked confused and stunned. Before she could gain her bearings, the malevolent host strode forward and grasped her in his arms. She screamed, and a few men in the audience responded with laughs. The host lifted the girl onto the settee and then his hands performed a terrible dance upon her body. As her screams grew more desperate, the laughter in the room rose, and so, too, did sounds of encouragement and goading. I felt a psychic hunger course through the audience as the host held a dagger in his hand and, with great precision, sliced the girl's dress open slowly and methodically, then, after excruciating minutes of this, pulled the dress from her trembling body. It was then that we all saw that this was not, in fact, a young girl, but a young boy—and the men in the audience screamed their approval as the host slit and removed the last garments from the unfortunate boy's frame and then held him aloft like a prize calf. He held the boy before the man in the front row, who nodded his approval without touching the chaste, white, shivering body.

I was about to enact the climax of my plan when two men wearing masks of the *commedia dell'arte* style appeared, carried a small ivory casket onto the stage, and opened it. I stayed my hand because of a moment's fascination. The host then placed the naked and whimpering boy into the casket and closed it. The casket had been fit with locks, and the cover was thick enough to muffle the boy's terrified screams. The host gestured to the audience to enjoy the screams. It was what they had assembled for—not merely the sight of the boy being degraded and abused, but for the pleasure of his terror.

I couldn't keep watching. I stood, withdrew a pistol, and shot the host in the chest. The audience thought this was part of the entertainment, and they applauded and cheered. Only the man in the front row seemed to understand that something was wrong, and he stood up. I moved forward, keeping the pistol aimed at his head. "Do you know me?" I said. "Do you?"

He stared at me, and then recognition dawned across his face.

The pistol now pressed against his forehead, I repeated, "Do you know me?"

"Yes."

The shot would have cracked his skull open, but at the last moment my hand wavered and I merely fired past his ear—the shock and noise enough to make him fall to the ground, thick red blood oozing from inside his ear, but very much alive.

The men who had guarded the front doors rushed into the room, and the audience had now figured out that something was amiss, but they were paralyzed by shock and confusion.

I pushed the bleeding body of the host away from the casket, its ivory now decorated with blood. I sprung the locks, opened the lid, pulled the terrified boy out, and wrapped him in my cloak. "Hold onto my hand," I told him. "Don't let go."

As the guardsmen and the audience approached, I tossed bags of gunpowder toward the candles in front of them, bringing loud, acrid explosions that blinded them and robbed them of breath. I whisked the boy out of the room, down the corridor and stairs, and then outside, where my carriage waited around a corner. I attempted to hasten him into the carriage, but his terror gave him new strength, and he was unable to distinguish my care from the abuses of the men in the mansion, and so he struggled and fought until he was free of my grip and my cloak, and he ran, naked and screaming, into the night. I knew that the noise of my guns, perhaps, and the boy's screams, almost certainly, would alert neighbors and elicit eyes at windows, so I gave the boy no more thought and jumped into my carriage and we hurried away.

I learned much later that, shortly after I proved unable to shoot him in the head, the man I had previously thought of as my savior showed up drunk and sick in Baltimore, where he died. His literary work gained fame and notoriety in the following years, but I have always refused to read a word of it.

As I alluded above, I was able to make a new life for myself thanks to my own cleverness and determination, and to acquire something of a reputation as a philanthropist and an advocate for the preservation of Saxon strength through careful, deliberate habits of breeding—I am pleased that my pedagogical historical narrative *Hengst and Horsa, or, The Saxon Men* sold extremely well some years ago under one of my *noms de plume*. But I am an old and ailing man, now, and my time is limited, and as I have always devoted my life to the truth, I feel I must pen this manuscript, for fear that I will disappear otherwise into the vortex of time without having expressed the truths of my life—truths which, for all their apparent wonder and horror, I trust will speak their veracity to you, dear reader.

> "In me didst thou exist—and, in my death, see by this image, which is thine own, how utterly thou hast murdered thyself."
> —EDGAR ALLAN POE, "William Wilson"

It is not the ending I intended. I had been struggling with it for a week or so, failing to create the tone I wanted, trying out a bunch of things to give it both a sense of verisimilitude and drama, never achieving it—and then three days ago got a call from Ginny with the news that Adam is dead.

I was going to try to revise the ending, but why bother now? I secretly hoped he would read the story and like it, or even hate it but be amused. I thought he would see that I understood how hard he worked, how talented he was, the worth of stories and storytelling. Or something. I don't know. Maybe my intentions were less noble or naïve. I don't know.

What I know is that now there is no point. Words are not magic. If there is truth, it lurks between the lines, unreachable, silent, lost like the truth of whatever happened to Poe in the last week of September 1849. Lost. We can imagine stories, but that is all they are: imagined.

LACUNA

I was writing this story for myself, I thought, but really I was writing it for him, and so I wrote it for nothing. It is here now, it exists, like me, alone, unfinished, a testament to nothing but itself.

I've read so many interviews with writers and artists who say they create to have a sense of immortality, of leaving something behind after they go. Adam said that sometimes. His stories, he said, were his children, his legacy, his history, his immortality. Even if he wasn't rich and famous, at least he had books on shelves and maybe one day in the future somebody would stumble on one in a library or a bookstore and his words would live in their mind. His work would live on. But what good is posterity? You're still dead.

Words are not magic. Stories are not truth; they are evasions, misdirections.

He took a couple Valium, drank most of a bottle of vodka, loaded his father's old Colt 1911 pistol, put it in his mouth, and pulled the trigger.

Those are the facts. End of story.

The Most High looked from one of them, beauty and virility made flesh, to the other, some other thing, and then back at Cianco. "So this your boy, huh?"

SUPERBASS

Kai Ashante Wilson

*We have been down together in my sleep, unbuckling helms, fisting each
other's throat, and waked half half-dead with nothing.*

Gian stole into the house. From the back garden, a work-song:
soprano led two deeper voices, who called the responses. There
was the big wooden box, under the worktable. Gian went to it,
pulled the box out, and rummaged its contents. He plucked gold from
his ears and put in disks of mother-of-pearl. He lifted off his military
beads, all the commendations he'd won in the Kingdom's wars as *one
who stood* When the River Ran Red, and restrung his neck with clatter-
ing necklaces of polished white stones and shell nacre. Silence fell in the
garden. Shadows blocked the good light. Busted!

The shadow up front leaned from brightness, peering into the dark—a
sudden movement. Used to blows, Gian flinched. *Still?* No one alive
could or would knock him around, and Milord the Marshal had gone
down in the river, one of countless who'd bloodied the waters.

"That's your sister's."

Black Daddy stood at the back doorway. In their scarves and broad-
brimmed straw hats, Mama and White Daddy crowded close behind
him.

"I *asked*," Gian said. "She said I could borrow it."

"There's no bembe up at our temple today." Black Daddy came into the house. "So what you dressing in daytime regalia for?"

"Somebody asked me to go somewhere with them, that's all."

"Somebody, *huh?*" Black Daddy invested huh with deep, wry knowledge. "Everywhere we go, Gianni, all this last season, people keep telling us how they just now bumped into you somewhere around the hills of Sea-john. Always with the same good-looking fella. People can't remember when they last *seen* somebody so much in love. All of them say how happy they are to see you doing so much better now, than when you first got back from the wars. But why you never bring your man by here, Gianni? We could make dinner for him; he could meet your mamas-and-papas. Everybody could say hello to each other."

"I can't right now, Daddy...I gotta go somewhere." Gian shimmied from his everyday shirt, bright-dyed and fitted. He drew on his sister's, loose and white. "But soon, all right? Real soon."

"You ashamed of us, Gianni? We too poor? You don't want your fine man seeing what you come from?"

"No!" Gian thumbed loose the knot at his waist. "It ain't like that." His wraparound pooled at his ankles. "He's just like us—nobody high and mighty. Feet on the ground, not nose up in the air." Nothing like Milord whom he'd served the last decade, in other words. Gian rewrapped his waist and legs with the length of white cotton, expensively well-bleached. As was his wont, he tied off the wraparound girl-style, rather than just folded over, then buckled back on his belt and scabbard. "He's just a plain ole Johnny from Sea-john, same as us."

"Well, who his people, then? What hill they live on? Which parish? What the boy name?"

"Black Daddy...!" Gian exclaimed in exasperation; he swept up the loose flowers he'd laid atop the table.

"We can't hardly step in the street, but somebody don't stop us to say they just now seen you, hugged up with some fella we ain't even met *once.* Now, all of a sudden, you going to services out of parish. What it *feel* like, Gianni, is you cutting out the people who love you best."

"No, no; me and him just been busy, that's all." Gian desperately bundled his clothes and things together. "Soon as things get settled some, we'll all do something nice. I promise." No slipping out—he *must* say good-bye properly.

Mama and White Daddy weren't dumb: of course not. But they were so ashamed of their accents, mostly Black Daddy spoke for them if he was around. And since sturdy rope and a team of horses would never tear them loose from his side, it was *no wonder* they couldn't speak Johnny worth spit after a quarter century living in Sea-john. Black Daddy had learned *their* foreign jabber. Gian sucked his teeth softly, glancing down so his parents wouldn't see him roll his eyes. He leaned up to kiss Black Daddy's cheek, and touched Mama's hand, then White Daddy's. He fled the house.

After the indoor shadows, the flood of morning light was nearly blinding. Gian turned up a hand to shade his view, squinting down the block. *There* he was! At the southwest side of the parish temple, in the last patch of semi-shadow, stood a silhouette well-known by stature, breadth of shoulders, and locks twined to a turban atop the head—waiting right where the eyes sought first. Gian dashed that way.

"You musta been talking to somebody." Cianco laughed and took the flowers. "But *you* didn't need to bring flowers, or wear regalia, either— that's just the rest of them. It's something else you gotta do. Now let's get going: we got nigh on three hundred folk waiting for us." He looked up suddenly, back down the street. Gian turned.

Three can marry in Sea-john but not two, not six, not any number but three: his parents stood at the doorway of the house, two under hats, and Black Daddy's hand at his brow against the glare. There wasn't much you could make out of them at this distance, except who was nearly as tall as Cianco, who as short as Gian, who was man, who woman, who—"I thought you said we were in a hurry." Gian tried to draw Cianco away, who didn't budge.

"That's them, ain't it? Your mamas-and-papas."

"Yes." Gian embraced Cianco's arm. "But won't the priests be wondering where we at about now? Can't keep everybody waiting."

"They look like real good people, your folks." Cianco broke into a grin. "I'ma go say hi to them!"

"*It ain't right*"—Gian made himself heavy, both hands gripping Cianco's arm—"making all those people wait!"

Cianco looked at him. "You don't want me meeting your folks."

175

"It's not that. Really, pop. Just...next time, all right?" Gian tugged without effect: no one made Cianco do anything, not by force. "We can have us a good visit next time around. Promise."

Cianco stared and stared. Gian fought not to shuffle and grin like a liar about to be called out—but at last Cianco nodded. He turned and raised a hand in greeting. Far up the block three hands waved back. Then he let his lover nudge him into motion and drag them hustling the other way.

They went downhill and up into the next. "So, Gianni-mi—listen up," Cianco said. "I'm gonna change and be all strange and different today, but still myself, all right? And if the congregation calls you the hallowed boy, or Summer King's lover, don't worry about it. Understand?" Not really, no; but Gian nodded. Cianco led them around back of a temple. "And she's tough and hard-headed; she *always* gets her own way. But just for today, the one she chose for Summer King knows better. That's me."

She? "Who?" Gian said.

The Most High stood in the street outside the temple; she said, "Drink this. More! Now pass it to your boy." She snatched the chrysanthemums from Cianco, and made them both gulp from a flask of infused spirits (*oh*...the world tipped giddily; Gian hadn't yet broken the fast) and hustled them the back way into the temple, by a little postern door. "Man, why on *earth* did you dress your boy like another petitioner?"

Cianco could have exclaimed without injustice, "'Ain't nobody told him to dress like that—*he* put them clothes on!'" but he said, "My baby's pretty in white. I like him like this."

The answer satisfied her. At Gian's parish temple the Most High was a short elderly woman, too kind if anything—she'd always let him get away with things, including never attending services. Not the boss priestess here! This Most High was another Johnny giant, *more* robust in middle years than anyone younger. Abrupt and sharp-eyed, she managed to say with one glance, *I'm well aware of your foolishness; soon there will be a reckoning.*

Inside the temple drawing breath was *work*, the aromas thickening the air were so bitter, sweet, and noxious. Sage smoked from braziers. The fragrance of flowers commingled and clashed. Up in there reeking was the old standby stench too, savory with death, rusty and wet: a flock of beheaded fowl hung from trussed feet overtop stone deities, knee-deep in slopping tureens. The feathered bouquets wept clotted black drops still. Nausea watered Gian's mouth. A hand clasped the back of his neck, rested with affectionate weight, and let go. The touch steadied Gian, on bad footing at the river's brink. A fossil of memory jostled him in passing, and was borne away on the ruddy current: some soldier face down, arrow ridden.

Gian looked up. Cianco's eyes weren't on him; they admired the temple's spectacular door of flowers. Often enough his lover had said, "I get so lonely for you, Gianni. Sometimes when you're right here by me." And then would come the bulwark of a hand, supportive somewhere on the back of Gian's body.

The massive doors were thrown wide, yet nothing could be seen of the courtyard fronting the temple. Dozens on dozens of garlands hung in a curtain, blocking the view. The light broke up among flower petals, scattering on the temple floor as dimly luminous confetti, in peacock colors, and toucan.

"*Jump*, dammit!" The Most High snapped her fingers at the women and sissies attending her. They hustled forward with a crown of marigolds and tiger lilies, a crimson mantle, a green wraparound all stiff with gold brocade, and some fancy sandals of the sort nobility wore in the Kingdom. They stripped and redressed Cianco. With the nimble truant immobilized, and preparations underway, the Most High could now light into him properly. "*You* got some nerve," she snapped, "falling up in here late like this."

"But…" Cianco blinked, head shaking slowly, and smiled. "…I ain't though." That way he had, that voice, all caramel and languor, could awake such love in hearts, or—"You know me, Aunty: always on time."—such fury.

She put her finger in his face. "*Tu, m'iamas 'Laltissima'!*"

Cianco gently took the hand and softly kissed it. "I'm right on time, Most High."

She snatched it back. "A couple hundred people out there waiting. They get *one* chance, *once* a year." The Most High slapped his chest at *one* and *once*. "King comes at noon and he's *going* at first quarter of the night—"

"Let's don't waste no time, then." Cianco pointed at a hole in the ceiling, falling from which a narrow sunbeam struck a brass plate atop the altar. The endpoint sparkle had crept nearly dead center the plate's much-etched symbology. (Sweet as nectar to the bees, so were the many splendors of Cianco to the sissies. He was muscled and manful, full of mellow charm—and oh it took the *breath* away, that print of bird! Gian felt himself in warm fellowship with his sisterly brethren, and so tolerated more foolishness than others might. Even so, one of the Most High's attendants began to work his nerves with all the fluffing, and tweaking, and smoothing of the lay of Cianco's mantle and regalia. It was just *way* too much. Gian muttered with soft vehemence: "All right, you done here"—plucking off those hands in favor of some having a right to that work, *his own*—"My man *got him* a sissy for this." Licked wet, his thumb wiped away crystals left from sleep at the corner of Cianco's eye.)

The Most High looked from one of them, beauty and virility made flesh, to the other, some other thing, and then back at Cianco. "So this your boy, huh?"

Of course she would have thought Gian born unpainted at first glance. Everyone did. Now he watched her eyes dismiss him into a familiar exile, deciding Gian's origins must lie not off the hills of Sea-john so much as off the continent itself. His younger brother and sister never suffered such skeptical looks: they were both tall, both born tawny, and nicely browner still after a lifetime of equatorial sun. Proper hair too.

"Yes," Cianco said, and with no little peck; with tongue, at length, he proved it. "Love me some him!"

"But…is he Johnny, though? Power comes down best for the young, *los formozi*, for somebody born up here in the hills, Sea-john."

"You can talk to *him*, Most High. He standing right here, ain't he? And he just as beautiful and Johnny as you or me, or anybody."

Gian's hair was tied back. With a winkling finger, the Most High loosed some strands for examination. *What rufous stuff is this?* Her thumb and index worried at the lock. *And so lank!* She, like most Johnnys, was very tall; nowadays though, with his hair grown long, the monstrous scar some arrowhead had torn across Gian's scalp could be hidden, never seen by anyone but a lover. But the Most High mussed the monster out. Grimacing, she looked down, and demanded: "What hill? What parish?"

"Born and raised up on Mevilla hill," Gian said. "Toretta deldio"—he gave her the parish-sign—"represent!" The hills of Sea-john all spoke different dialects, every parish another accent.

She frowned skeptically, but there was no arguing with the evidence of her own ears. Next she asked, "How old are you?"

The wars had weathered him. So a young man came by so many scars, fine lines, and old man's shadows in his eyes. "Twenty-three," Gian said. Despite the truth's implausibility, he spoke with a steady voice because of the hand stroking down his back. It cupped his ass...and dropped away.

The Most High grunted, the skepticism given voice this time. She snapped fingers at her priestly cronies again. "Y'all bring me La Pablo in here."

They brought in a tall youth, shirt open, skin glossy as oiled obsidian; he smiled, seeing Cianco, and didn't see Gian at all. Was this preferred boy good-looking? Halfway cute? Just all right, if you liked that sort of thing?

La Pablo was *gorgeous*.

A creepy-crawly sensation, hotness too—half a blush and half swarming ants— itched and burned Gian's face and back, all up and down his arms. Cianco happily scooped the lovely La Pablo close to his left side and, lips upon ear, murmured to him tenderly. If one of the luminaries should condescend, then the homely lover, plain of face, knows damn well to choose some modest number, and then begin counting down the days of love. Beauty seeks after beauty, like goes with like; forever this was the way of things, world without end. Recognizing the moment long dreaded had come, and feeling a fatalist's relief as much as dizzying humiliation, Gian eased back toward the postern door and...

...was caught by Cianco's free hand, of course: reeled in close under his right arm. "Two!" said the Summer King, grinning at His bounty. He hustled Himself and armfuls out through the door of flowers. In the high noon outside, the Summer King shouted: "Look what I got, y'all!" brandishing His right and left arms. The crowd roared approval.

And well they should adore Him. The Summer King was man no longer but Someone greater. The folk clapped and stomped, hailing Him with joyful noise, the song palpable in its cadent thunder. He put forth radiance outshining the tropical sun at meridian. No one closer in the embrace of that glare, Gian squinted his eyes, a little shaken.

Priestesses stood round enormous drums beating the invocation. White-clad and chanting, the congregation held all manner of flowers. Most had come with wreaths of bright wild flowers and pretty weeds. The poorest held branches broken from magnolia trees, or jacaranda. A few folk held singular blooms, a rare lily or strange orchid, for which they must have foraged the bush, or nurtured in home gardens, against this very day. All had come with their best. The stout daughters of the richest family propped up between them a huge folly of flowers, bear-shaped and sized. Father and a younger sibling lay at their feet shivering on pallets, given to drinks and brows wiped dry by two mothers.

The people were crammed along the walls of the sacred compound, to clear a space before the door of flowers. In that dusty clearing awaited the throne. It was a huge stool of carven hardwood, shiny black from age and oiled care.

"*Atuandicy, Pablihno,*" said the Summer King, when they'd reached the stool. He put the pretty boy standing at the stool's left side. Gian moved toward the right, but oh no, he'd got it wrong again. Taking seat upon His throne, the Summer King dragged Gian down upon one thigh. Big and smaller man fit their seats just fine, one a full foot taller and half again as heavy as the other; the stool, immense.

The drumbeat changed and folk quieted. "Who first?" called the Summer King. His voice, sonorous and rumbling just a moment ago, now eerily rang out as tenor, a bell tone.

A girlchild, four years old, stepped into the dusty amphitheater from the encircling throngs. While approaching the throne, she cast back frightened looks to a woman, two men, and three older children who nodded, flapped their hands, and smiled encouragement of the girl's every reluctant step forward. She was called "Patri," for with that name the family urged her on. And they cried, "Go on, baby. Keep going." In her hand, she bore the flowering bough of a flame-of-the-forest tree, with blossoms red as mango pits, orange as that fruit. And full of fish, the jowls of some pelican rising from a sea dive might bulge too, as immensely as did this child's, goitered or scrofulous.

"Put that there, little mama," said the Summer King. The girl stooped to lay her flowering branch at La Pablo's feet. "Now come here," He said; the girl stepped just between the sprawled knees. He set a hand on her shoulder (the other palming the small of Gian's back). To the crowd He said, "Bring down some power, y'all," and the people began to sing; but quieted when He lifted His hand. "Oh, no, mamita. I need sure 'nough strength for this." The Summer King shook His head sadly. "The flowers are good, but why didn't you bring me some rum?"

The child stared, mouth ajar, knowing His question was owed some answer but not knowing what. Her eyes shone, and lips trembled. From along the walls her mamas-and-papas, sisters and brother cried pardon for their family's poverty.

A cripple was leaning on his crutch at the edge of the crowd: to him, the Summer King called, "Can't grow back that foot of yours, pa!"

Calling back, "No?" the old man said, "How come? Summer King could do anything, I thought."

"Man, you been coming ever since that shark bit you. Every year the Summer King say the same damn thing: ain't no growing back hands, feet, or nothing like that. What's gone is gone. You *been* knowing it!"

"Yeah, well." The old man scratched his beard, rooting in the grizzled scruff. "Man can hope, cain't he? But, Summer King, not *nothing*? Can't maybe grow me *half* a foot? Then, see, I could come back next year and get—"

"No," said the Summer King. "It ain't no half feet, either. So why don't you just give that rum you holding to this little girl right here."

The freckled old man, redbone, whitened with rage. Selfish spleen contorted his face, but as he looked at the pickney, inflamed eggs bloating her underchin, his sneer fell away. "Yeah." He made a sheepish face, ducking his chin. "You right, you right." The old man held out his gourd.

The child looked to the Summer King; He said, "Go 'head, little mama," and she fetched the rum back to Him.

The Summer King unstoppered and drank. His body always blazed with more than ordinary heat—such that after making love, after caresses, after the whispers, on sweltering nights Gian needed to roll to the farthest edge of the long pillow for relief and sleep. Now those inner flames surged, and the flesh where Gian sat warmed up *hot*; sweat beaded his brow and sluiced down his back. The Summer King tossed the emptied gourd aside, and cupped the child's cheek in His hand. She cried out, thin and high. Her body seized and shook. The little girl crumpled into the dust when He let her go. "Patrízia," shouted one of her papas, who ran from the crowd.

The father knelt. His daughter woke and he lifted her in his arms. Laughing rapturously, he spun the child around, held aloft for the crowd to see—her chin and neck were sharply defined, the swelling gone.

So they made petition, one after another, until the enthroned sat knee-deep in flowers. There came grievous wounds and mortal illnesses. A woman bared a breast purple and deeply ulcered, a man held his testicle, gigantic and misshapen, cradled heavily in both hands. Infection turned brown-skinned toes, a golden shank, one damaged cheek the dark twin of which was perfect, into smelly black and verdigris sponge, all nibbled at by gangrene. For *them*, no, the beating drums, the crowd raised to unison chant, the proffered flowers, and even rum for the Summer King weren't enough. "Hold on," the Summer King bade these petitioners: "For this, I need some *love*." And Gian's role in the proceedings came clear: he must give the Summer King his kiss. At night on the long pillow, with the shutters closed and portieres drawn, naked in the midst of love, Gian felt passion for this man so surpassing fondness or desire he'd felt before, what else but to admit he'd known nothing of love whatsoever, was learning *now*. And those lessons had their time and place...surely not *here*? Yet, here, the merest brush of his lips to His raised the same ecstasies in Gian as the most intimate acts, and if the sacred kiss should become wet, and the Summer King slip His tongue...

It fell to lovely La Pablo to distract the sick and wounded. With the kindest fluency, his chatter did so whenever kisses ran long. Finally, the Summer King would free Gian to sit upright, then pass His hand over the crown of Gian's head to draw off the blazing overspill of emotion, heady and hot and half-brokenhearted, stoked by their kisses. With the aid of "love" He could make even the worst-off well.

By the dozens they were healed, only four or five turned away.

To one of these the Summer King said, "No, grandfather. You belong to the Crow Sisters. I can't give you but a little comfort. Want it?"

The old man wept, and said, "Yes."

The Summer King whispered in the old man's ear, and whatever He said smoothed a few hard lines of pain from the old man's brow, and raised a wavering smile to his mouth. That petitioner went away content.

All those others denied had had truck with witches: they'd entered into pacts from which they now sought escape. All of them made the same report, that the price of witchcraft proves too high...*everything*! Each in turn, the Summer King suffered to speak her piece, or cry his repentance, but always He shook His head at the end and said, "No." Here was neither comfort nor aid, for man or woman who'd gone to witches.

Third of those refused was a woman frail and aged, her scalp darkly gleaming beneath wisps of cotton. Oh, *she* moved Gian! The hunched carriage of her shoulders, her haunted eyes, the hopeless slackness of her mouth, half-open and gasping: all was reminiscent of soldiers who'd come through the hottest action alive, yet afterward could find no good in life. Haltingly, the woman gave an account of the perfidy of witches that raised the hair on Gian's arm. To hear how they'd tricked her turned his stomach—they'd taken so much for just a little luck in finances! Sent unsuccored back to the arms of her two wives, the woman let go such rough sobs Gian couldn't bear them. He turned, and his own eyes full, said, "Won't you?"

In the dusty courtyard were hundreds, and none missed this petition. The drums fell off, all noise from the crowd, saving the wives who wept together. In that lull, only after he'd asked, did Gian recall that every favor comes at some cost.

Sweeping Gian off His knee and embracing him close, the Summer King whispered in an ear: "To help her, say *yes*: before midnight, you'll tell me what happened When the River Ran Red"—Gian's stomach clenched painfully—"and the whole truth of your service to Marshal Jaqash, peer of the Kingdom, wasn't he, who fell in the river. Of course he did! Cruel but no coward, Milord always led the corps from the front, didn't he, and you there right beside him. The lesser soldiery said about you corpsmen: 'Spilling blood gets 'em drunk.' Yeah, you few up in the van they called Blood Drunkards. Heaven has plans for you, Gianni-mi, but you're no good to yourself or the world all walled up in secrets."

Afraid of questions—afraid of his own answers, rather—Gian never spoke about the years of his conscription. It was a horrible shock, then, hearing unuttered confidences pour from another's mouth. Bitterly he said, "You know everything already!"

"No," whispered the Summer King. "This is your own heart talking to you—your poor lover knows nothing."

It was Gian's pleasure to be handled and grabbed by these hands; but sometimes his body must signal the contrary, for the grip always knew when to loosen, as now. Gian stood and met the gaze of the accurst woman, needing his eyes full of the sight of her suffering, if his mouth were to say yes. She stood between wives, gripping their hands, her eyes terrible with hope. Neither wife was older than Gian, yet the toll of tribulations had croned the woman who'd gone to witches.

Gian said, "All right, pop."

The Summer King beckoned the woman back. He said, "Lean close," and the words whispered into her ear dried up every tear, and straightened her back, and her hands clenched and opened as she listened. Her countenance was no longer woebegone, but became charged with fearful awe. After the whispers, much-shaken, the woman gave the promissory nod. The Summer King accepted her flowers and drank her rum and she stepped away, that Gian could give the kiss. Tasting only of the fruit juices Johnnys mixed into rum and called *Jaúndi mar libre*, there was no breath of spirits in the Summer King's mouth.

Gian had been waiting for this so long.

Thirteen years old, and taught marksmanship by shooting bound felons full of arrows, the boy he'd been had thought, *A long time from now when I get home to Sea-john, I won't kill again or hurt anybody. I'll have friends. I won't be alone.* Eighteen years old, and favorite of the Marshal himself, Gian had been the corpsman most envied of the vanguard, despite the hard use everyone saw, and the harder still none did: that Gian had dreamed, *This won't be for always. I'll go home one day, and there'll be some Johnny man, better and kind to me....* Later on, under hard black rain, the torrents made of iron and each drop some man's death in the river, Gian had splashed on past the upreaching hands of drowners, the faces breaking the surface with a gasp only to go down again, and across the river on the far shore he'd caught sight of enemies who would die once he and this spear reached them—and they reached them, and they killed them, as many falling at his hand, quite possibly, as legend claimed. *This is your work now,* Gian had thought, strewing death about him, *but only live and some day, home again, turn your hand to something better, and in Sea-john life will be good, and safe, and full of love—*

The kiss broke. Gian sat up dazed and the Summer King gathered up the heart's hot surfeit in His hand. With it, he broke the witches' curse upon the woman.

Catastrophe, it's said, can bleach a suffering head overnight. What Gian saw then was hair, sparse and white, turn instantly black and thick, blooming about the woman's head heavy and dark as some thundercloud.

Her brow smoothed, and the corners of her eyes. Her hands softened, and gaunt limbs grew plump and strong. Everyone in the temple court-yard knew the moment her baby, fallen quiet these last days, kicked with sudden life: the woman clapped both hands to her heavy belly, and joy beyond joy lit up her face. In the arms of her wives again, she cried still, but not as before. Gian wept too.

Lastly there came a petitioner uncalled-for. This man smiled, whole-some of aspect, and handsome. In his hand he bore a lily rich in color as the deepest tissues of the body laid bare. When he set the flower down, its petals brushed Gian's ankle, soft and downy, only a little cooler than living flesh. A hue and cry broke out among the congregation, for no few at the bembe knew this man. He was Sea-john's greatest villain. How had he passed unseen in the courtyard until this moment? The drums quieted and none would sing for him. Sing? "Throw him out!" "Strike him down!" "You be careful there, Summer King. Watch him close, beware!" The ful-minations of the people went on and on, until at last the Summer King said, "Be still, all you! I'll hear him just the same as anybody." Deep was the hush that fell then, and all hearkened to the hideous truths spoken before the throne.

This man had once been the lover of a famed beauty who in the end had chosen to marry others. So the man had gone to witches for a ven-geance. Before the next dark-of-the-moon, both husband and wife of his former lover had met with gruesome misadventure: the one scalded dead when a vat of boiling laundry overturned, the other caught out some night without talisman by the wild dog packs. Indeed, the famous beauty too was dead now: throttled and drowned, by this man, while bathing. Crimes enough, anyone would have thought, when the man owned up to these murders, then quieted. Yet indignant voices from the crowd picked up the tale, and called out further iniquities. The mamas-and-papas of the beauty: found mutilated and dead. An orphaned infant: snatched from aunty's arms; dashed against a wall. And more, and worse.

When the chorus had at last rendered a full accounting, the man hung his head. "Those things…" he said sorrowfully, "…happened. It's true"; but all this evil owed to the whispering devil perched on his shoulder, the man said. The witches had put it there, and even now he felt hot breath blowing on his ear. Though no one else could glimpse it, and none but him hear, the fiend was always with him, suggesting fresh abominations.

That lickle child, your knife: kill her, it might say, or, *Sex that man there; choke him dead in the throes of love.* Only to make amends for past evils did he now beg freedom from this demon, goading him always deeper into damnation. You were hard of heart not to suffer some doubt then, not to wonder whether this man could really author such grisly wrongs, seeing his soft brown eyes glitter so, full of tears.

And yet to him, as to those others, the Summer King said, "No."

The man turned to Gian. "*Ó Sãozinho,* will you speak for me?"

Uneasy, Gian shook his head slowly.

The breathable ethers grew spiteful, pungent to the tongue and nose and eyes, as when chilies strike hot oil. La Pablo *si beau* screamed; for the man's face convulsed with demoniacal rage. A hidden dagger drawn, a hand thrown back only to stab down—and the villain lunged. (Gian had in fact shifted weight from his perch already, and set his feet in readiness, watching this man hawkishly all along. Gentlier. More gently, he might have caught the murderer's hand in its descent, crushed the fine wrist bones in his grip until the fingers sprang apart, loosing the blade, or else wrenched the man forward faster still and sent him hurtling past the throne to a stunning fall. More roughly, there were easy openings for a killing blow to the throat, or else for slitting it wide, should he swipe out the knife from his own belt. But in the event, rough or gentle wasn't Gian's to choose.) Some dry leaf blows into a campfire well-stoked and drawing well. What follows? That leaf catches at once, swiftly is consumed, a shadow withering briefly in the fierce light, and thereafter little remains, not cinder and ash so much as smudges of char. Thus for that man bewitched: where he'd stood, a whorl of soot came floating down, a scorched funk already dispersing from the air. The mortal whole of him had burned, unto teeth, bone, and the knife.

The Summer King lowered his shining hand, and it fell dark. Become Cianco the man again, he stood up with Gian, and celebrations began.

The hymns and holy drumbeats turned worldly, the dancing fast and loose. Everyone feasted. Long after dark, beloved hands plucked Gian mid-dance from amidst a sweaty grind of women, and he clung to Cianco as the dizzy world spun still, he'd drunk so much. Overhead, his lover said to the wives: "Getting late, y'all. Me and baby need to head out." After some hugs and kisses for Gian, they left.

Cianco walked with purpose while Gian straggled after, a finger hooked in his lover's belt. They came over the hill, seaside, where breezes freshened off the waters—this wasn't the way to Cianco's house. Nor were they heading down to the beach to sleep, as they did every so often.

"Where we going?" asked Gian.

"I want you to meet somebody" was the answer.

Salty air stirred and Gian stopped. He closed his eyes and stood, swaying as wind cooled the rummy sweat slicking his skin. That thunder in the distance, rolling and rolling, was only the ocean downhill: with loud-mouth Johnnys all gone to bed, the sounds of breakers hitting the beach reached up into the hills. An arm encircled him. "Come on now." A deep voice, warmly fond. "Come on, with your drunk ass." Basso and arm chivvied him into motion and kept him moving. "Moon's setting," Cianco said.

"Mmm," said Gian, keeping his eyes closed; he trusted to the arm's guidance. Gulls cried overhead.

"We'll hear 'em ring soon—midnight bells from over in the Kingdom."

At *midnight*, the memory of his promise returned. Gian's eyes sprang open.

"Ready to tell me what you got to say?" Cianco said. "It's a long walk."

Stopping sometimes for Gian to catch his breath, they walked the length of several parishes. When he'd told everything, though expecting to feel lighter and unburdened, Gian felt only tender and undone, none the better.

"Sit here," Cianco said, with hands upon Gian's shoulders to urge him down beside some parish well. With satiric looks—inspiring shy smiles—Cianco made a parody of the nuptial rite. He drew up water and gave it to Gian to drink; kneeling, he rinsed Gian's hands and feet. But whom did the joke mock? Hard to say, with nothing but the real thing in his care. Gian's heart knocked painfully. He must still carry the past with him and the river might never run clear again. Love doesn't take the burdens away, only makes them worth bearing.

In a temple across the square, drums of a nighttime bembe had this whole parish bumping; and suddenly they ceased. Behind the walls, a voice spoke in the silence, pure and clear as ocean shallows, that woman's voice—until it turned, mid-word, to smoke and gravel, the deepest bass of the most ancient grandfather. If they were only just getting to the invocation, this other congregation would be *all night*, Gian thought. He yawned. And it finally dawned on him to ask, "Pop, where are you taking me? And who we dropping in on, this late?"

"End of the block, right there." Cianco pointed. "And she's a nightbird. 'I'll be up whenever you get here,' she said." He pulled Gian to his feet. "My woman I go see every day I ain't with you." Midnight bells rang over in the Kingdom. "About time the both of you met. It's something all three of us together got to talk about."

When the window was clean enough
to reflect the dark shadow of his
face and the silver sea behind him,
Feetmeat scuttled down the side
of the Teeth Tower. Below, he saw
a flash of yellow through the trees,
moving back toward the Scroll Tower
through the connecting garden. He
might not be too late.

MIDNIGHT AT THE FEET OF THE CARYATIDES

Cory Skerry

Feetmeat scurried up the cool stone bricks of the Teeth Tower, his toes splayed out over stone fruit and leaves, his fingers digging into the spaces between gargoyles' teeth.

Everyone agreed Teeth Tower was the tallest, though Feetmeat wasn't sure how they'd know. The towers reached so high that no one in recorded history had ever visited the attics. Every expedition, even using the indoor staircases, had turned back when they ran out of supplies.

Teeth Tower was also the easiest to climb on the outside—for fifteen stories, until the baroque style was replaced by austere Greek columns. The vandals who called themselves the Court consistently marked their territory below that line, unable to scale smoother stones the way Feet-meat could.

And the Court's vandalism was why he was headed for the ninth-story classroom window, where they'd left their latest painted gift. He reveled in how the climb stretched his muscles and the wind tested his grip. He fancied the building knew he was there to clean off the obscenities, that it welcomed his visit.

Even with that imagined benevolence, the ascent had its perils. He edged past a row of spikes placed on the cornice long ago to prevent pigeons from nesting. It worked, but it also attracted raptors from the desert to the east and the sea to the west, swooping in with fish or rabbits and dropping them onto the spikes.

When he reached the ninth-story ledge, he rested for a few moments, his back against a gargoyle. Its claws had been sculpted so that they dug into the cornice; if upon each of Feetmeat's visits the gargoyle's grip seemed to have changed, or if sometimes there were gnawed bones lying on the ledge, it was no business of Feetmeat's.

The school and its Towers held many secrets, and Feetmeat reasoned that he didn't want to know most of them.

After all, there were plenty of daylight atrocities. Every student was a blue-blooded heir to varying degrees of fortune, and some of them seemed poisoned by it rather than blessed. Feetmeat couldn't help but wonder if things would have been different with money, with a powerful family. His face was handsome enough, he thought; he had eyes as green and slanted as a cat's, a gentle hill of a nose, smooth skin the color of the desert to the east. His arms were nearly the size of other men his age, muscled from trips up and down the towers. But the chest that anchored them was the size of a pubescent child's, and his short legs each bowed inward so severely that if he stood up straight, he must walk upon the sides of his feet.

Most of the school only ignored and avoided him, but four of the richest and vilest students had made it their mission to torment him whenever they could catch him. He was sure it was only his knowledge of the best ways to climb that had convinced these four, the Court, to spare him so far. Otherwise, they might have already beaten him as they did with select students, or even killed him, as they had done with too-friendly cats.

Last night, the Court had scrawled a lewd act on the window in crimson paint: a woman with a crown being used as a conduit between two men, one of whom had a large hat, the other with tiny dashes for eyes. The students didn't fraternize with Feetmeat, even though they were his age, so the caricatures meant nothing to him, but he had a feeling their identities were clear to everyone else.

He slipped out his flask—not whiskey, but turpentine—and wetted an old sock. The paint came off the glass reluctantly, revealing a Lector in the classroom beyond, flapping her mouth soundlessly. Before her, seated at desks arrayed in a half-moon, the students scratched black wounds into paper with sharp quills and cold fingers. Their disinterest in Feetmeat's arrival was to be expected—to most of them, he was of no more consequence than the school's many ghosts.

The door opened, beyond the Lector, and there was a flash of yellow. Feetmeat paused, pressing his face so close that his eyes and sinuses stung from the turpentine fumes, but he couldn't let the overcast sky's reflection get in the way.

It was *his* library aide, the boy with the halo of black curls. The aide handed the Lector a stack of books, as confidently as if he approached an equal. Feetmeat's heart beat a fierce rhythm, like the drums in the caravan where he'd lived before the school. The aides rarely left the libraries in the Scroll Tower, and he'd never seen the object of his affections venture out before.

If he finished this quickly, he could climb down and…. Well, he was too shy to approach the aide, but the idea of seeing him without glass between them would be euphoric.

Feetmeat scrubbed at the graffiti with reckless fury, as if it was intentionally obstructing him. The vandals had used long-handled brushes this time, and Feetmeat had to climb onto a gargoyle to reach the highest daubs of paint. He strained, because if he had to climb another story and dangle on a rope, he would never make it down in time to see the aide.

His toes slipped off the gargoyle's pate, and he fell toward the spikes below.

He grasped at the ledge, catching it with both hands. The impact stung his palms, and his fingers slid off.

His descent stopped with a sudden yank, his rope belt digging into his gut. He breathed hard through his nose. Below him, past bare feet that were too warped to fit into any shoes, the spikes waited.

He reached up and grabbed at the gargoyle; his belt had caught on its curled tail. The muscles in Feetmeat's arms burned as he clambered up the statue and back onto the ledge. If he'd been an average-sized man, he wouldn't have had the strength to lift himself. It was a thought he held gingerly, because it felt strange in his mind.

His sides prickled with fear-sweat, the sour odor stronger even than the paint thinner. He picked up the sock where it had fallen and began scrubbing again. His cheeks burned, even though no students had come to the window to witness his struggle.

Skerry

A ghost had. She looked just like all the other phantoms trapped in the school's towers: pale, hole-eyed wisps of young men and women whose hands ended before their fingertips and whose mouths held no teeth or tongues, as if in death they had forgotten some of what they were.

There was no way to tell how she had died, whether it had been inflicted by a cruel classmate or a bad decision. He knew she hadn't jumped or fallen: no one ever died that way on school grounds. There were dark rumors of past students and even Lectors who had tried, each of them saved by a sudden wind. Saved from death—but not necessarily from paralysis.

When the window was clean enough to reflect the dark shadow of his face and the silver sea behind him, Feetmeat scuttled down the side of the Teeth Tower. Below, he saw a flash of yellow through the trees, moving back toward the Scroll Tower through the connecting garden. He might not be too late.

He hobbled along the path, now angry at his tiny body, as if he hadn't been glad of it minutes before. Maybe he was light enough to climb well, but his stride fell far short of the aide's, and the rough gravel abraded his deformed feet.

As he neared the last garden, he heard the Court ahead.

He stopped behind a hedge, one gate away from running into the four psychotics. They'd smell the turpentine, know that he'd just come back from ruining their night's work. He wished it was anyone else between him and his aide, but there was no mistaking the distinctive honk of Bestra and Bulgar's laughter.

He would have to turn back and look for a place to hide. Silently. The Court had cat ears that listened for the sounds of hiding and retreating, and they had jackal hearts, their greatest joy derived from the hunt and its grisly end.

"Where's the key, fussy little mouse?" called another familiar voice, like a badly-played violin. Genevieve.

"We want to *improve* on those dusty old books," Bestra sneered.

Feetmeat froze as he realized they weren't talking to one another, but to a victim. Someone who had a connection to books.

The library aide.

A shriek cut the air, followed by the wet meat noises of impact-tested flesh.

Feetmeat knew he should flee, but instead, he crept up to the gate. Through the iron filigree, he watched the Court brace themselves on their strong, fit legs as they pummeled a blur of brown and yellow.

The aide. *His* library aide, with the beautiful brown eyes and curly black hair and huge, plush lips. His robes had always looked bright and noble through the windows, but now, in the apathetic daylight, the cloth seemed as dingy as weathered bones.

"Give us your key," demanded Ansimus King, the leader of the delinquent Court. Even the other spoiled nobles who attended class in the Towers avoided angering King. Whether he was telling a joke or breaking someone's fingers, he rarely changed expression, like a statue carved from a block of cold hatred.

The aide reached into his pocket—and just as quickly, pressed a glinting piece of metal into his mouth. His throat flexed. He looked up at his captors, smiling a gallows smile.

The Court cackled, as if it was a funny enough prank to get him to swallow a key, except for King.

"We'll have that back," he said.

Bulgar punched the aide in his stomach, but he only moaned—nothing came up.

"Not that way. It's between classes—no one to see if we do a bit of *excavation*. Hold him," King said, and he flicked out a blade. Genevieve slipped the scarf from her neck and worked it into the aide's mouth, drawing back on it like reins so he could only choke instead of cry out.

King sliced away the aide's robe, baring a smooth brown belly.

"You'll get blood all over you, and they'll catch us," Bestra said. She sounded frightened, and for a moment, Feetmeat had hope.

"I've done it before. If you cut slow enough, it all bleeds down instead of out," King said, and crouched in front of the squirming aide. If the others had qualms, they were too afraid of King with a knife in his hands to mention them aloud.

Feetmeat gripped the ironwork of the garden gate with his fingers and rattled it as noisily as he could. When he turned the handle, the gate swung open, with him riding it at an average man's height.

The other three turned to stare at Feetmeat, and King stuck the blade in just enough to squeeze out a few beads of blood. The aide stopped struggling, held himself motionless, but quivered with the effort.

"We're busy, Feetmeat," King said, as if he was only carving a holiday gourd.

"I have something that might interest you," Feetmeat called. More than once, he'd traded a secret climbing route for mercy. He hoped they hadn't tired of his bargains.

"You going to tattle on us to the Administration, Monkeyman?" called Genevieve. She had the same dark brown skin as the aide, but where his was silken, her flaccid cheeks and short forehead held a sheen of grease. Her overbite was so pronounced she couldn't close her mouth all the way, and in consequence, her own damp breath kept her lower lip and chin slick and shiny. Feetmeat wondered how she could laugh at the way he walked, how she thought his fish-hook-shaped legs were any worse than her shark mouth.

"Leave him," Feetmeat said, "and I'll show you a better place to make your marks."

"We're bored of your places," said King. "We want somewhere new, and he's got it. The inside of the library can't be cleaned with turpentine."

"This place," Feetmeat said, spacing his words out to emphasize each, "is both familiar and unknown. Why paint the books, where only a few scribes will see, when you could paint a place everyone can see, from every classroom in Teeth Tower?"

They dropped the library aide. Bestra and Bulgar stared with dry red eyes while King stepped closer.

"You mean the library windows, the ones held up by those statues who've each got one titty hanging out," he said. He seemed close to genuine reverence.

"Yes. I can take you to the caryatides, but I'm too short to reach what you paint, and no one can climb higher than the windows, not even me, so your marks will remain, even long after you've left the school."

King regained his feet. He commanded the others from the peak of wealth, the peak of cruelty, and the peak of beauty. King had a square jaw with a dust of early stubble, dark-lashed blue eyes, and strangely small but perfectly aligned white teeth. Feetmeat had thought him handsome, the first time he saw him, but a few minutes in King's company and that changed forever.

"Usually if we want help, we have to catch you," King challenged, his voice low and soft.

Feetmeat's story poured out with all the bitterness he would have felt if it had actually happened. "I asked to live in the dorms, with warmth and the other youths, and they said never, not even in the worst blizzard, not even if wolves stalk the grounds and the ocean chews at the front steps."

"And a good thing," Genevieve said.

King's eyes glistened, unfocused as he no doubt imagined desecrating the Scroll Tower, the center tower, which could be seen from nearly everywhere on the school grounds. In all the years the Towers had been a school, no other student had ever managed to paint so high or prominent a place.

In the ensuing silence, Feetmeat thought only of ghosts pressing their spongy noses against the windows, scratching with their stumps. He would never ask to live inside. It seemed absurd that the Court and their ilk, who made the ghosts directly with their hands and indirectly with their words, would believe anyone wanted to trap themselves inside that world.

But though Feetmeat clung to the gate like a frog on a wall in summer, ready to snatch insects that ventured too close to the door lamps, they saw only that he was small—not that he was hungry. To them he was only fragile bones and bumbling steps, a child-sized tragedy.

"We'll need more paint," declared King. "We'll meet you here, four days hence. Veneris, at dusk?"

"Yes, Veneris," Feetmeat said. "Bring old clothes that we can blacken, and climbing harnesses with the longest ropes."

"If you're not here, we'll break the neck of every cat we see and tell the Administration we saw you do it," Genevieve said.

"I'll be here," Feetmeat said. He tried not to think of the cats who sheltered in the toolshed where he lived, their purring silenced by cruel hands. He remained on the gate, swinging slightly with the breeze, until they dropped the library aide and passed out of sight.

The boy's soft halo of curly black hair was mashed with mud and stuck all over with twigs and thorns. Normally there was a quill tucked behind his ear on either side, but those tiny wings were missing now. The corners of his mouth bled where Genevieve's scarf had abraded him.

Sometimes, when Feetmeat washed the library windows on the first seven floors, he would see this aide sneaking short reads as he reshelved books. His long, fine fingers splayed over the lines of text with such grace that Feetmeat had imagined those hands fluttering over his skin, reading him with the same fierce curiosity that drove them to turn pages. He knew that wished-for lust was impossible, that everyone saw him as an animal or a monster, or if he was lucky, as a child.

"Thank you," the aide rasped. They must have hit him in the throat. "They were going to...like a *fish*—"

"I know," Feetmeat said. He reached out a hand, intending to help the aide to his feet, and realized only too late that his gallant gesture was laughable. The aide did smile, but he held out his hand as well, and shook it once in greeting. His fingers were gentle and cold.

"Felipe," the aide wheezed.

Feetmeat was silent.

"Do you have a name, heroic window-washer?"

Feetmeat had come here as the barely-tolerated freak in a visiting caravan, and when their negotiations with the Administration of the school hadn't gone well, they'd decided Feetmeat was the cause of all their bad luck. They'd tried to burn him. A long-dead janitor had saved him, but the man wasn't much more sensitive than the caravan folk. "Feetmeat" was what the janitor called him, and in time, so did everyone else. He couldn't bear to say this memory-tarnished name aloud. "Not yet," he said.

Felipe struggled to his feet and headed through a side gate shrouded in foliage. Felipe walked slowly; whether from pain or to allow Feetmeat to keep pace, it wasn't clear. They wended through the garden, wet and fragrant with rose blossoms and mint, until they passed through one of the western gates onto the cliffs that held back the roiling sea.

Feetmeat's dread grew with each of Felipe's steps.

When Felipe neared the eroded edge, Feetmeat cried, "Don't!" and hobbled forward as fast as he could. He flung out a hand, intending to snag the scraps of robe as Felipe tumbled over the edge. Instead, Felipe's hand swept down and landed in his with the precision of a bird.

"I'm not going to jump," Felipe said. His laugh turned into a cough. They gazed down the jagged slope at the rocks below, where the sea thrashed and foamed. Felipe's one exposed nipple protested the bitter wind, as hard as Feetmeat's cock.

No one had ever held him with such charity—once a doctor, for money, and once a crowd, in the attempt to burn him. This warm touch, made all the more intense by the cold air, was like petting a fallen star. He was afraid his callused grip would extinguish its light, but he clung tightly nonetheless.

Felipe's injured voice frayed in the wind, but the connection of their palms seemed to amplify the words.

"Thank you. You saved me, but also my books. I wanted to work in the Scroll Tower since I was first admitted to the school. It's the only place I belong."

Feetmeat belonged on the outside of the towers, with the birds and the carvings, but he couldn't trust his voice. He squeezed slightly to show he understood.

Felipe let go, and cold wind filled Feetmeat's palm. "But I should jump. They'll find me again, and they'll take my key. The Administration would rather lose me or a roomful of rare books than anger those monsters and their influential families."

He didn't move. The wind made flags of his tattered garments, and his crown of muddy hair blew straight back from his face as he stared at the furious ocean.

"I care about…the books," Feetmeat said, and again he squeezed Felipe's hand.

"You're fierce," Felipe said. "All *books* should be so lucky, to have a strong gargoyle like you."

He smiled without joy.

Feetmeat's chest tightened, and tears burned his eyes as he thought of the gnarled stone creatures with their snaggle-teeth and bulging eyes. He should have known better than to let himself hope. He turned, because he would rather leave Felipe now, before he saw him cry.

Felipe suddenly went to one knee, so they were eye to eye. He grabbed Feetmeat's hand again, with both his own, and held him in place. "You misunderstand me," he said. "You know why the gargoyles are there?"

To scare away pigeons and rats, Feetmeat thought, but he only shook his head.

"Historically, gargoyles are placed as guardians. They chase away evil. You did that, today, and if I heard right, you've done it before. So yes, maybe you're not shaped as men expect to see; but every part of you is only mismatched so that you're the size and shape you need to be who you are. Behind those beautiful green eyes, you are as tough as stone."

Felipe smiled and pulled one hand away, revealing Feetmeat's callused palm. "Tough as stone doesn't mean it can't be a beautiful sculpture."

For long seconds, Feetmeat tried to enjoy this moment. Instead he panicked, knowing that somehow this would end. Nothing good lasted—not for long. Not for Feetmeat.

He remembered the ghost in the attic of the Shadow Tower, the only one of the school's five towers which was short enough that he had been able to climb all the way to the roof. This dead girl had been blonde, with prevalent freckles made even darker by death. Her ghost hadn't looked out the window, but had instead gazed at her desiccated body, curled like a spider in the corner where she'd slit her wrists. Her cavernous eyes swallowed the sorrow of her own death for such a long time that Feetmeat had fallen asleep against the glass as he watched her.

He thought of Felipe with hole eyes, with his long graceful fingers frayed into smoke at the first knuckles, staring at his own open chest cavity on a forgotten landing in a disused stairwell—or of his body smashed against the rocks below, his ghost flown away so that Feetmeat couldn't even have that much of him.

Felipe was right. The Court would get to him, one way or the other. They were the thing that would ruin this moment, that could flay the dedicated grip on his hand, that could dim these brown eyes so they no longer glowed with admiration.

"I would like to borrow your key," Feetmeat said. "I'll use it to save the books again. This time, forever."

"I owe you a favor. If it's my key, so be it," Felipe said.

"I may need more from you," Feetmeat admitted. "We may need to sacrifice the Scroll Tower's clock."

Felipe shrugged. "The worst—and only—noise in the library is the clock upon the hour."

Each of the next four nights, Feetmeat climbed the Scroll Tower in a different way, carrying a heavy coil of chain in his haversack.

The Scroll Tower's twenty-seventh story was a giant clock, floating about the twenty-sixth story, which was a solid ring of giant windows, impossible to climb. This glass level was held aloft by a circle of languid, willowy caryatides on the twenty-fifth story. Each of them held a vase, lyre, or switch in one hand, the other above her head to support the windows.

Feetmeat wired the chains among the feet of the caryatides into a safety net wide enough to support all of the Court. If anyone noticed the chains during the day, no matter—they wouldn't be there long.

On Jovis, the night before he was to guide the Court up to the ring of caryatides, he used Felipe's key and climbed the stairs inside the tower. After hours of wrestling with steps built for a different shape of legs, lugging a sackful of tools pilfered from the gardener's shed, he finally emerged inside the giant clock. It faced north, toward the Teeth Tower, where the lectures were attended.

He finished just before dawn.

When the clock next struck midnight, the hour hand would wind up the last of the rope, and the rope would pull the holding pin, and The Court would be cinched into a net of chains. Feetmeat didn't look forward to what he had to do—in fact, he wasn't entirely sure he could do it—because taking care of evil was an evil in itself.

But he knew what was required of a protector, and if he was also caught in the net, he was prepared to burn himself as well.

When Feetmeat thumped down onto the roof of the toolshed where he lived, he barely had the strength to swing into the loft window and land on his bed. He still had work to do, however.

When his hands regained their strength, he penned a note to Felipe. He stuck the key to it with grey wax, made from stolen candle ends.

"Yours in flesh and heart," he signed, and below that, in lieu of a name, he wrote simply, "Not Yet."

He crept into the vestibule of the dormitory and placed the missive in Felipe's box. Now that he knew his love's name, if he survived, he could write more letters.

Maybe he would write entire books.

King, Genevieve, Bestra and Bulgar arrived late, nearly an hour past dusk.

"We must hurry," Feetmeat whispered. "If we're to climb all the way to the great windows, we'll need time."

"Relax, Feetmeat," said King. "We're faster than you think. After all, we can use our legs." Genevieve tittered. Bestra and Bulgar waited for orders from King, as always. And the clock on the Scroll Tower struck nine.

Feetmeat began dragging supplies from the bushes. Pails with tin lids, brushes and palm-sized sacks of powder. He gestured to their clothing.

"The moonlight is already against us—tar your clothes, that we might pass the sentinels in peace."

"Sentinels?" King scoffed. "What sentinels?"

"I said I would take you where you'd never gone," Feetmeat said, his heart thumping. Tar was more flammable than their clothes. "If you want to reach the caryatides, and paint the windows they hold, you'll find it takes more cunning than throwing a rope around a gargoyle's horns and scrabbling up."

"I'll do no such thing. The Admins are all asleep anyway, and even if they woke up, who cares if they see us?" King said.

Feetmeat still had a flask of turpentine to pour on them, once they were trussed into the chains, and that would have to be enough. Perhaps it was best that they delay no longer—they still had several gardens to traverse before they reached the foot of the tower.

"Fine, then let's hurry," Feetmeat urged.

"Bulgar, he's right," said King. "Carry our twisted little friend that we might make better time."

Feetmeat protested, but Bulgar leaned down and scooped him up, holding him like a babe. He didn't struggle, lest Bulgar accidentally snap his bones. The boy's breath smelled like wine and wet dog.

"Where are your stencils?" Feetmeat asked, afraid they had left them and would need to go back.

King chuckled and pointed to Genevieve. "Tonight, we need only words, and Genna has a fine hand."

"Words, to go on the library," Bestra said, as if she was explaining something profound that a mere window washer might not understand. Genevieve pinched her, and she was quiet.

Feetmeat endured the journey in silence, sick with second thoughts. They were wicked, but perhaps not evil, not enough for the cruel example he planned to make of them.

When they reached the base of the Scroll Tower, Bulgar flipped him around like a doll, one arm crossing over Feetmeat's chest and arms, the other reaching between Feetmeat's legs and roughly palpating his privates. "What would you need all this for? Seems a waste."

Feetmeat kicked as the others howled with laughter, but he couldn't get free.

"Book boys, is what he needs 'em for," Genevieve added. "Maybe they'll make little babies, little butthole babies!" Her giggles took flight like bats, shrieking up the side of the tower.

"Let me go," Feetmeat snarled.

"You couldn't keep up with us, not on the stairs," said King, and he held up something that glinted in the moonlight. A key.

"Turns out another bookboy was more agreeable. So we changed our minds."

He unlocked a small side-door, and the Court filed in after him, Bulgar last.

Feetmeat's chest seized. He thought of the note he'd left Felipe that morning:

> Your regard for me is more than I could have ever hoped, even if only as a protector. I fear the price of being a gargoyle, however, is that one must also be a monster. Perhaps you can be my friend even after I become what I must; perhaps not. We shall see what you make of me, if you meet me at the library's northern window at midnight.

He'd intended to wave through the glass, to deal with evil the way they had in the caravan, to see if Felipe could still look at him the same afterward. Now, Felipe would walk right into the library as the Court was destroying it, and there was no doubt they would be happy to vandalize his body along with his beloved books.

Feetmeat struggled, but Bulgar wrestled him sideways, one arm still gripping his chest, pinning his hands to his sides, and one arm around his legs, so he could no longer kick.

The dark stairwell coiled like a snake. As they passed the dormitory doors on the first three floors, Feetmeat thought about screaming for help, but he knew they'd toss him down the stairs and say that's why he'd yelled. They'd make sure his neck was broken before an Administrator got close.

Skerry

If he didn't come up with a plan, he would end up broken anyway. He stared at the dark wall as it passed, his stomach clenched as he bounced with Bulgar's footfalls and eternally leaned to the right as they followed the steps. He was too small, too weak.

Every four turns, a window poured harsh moonlight into the stairwell, and then they marched back into darkness. The fifth window they passed illuminated a drab ghost, her white skin clay-like in the harsh moonlight. She looked out the window, her posture haughty, uninterested in the living. The Court had no use for a dead victim when they still had a live one, so they ignored her as well. As Bulgar passed her, Feetmeat's face went through her shoulders.

Cold air burned his eyes, stung the inside of his nose, raked over his brain like a cat's claws. Her memories settled into his brain like leaves sinking into a pond. His despair grew heavier, and he tried not to think about what they might do to him, even as he remembered what some other long-ago bullies had done to her.

She'd been proud, though. She refused to give in, had thought it meant something that she never cried or begged. She endured, and then she poisoned herself.

Feetmeat would rather be alive than be proud.

He counted ten more windows, just to be sure they couldn't go down the stairs quickly. On the fifteenth floor, he pissed all over Bulgar, who predictably dropped him with a shriek of rage.

Feetmeat swung out the window faster than they could grab him, trusting the tower to save him. He caught himself on a stone vine, his fingers cupped over the slick leaves, and then he climbed faster than he had in his life.

Their hooks and harnesses clacked against the stone near him as they tried to snag him. He climbed up, so it would be harder for them to swing their equipment toward him. Once they gave up and retreated to the stairs, he would climb down and wait by the fourth-story window to warn Felipe. To tattle on the Court to the Administration would be suicide—they would force Feetmeat to swallow every key they could find and then cut them all out with separate holes—but he could at least prevent them from having a human victim to go with the library.

When they disappeared back into the stairwell, their whispered curses still skittering like insects in the night air, he began his descent, only to seize in horror.

There was a small glow by one of the library windows far above him, like that of a single candle.

Feetmeat climbed at speeds he usually didn't dare. He stopped just short of true recklessness—some voice in his head reminded him that he couldn't warn Felipe if he was motionless on the ground below—but he barely paused to wipe the sweat from his hands or mentally map his hand- and foot-holds.

However fast he climbed, there was the risk that the Court would have climbed the stairs quicker.

When he arrived at the feet of the caryatides, slicked in sweat and breathing hard, he still couldn't see who was behind the glow.

He grasped the stone tunic of the nearest caryatid. The folds were smooth and he didn't have the best purchase, but it was the only way to reach the window on this side—the chain he'd left dangling from the clock was on the north face, and the stairwell went up the west, the side that faced no other buildings, only the sea. When he reached the window, his stomach sank. He'd hoped it was a cranky Administrator who'd fallen asleep at a window desk, but of course it was Felipe, who jumped when Feetmeat knocked on the glass.

"The Court is coming," he said. Felipe shook his head, and Feetmeat said it louder. Screamed.

The glass from the windows was too thick.

Shaking, Feetmeat slipped his small knife from his belt and held it in his teeth so he could slice the pad of his index finger. Using his blood as paint, he wrote *Hide* backwards across the glass.

Recognition dawned on Felipe's features, but it was too late.

He jerked his head, drawn by some commotion Feetmeat couldn't hear, and dashed off into the stacks.

"The candle!" Feetmeat yelled, but moments later, King appeared. He saw the candle first, then the message in blood on the window, then Feetmeat's face.

King's blank face stretched into its first smile. He walked off the way Felipe had gone.

Skerry

Feetmeat clung to the caryatid's arm like a bug on a branch, motionless even with the predators behind glass. He could never wake an Administrator before it was too late. If he climbed his way down to the stair window and back inside, it might still be too late. Besides, he was barely four feet tall. There wasn't much he could do.

The Court punctuated his failure by returning with Felipe squirming in their midst. Bulgar and King pressed him onto the desk while Genevieve snatched up the candle. She singed his hair.

Something cool touched Feetmeat's leg, and he glanced down to find a pale hand offering him a stone jug. The caryatid looked at him with eyes as blank as King's, and though Feetmeat should have been afraid, her stone face was gentler than King's flesh.

Feetmeat grasped the jug by the handle, and she released it, placing her free hand out to form a second foot-hold. Feetmeat looked down at the other caryatides. Their faces were all turned toward him, and below them, all down the building, the gargoyles faced his direction as well, baring their teeth. One flexed its wings; another lashed its tail. They seemed to guess he was about to destroy part of their home.

"I'm sorry," he said. "If it helps, I won't last long after I do it. But the tower can be fixed, and Felipe can't."

He swung the jug and smashed it into the glass window. That drew the attention of the Court for a moment, but King narrowed his eyes and shrugged.

Feetmeat imagined King's foot connecting with his chin, knocking him out into the air, just as he knew King was imagining it. It didn't matter. He wouldn't sit here and do nothing, and he wouldn't retreat. Felipe was going to die either way; he deserved to know someone cared enough to go with him.

The stone jug shattered the window on the fourth hit. Feetmeat used it to knock aside the largest shards. Bestra, who was closest to the window, was still shaking off her shirt when Feetmeat stepped onto the shard-strewn carpet.

He swung the jug into her left knee, and the sound was quieter than the breaking window, but loud enough to hear. That one moment of triumph blossomed: if Feetmeat could just injure each of them, just slow them down, Felipe could carry him down the stairs in time to get away.

His fantasy lasted less than second before Genevieve hit him in the head with a book and dragged him across the glass by the back of his shirt. She rolled him off the sill.

The caryatid reached out with the arm that didn't hold the window, tried to catch him, but the impact was too much, and her arm snapped off. Feetmeat plummeted toward the garden below, struggling to catch himself on something. He needed to get back, to distract the Court from Felipe.

His belt yanked tight around his waist. He almost vomited from the sudden squeeze, and then he was falling sideways. He opened his eyes, amazed to see tiny bits of glass falling like snow from his hair and clothes, sparkling in the moonlight.

Two stone paws hung in front of his head, their talons curled back toward him. The gargoyle that clutched his belt swung around, gently sweeping its way toward the ground.

"No," Feetmeat gasped. "Back to the window. I don't care if they kill me. I'm not leaving him."

He wasn't sure if it understood. Maybe it didn't care, and would rather have someone to clean pigeon shit from its feathers than some human it had never seen.

But after a moment of flapping in place, it banked right, then began to rise. When it swooped toward the window, Feetmeat spotted Bestra curled on the floor, clutching her knee. As soon as the gargoyle's shadow flickered over them, the others glanced out.

It swept in, its great stone wings knocking more glass from the frame, and gently placed Feetmeat on top of a standalone bookshelf. It grabbed Bestra in its hind claws and leapt off into the sky, her scream echoing back as it flew off to its perch.

Bulgar bellowed, like the camels in the caravan. He and King both let go of Felipe. Bulgar thundered toward Feetmeat, his fingers hooked like claws. Feetmeat tossed a book at him, but he didn't even notice. A dark shadow flitted across the moonlit floor once more, and this time, King grabbed the stone jug from the floor where Feetmeat had dropped it.

When the gargoyle flew in, King swung the jug, snapping off some of its feathers. It whirled on him in silent fury, even as more gargoyles crawled and flew in through the window. One by one, the Court were dragged screaming from the room.

Skerry

The last gargoyle looked closely at Felipe, where he crouched motionless on the table.

"Please," Feetmeat said hoarsely. "He's my friend."

The gargoyle turned and took wing. It dipped down below the window sill.

Feetmeat clambered down off the bookshelf, suddenly aware of every place where glass had lodged in his skin. Felipe, who wore slippers, hurried off of the desk and over to Feetmeat, who sagged against the books.

"I'm sorry. Bleeding all over. And the window…. If it rains, the books will get wet," Feetmeat said, his voice as hoarse as if he'd swallowed the glass. He didn't know what else to say.

Felipe wrapped Feetmeat in his strong arms.

"How did you do that," he whispered. It didn't sound like a question.

Feetmeat shook his head. "I'm sure if the books could have, they would have defended you. It just turns out the place I belong has more teeth."

Felipe laughed, all relief and little humor. After a moment, he released Feetmeat. "Thank you," he said, but instead of getting up and leaving, he leaned toward Feetmeat once more. This time he pressed his swollen, bleeding lips against Feetmeat's. Soft but unyielding, he kissed Feetmeat until neither of their mouths tasted of blood.

"Now, whose lips are these?" Felipe asked, outlining Feetmeat's mouth with one gentle finger.

Feetmeat thought of what he'd done, of the burden he'd taken upon himself, of the friends he hadn't known he had, and most of all, the caryatides watching his combined sins and heroism with their implacable stone gaze.

"Telamon," he said. "That is my name."

Wilde accepts their praise, acknowledging his growing reputation as the knight-errant of this, the disturbed Exposition Universelle. It is as if no one remembers his dank, weary form haunting the city's cheapest cafés, a penniless, friendless alcoholic and shamed bugger, embracing a long and pathetic public suicide. Most likely some of these same women spat at him on the street only a month ago as their fine, intact parasols darkened him with shadow.

THE REVENGE OF OSCAR WILDE

Sean Eads

"*C'est lui! Dieu merci!*"

"*Je vous remercie, Saints, pour la santé de Monsieur O.W.!*"

He bows to acknowledge the appreciation from eight pretty damsels in distress. Two divergent groups of shambling, decomposing Lazarus men have herded them into a terrible trap in the narrow street between the Panorama du Congo and the massive, barricading left wing of the Palais du Trocadero. An hour ago, they were modern, self-assured young ladies quite unwilling to let the men, their fathers and brothers and husbands, sequester them further. They were *armed*, after all, and no doubt confident in the sturdiness of their parasols. Now the skeletal remains of those umbrellas lecture them on their foolishness. Shreds of fine vibrant fabric flutter off the broken, twisted ribs, mimicking the crisp, massive flags high overhead on the Palais spires. But the women's gaze is not heavenward. If there is a god to them now, he walks this earth and his name is Oscar Wilde.

He has appeared seemingly out of nowhere and stands resplendent in an orange topcoat, a sunflower in the uppermost buttonhole and an elegant Webley Royal Irish 450 CF revolver in his right hand—the weapon a gift from his lover Bosie, the pretty poison he has picked and died from years ago. Wilde's head is bared to the breeze, his brown hair long and unkempt as in his younger days. Standing beside him, significantly shorter and appropriately serious and somehow vibrant in matching gray pants and shirt, is Albert Ayat—as of fifteen days ago the gold medalist in fencing at this, the 1900 Olympics here in Paris.

The sword Ayat lifts in salute to the ladies now is sturdier than a traditional foil but his accuracy and speed with it are unchallenged and deadlier for the heft. It cuts a nifty whistle in the air when his wrists flick it just so.

"I do not believe any of these Lazari include the one who bit poor Bosie, Ayat. Nevertheless the ladies require our attention—how dreadful."

"There are ten threatening from the left. I will take them," Ayat says. Wilde listens, slow on the translation. Ayat is difficult to understand when he's almost breathless. Wilde himself is nearly breathless just from looking at Ayat. But all that must wait. Ayat maneuvers toward the larger group of Lazarus men in that peculiar fencer's stance that seems both noble and ridiculous. Wilde turns, his sigh quickly changing to a gasp as he weaves away from one clumsy hand. Decaying fingernails rip the sunflower from his chest and crush the petals. Three lumbering creatures growl at him and close.

Wilde recomposes himself, brushes the flower's remains from the buttonhole and retreats several steps, coolly checking the Webley to find it loaded and in good working order. In the days before his downfall in England, when Bosie's father the Marquess of Queensberry threatened to assault him, Wilde threatened in turn to shoot him on sight. It had been a bluff—and Wilde was a very good bluffer. There was genuine fear in the little old bully's eyes when he thought the towering Irishman might kill him there and then. *I should have*, Wilde thinks. But in 1893 he was another man, civilized, Bosie's devoted fool. Wilde has been—and been with—many different men since then. Every dead incarnation of his being lives in whatever man he is now. But perhaps men always remain, inside, with the first person they ever loved, and remain the men they were at the time of that love's experiencing. Why else is he out here once more avenging Bosie's honor?

Bosie's father died many months ago. His passing did nothing to ease Wilde's troubles at the time. It did not elicit the strange recall to life he feels now. His greatest pleasure, before he shoots the nearest Lazarus man in the head, is imagining it is 1893 again and that Queensberry is charging toward him. A bullet would have undone much misery.

Wilde smiles and returns the first resurrected man to his rest. He dispatches the second and third attacker in short order, aiming at Queensberry's face each time. It will take more than Christ to bring these Lazari back now. But perhaps resurrection was always the devil's own work.

Behind him, Ayat has troubles. He is a genius with the blade and a fine physical specimen, though Wilde cares little for the curly moustaches that age the Frenchman's face past its twenty-four years, hanging off his lips like wilted petals on an otherwise vibrant flower. Careful and strategic in most circumstances, diagonal in his feints and parries—a chess-piece bishop with the sword of a chess-piece knight—Ayat has miscalculated. Wilde knows the root of his difficulties is the ladies and his eagerness to impress them. The young fencer leapt into the fray without realizing how the narrow confines and the Lazari's sheer numbers cheat his sword of its principal attribute—length. Now nearly encircled, he cannot swing or stab his way free. *A smitten fool,* Wilde thinks. But Ayat looks too wholesome and fresh to garner further opprobrium. The fencer's youth and vitality have made Wilde's heart his *Piste.*

He reaches into his left coat pocket for bullets to feed the Webley and then steps forward unflinching, gun outstretched. He sees Queensberry's right and left profile; he sees the back of Queensberry's head. Imagining well is the best revenge and the Lazari sate his imagination. Several minutes later, when the last resurrected man is returned to the dust, Wilde can only marvel at the Webley, saying, "The pen may be mightier than the sword, Ayat, but I believe I should like to compose only with this henceforth. There are several critics I have been meaning to send letters."

"Must you be so impossible, Oscar?"

"It is an impossible situation, Ayat."

The ladies rush toward them, their white gloved hands waving in welcome little surrenders to both men. The French women are very unlike the British, Wilde notes, especially in moments of excitement. Their initial hysterias are the same, but French ladies seem immune to fainting spells and are surprisingly adaptive to scenes of gore. Consider how they stand around these rotting corpses unfazed now that the danger has passed. Wilde accepts their praise, acknowledging his growing reputation as the knight-errant of this, the disturbed Exposition Universelle. It is as if no one remembers his dank, weary form haunting the city's cheapest cafés, a penniless, friendless alcoholic and shamed bugger, embracing a long and pathetic public suicide. Most likely some of these same women spat at him on the street only a month ago as their fine, intact parasols darkened him with shadow.

Their scorn was well deserved and earned, Wilde thinks, shuddering at an image he conjures of himself lying insensate in a gutter. It has been over three years since he completed the jail sentence that destroyed his soul. Disgraced, humiliated, divorced, he has lived these years in European exile, determined to conclude it here in Paris. There had been presumptive talk among his friends that he should write again—that his wit would be a magic balm to erase the past and soar him to even greater heights. None of them understood, not even his dear and loyal friend Robbie Ross, the impish boy who first seduced Wilde and unlocked the key of his being, stirring fresh life from an existence that was dead for reasons Wilde could not articulate to himself. He had a wife and darling children and yet he was not a living man until Robbie embraced him— Robbie who seemed to understand everything in the world in spite of his youth, or perhaps because of it. No, not even Robbie understood the prison experience, the years of hard labor, the hideous conditions that yet held sway over his mind. When Wilde dreams, he is there again, in the prison yard watching fair-haired youths bruised and worked until they shamble about so very much like the creatures he and Ayat just put down.

> *Yet each man kills the thing he loves*
> *By each let this be heard.*
> *Some do it with a bitter look,*
> *Some with a flattering word.*
> *The coward does it with a kiss,*
> *The brave man with a sword!*

Wilde shudders again and the women mistake it for something else and offer their comfort. A glance at Ayat's dripping blade makes him remember the conclusion of his poem, his only attempt at writing since his release. "The Ballad of Reading Gaol" had been an anonymous hit with the public and it had pleased him, the master of paradoxes, that everyone had missed the poem's ultimate paradox. Even Robbie and Bosie had missed the intent of that line—*For each man kills the thing he loves.* Had Wilde not also said, "To love oneself is the start of a lifelong romance?" The poem was a statement of intention, a suicide note that announced he planned to kill himself by living.

He had embarked on this plan by drinking and whoring as much as he could, each day a meaningless and wincing preamble to a long and stuporous night. He wanted only to rot where he stood and decay as he walked, until nothing remained. Yes, it was a prolonged suicide, and a successful one until the phenomenon of the Lazarus men. Wilde may have seen the very first of their kind, three weeks ago. He had fallen into a gutter across from a man who seemed quite dead, no doubt a murdered tourist. Wilde had even slurred a question to him about what it was like. Then the dead man rose and stumbled into the crowded night. A hallucination or mere mistake, Wilde thought at the time, though now he is certain it was a Lazarus man and he wonders if his drunken impotence then bears some responsibility for the present chaos. *And for poor Bosie's condition.*

"These ladies are lovely, are they not, Oscar?"

Ayat gallantly swipes the sword's blood across his right pants leg and then kisses the hand of the girl he has decided, Wilde assumes, is the loveliest. The ladies are quiet and indeed all of Paris seems so. How many of its citizens have been killed—and killed again? He thinks of Bosie, stripped half-naked and sweating in his sheets at the hotel, his throat bandaged from the bite that happened three days ago. He hears the young aristocrat calling out, fading away. The auditory vividness of it startles Wilde. *What am I doing out here, attempting to avenge a death that has not even happened—and won't happen!* He wonders if this self-assurance is a bluff or a mad reliance on a technicality. There is one point of universal agreement in these days of penumbral confusion: a Lazarus man's bite is fatally transformative. Bosie will die and yet he will *not* die.

Wilde considers how best to excuse himself. Ayat will want to accompany him. Even the allure of beautiful, willing women is not enough to sever the sudden warrior bond between them. They have now fought four battles together, Ayat having sought Wilde out for his renewed fame. Wilde was, of course, quite drunk when the first incidents occurred and multiplied. The attack at the Velodrome de Vincennes supposedly killed over three hundred people, though it had not proven easy to distinguish victims from attackers in many instances. Wilde realizes, from what little he can remember, that nothing short of divine providence acquitted his escape at the simultaneous attack on the Champ de Mars. For he had defended a child using the heavy cane of someone already felled. Wilde was a very large man, not athletic but powerful all the same. Fueled by alcohol and rage, a powerful anti-societal vengeance suddenly electric in his spine, Wilde bashed heads with such furor that no less than ten skulls were certified split open from his blows. Reflecting on it in later sobriety as he wittily held court before admiring Frenchmen and the child's injured mother (bitten, poor creature, but at the time this was no cause for alarm), he realized he had no idea if the people he had struck—men only, there was at least that balm—were innocent people or their resurrected assailants.

He has not touched a drop of alcohol since.

"See the ladies to safety, Ayat. I have urgent business elsewhere."

The Olympic fencer protests but there is nothing he can do. Wilde holds up an imposing, callused hand. "We will find each other later, dear boy. You may rest assured."

"Yes, Oscar."

Ayat is breathless now in a different way as he turns back to the women. Wilde smiles, wondering if the ladies are in even more danger now. But the Frenchman is young and no doubt lacks expertise. A pity, he thinks, checking the Webley again before starting off. Youth is wasted on the inexperienced.

He could expect a tedious walk to the Hôtel d'Alsace under normal circumstances, Paris's population having swelled by many thousands on account of Exposition and the Olympics. Now the streets are shockingly deserted and the Eiffel Tower, which Wilde considers an appropriate idol to worship if these are indeed the Last Days, stands a lonely sentinel's watch from across the way. He walks faster than he has in years and his heart feels it. He thinks of what he will say when he re-enters their room. He knows he must sound self-assured and fluid. Somehow he believes only a display of great confidence will keep Bosie alive. *Bosie, you must not die and you will not die as long as you have my love. Therefore, Bosie, I can assure you of a splendid immortality.*

Truth be told, while he has always been known as an amazing speaker, with wit at will, his speech is seldom as extemporaneous as it sounds. He has held imaginary conversations with himself since he was a boy, working on lines and rehearsing clever dialogue and bons mots to summon only slightly altered according to need. His employment and delivery is so quick and seamless that it truly feels spontaneous. But true ease in talking comes from art, not chance, to paraphrase Pope, and he believes Pope is always better paraphrased than taken directly. When faced with subjects he cannot even conceive of, much less practice for, Wilde knows he sounds like a stuttering fool, even a simpleton. Bosie's charming torment is his ability to create hour after unbroken hour of such instances, and Wilde humiliates himself in base incoherencies for the sake of love.

The entrance to the d'Alsace is like that of other hotels since the crisis, barricaded and patrolled by three armed and watchful men. Their guns train on Wilde before he is ever properly in shooting distance. Wilde stops and adjusts his posture and bearing to make sure neither in any way resembles the stumbling shuffle of the Lazari. He calls loudly to them in his Irish brogue and their fingers relax off the triggers. "Monsieur Wilde," one says, nods politely and clears a path for him.

"If only decent theatres could afford armed gunmen to keep out the public, plays might finally be performed in their perfection before absolutely no one. I've always said the unfortunate fact of drama is that it must be witnessed."

"*Oui, Monsieur,*" another guard says, and gives Wilde a glare that reminds him not everyone has buried his past with the risen dead.

He hurries up to their room—Bosie's room, really, since he pays for it with money inherited from his father's estate. In bed, Bosie's head thrashes right and left, dank blond tresses sweated heavily to his forehead. Death's skeletal hand has gift-wrapped his throat in thick white gauze over a necrotizing bite wound. The rest of his body does not move and this horrifies Wilde. It is as if the Death has asserted dominion everywhere else and what life there remains has gathered in Bosie's head for a doomed last stand.

Shots fire from outside the window. Wilde looks in that direction, sweating.

"So cold," Bosie says.

Wilde whips off his topcoat and presses it like a blanket of fire across the slight body.

"Dear boy," Wilde says. "Have you been unattended all this time? I left specific instructions—"

Eads

"Don't leave me again," Bosie whispers.

Wilde swallows. How those four words recall memories both tender and hard! Bosie once had the flu and Wilde nursed him devotedly, never leaving his side as he suffered. Then suddenly Bosie recovered and Oscar was stricken by the same malady. From the open window of his sickroom in their rented lakefront house, he endured the sound of his restored lover frolicking jubilantly with several local youths, Bosie having left him to sweat out his own illness in parched solitude.

Wilde forces his hands to open. He has clenched more fists in the last two weeks than he ever did during his three trials or even in prison itself, when the indignities and outrages he'd experienced built into a bitter torrent he directed entirely at Bosie—through a letter. The prison guards had finally allowed him to write something, and the resulting unsent letter presented an accusation, an entire trial and a sentencing of Bosie for his crimes. He had fallen so far, and for what? Bright blue eyes, a pretty face that launched and sank exactly one ship—Wilde's own? Writing the letter released a rage he would not know again until his moment on the Champ de Mars. *A love letter to my messiah*, Wilde thinks to himself in derision. It was longer than any letter composed by the Apostles. Here in bed before him is his love's Laodicean church.

"I can't breathe," Bosie says. His chest heaves in short demonstrative bursts.

Wilde touches the handsome youth's forehead. "Bosie, as long as you have my love, you will not die. I promise you immortality. Splendid immortality, Bosie."

"Oh, Oscar," Bosie says, coughs once, and dies.

Fifteen minutes later, men carry the body outside, Wilde protesting. There is fierce debate about what comes next. A German doctor staying at the d'Alsace wants the corpse left inside for observation. Wilde too wants Bosie left in bed. In truth, he is anxious to return the body upstairs because he intends to disrobe and sleep with it, holding Bosie until he feels the life return again. He has seen this happen with his own eyes. The resurrection starts with a tremendous shiver and shake, like the uncoiling of some terrific spring inside the body cavity. The arms shoot up and the knees bend as an extension of that energy. Meanwhile a hissing noise comes from the mouth as dry, inflexible and now unnecessary lungs try to fill. From Bosie's lips the hiss will sound soft as poetry.

One can survive everything, nowadays, except death. Wilde cannot remember when he said or wrote that. It does not matter—the Lazari have rendered it false.

Hurry back to me, Bosie.

"Le corps doit être brûlé."

Wilde stirs from his grief and hope, rethinks what he has just heard and translates. His hands move forward, shaking. "My Bosie is to be burned? I'll not allow that!"

"It is the government's orders. All dead must be cremated."

When I am dead cremate me.

Wilde rubs his temples, fighting unwanted memories of Bosie's father. Around him an argument ensues between the hotel's manager and the armed guards. The rapidity of the exchange and Wilde's inner distractions trouble his ability to understand. The gist is who shall take Bosie's corpse to the designated place of disposal. The crematorium is apparently not close and transportation has become exceedingly difficult and confused. The government has commandeered all the motor vehicles and there are things happening in the streets that have startled the horses. All serviceable horses are also government requisitioned, and the Lazari are known to prey on them when human meat does not present itself. A coach now out of the question, the one choice seems to be carrying Bosie across the city on a stretcher.

"I will not allow my staff to be exposed to such risks. I hired you specifically—"

"You hired us to guard the door. Well, we're guarding it."

"How much more do you want?"

"Couldn't pay us enough. Defending a fixed position is easy. Being out in the open, a moving target? Find yourself a few Americans. They seem foolish enough."

"Brave enough," Wilde says, bringing all attention where it properly belongs, on him. "I have been to that exotic land, gentlemen, and dwelt among their roughnecks. I have met recently a young man from a place called Arkansas—how I should love to flee there one day. Americans themselves do not flee. They are a people blessed by the music of Apollo and the ingenuity of Hephaestus. They—"

One of the gunmen strikes a match and holds it over Bosie's body. "No need to risk the crematorium. Get kerosene. We'll burn the body right here."

"In front of the Alsace? My god, the stench! No, my patrons cannot be exposed to such—"

The gunmen's leader just smiles. "To such what? Barbarism? Indelicacy? Inhumanity? It will be much worse when they see this thing rise to drink our blood."

"I believe you are confusing this hideous condition with vampirism. If you read the celebrated novel by my friend and countryman Stoker, you will realize they are not the same," Wilde says.

"He's an English aristocrat, isn't he? He was a vampire in life. What he returns as won't be so different. Get the kerosene."

Wilde's gaze shifts to the manager's reaction. The little Frenchman's forehead blisters with beads of sweat, telling Wilde that he has already decided to acquiesce. Before the manager can take a step, Wilde produces the Webley. The unexpected quickness of his hands combined with his great height and bulk stupefy them all. No guard even attempts to raise a weapon as Wilde's aim alternates fast before each face.

"If Lord Douglas must go, then so shall I."

"You'd carry him alone through these streets?"

"They seem quite deserted now."

The manager attempts to plead with him, though Wilde knows this is only for the sake of politeness. Removing the body is his chief concern and Wilde was a considerable headache to him before the crisis. In his view, if Wilde leaves with the body, so much the better.

Wilde holds the Webley out a moment longer and then pockets it. He stoops, gathers Bosie into his arms, and like some self-saddling mule Wilde slings him over his right shoulder. The weight stoops him and antagonizes his back, but Bosie feels most familiar to him as a burden to bear. Wilde realizes he did harder labor in prison and ponders that God laid him low in order to toughen him for the present nightmare. It is a perfectly Protestant fantasy, but Wilde is determined to die a Catholic. He takes one step and then another. It will be a slow journey but the weight is not manageable. Nothing truly is except for checking accounts.

"I shall entertain you, my dear resting Bosie," Wilde says some ten minutes into the journey. His pace is slowed even more because he stops constantly to turn and check his blind spots. The streets remain empty but the Lazari have a way of suddenly swarming in spaces that were clear only moments ago. They move with no grace at all, but so slow and inexorable that their footfalls are soundless. Those wearing shoes make a telltale scraping noise, but most come barefooted. The long dead come only on bone. *They lumber,* Wilde thinks. It is an odd word to describe a walking style and he wonders at its etymology. He assumes it means wooden and stiff, without joints, as how a tree might stalk its prey. But that association is too obvious, especially for English diction. Probably the meaning evolved from a root word long dead and resurrected in fifty other disparate expressions having little to do with one another. The paradox of dead meanings existing parasitical and hidden in living words pleases him.

Wilde smiles, remembering his promise to entertain Bosie. He begins to gallop a bit, as if he bore one of his own small children on his back (but no, he shall not think of them now, their mother is dead and it is too horrifying to imagine them alone in another country and surrounded by Lazari). His voice booms out, turning the street into a stage—

"Alas, poor Yorick! I knew him, Horatio: a fellow of infinite jest, of most excellent fancy: he hath borne me on his back a thousand times; and now, how abhorred in my imagination it is! my gorge rims at it."

Wilde stops, winded, and kneels to gentle Bosie's body to the ground. He pants for air as he strokes the angelic face and adjusts the white gauze that has slipped to reveal the wound. Looking at the purple and red gouge, Wilde only now realizes own lips were not the last to feel the heat and pulse of Bosie's throat before he died.

"Alas, poor Yorick," he whispers to himself. A famous speech from a play with many famous speeches—but why did his mind select *that* one? He is a living Yorick looking at his dead Hamlet. Suddenly he is certain the world has gone terribly wrong, that Bosie should live many decades more and that, by standing here breathing, Wilde is a resurrected man as unnatural as the Lazari. *I was dying and every part of me deserved the death.* He feels, even in the face of Bosie's end, the complete bloom of health and vitality. This flower he'll keep in his buttonhole at all costs. He looks down at his lover and repeats Hamlet's speech up to the point he set Bosie down. As Wilde's fingertips stray into Bosie's sweat-stiffened hair, he finishes: "Here hung those lips that I have kissed I know not how oft."

He bends to kiss them now and forces himself not to recoil at their cold, rubbery texture. Bosie's mouth does not open and Wilde's tongue encounters a barricade of teeth as perfect as prison bars.

"Come back to me, Bosie. *Wake.*"

How long will it take? Hours? *Days?* His pushes back from the body and ponders. Vaguely he hears the wounded gait of four, perhaps five, of the resurrected approaching from the east. Blinking away a few tears, Wilde straightens his back and turns to look over his right shoulder. Nine, he counts in astonishment. Six appear quite fresh—they wear fashionable clothes and are obviously recent victims of the very Lazari they have now become. The other three have spent at least ten decades in the ground, garbed as they are in shreds of Jacobin simplicity that doubtlessly resembled rags even a hundred years ago. Complete decomposition of the genitals at least manages to keep them from being altogether indecent.

As he stands, the Webley trembles in his grip. He has already imagined the prospect of reloading. His fingers rub against each other in the left coat pocket—the pocket is empty. He does not have enough bullets for the situation. *How could I have made such an oversight?* So many things never occur to him until it is too late; sometimes his life seems nothing more than a string of neglected chances at foresight and planning. He thinks of Ayat, leaping into action without thinking. *Who in Hades am I to criticize his judgment?*

Wilde closes one eye, raises the gun and prepares to duel. The pistol's strong recoil sends a bolt of pain through his broad wrist as the closest attacker drops, a third eye newly minted in its forehead. Wilde retreats three steps and then automatically circles closer, like an indecisively suicidal man. The brave imperative to assert himself between the Lazari and Bosie waxes and wanes against his terror.

His second shot isn't good enough—the shoulder. The impact flings the Lazarus woman onto her back and the entire right arm disconnects and shatters into splinters. Maybe it will be enough. But no—the remaining body rises a moment later, oblivious to its loss. The left arm juts out, fingers opening and closing, a hideous mimic of the creature's lipless mouth.

"You're nearly as stubborn as Sarah Bernhardt," Wilde says, firing his third shot into her head.

He shoots again and again, more careful with his aim. The bullets find and fell their targets. But five more Lazari approach.

And one bullet remains.

For myself, Wilde thinks, and even turns the gun around to stare down the barrel. A head shot will assure he stays down. But does he want that? The question surprises him so much he spares a second to consider it. In that space, he imagines himself rising, finding Bosie waiting on him. Is there love among the Lazari? There is clearly greed and gluttony and endless hunger. Is love so different than these things? Is love, as he's known it, any less base?

Sweat breaks across his face and pools on cheeks that have become sallow and pitted with age. So hideous, he thinks, staring at the monsters as he backpedals. The notion that he could become one of them willfully, that he would be mindless in his carnal pursuits…my God, he realizes: he already mirrors them. He has lived their existence even before his reputation and his fortune fractured. He had only better skin on a better public face.

The gun goes to his temple, his eyes wincing shut against the planned violence. Then he hears a familiar whistle and looks to see the head of the Lazari farthest from him go flying across the street. The decapitated body drops, revealing Ayat in all his glory, holding a sword so ostentatious that Wilde can only marvel. He brings the sword back to him and leaps into a pose—*à la coquille*. Wilde cries out, drops the Webley, falls to the ground and kicks away from a lunging Lazarus man. The remaining four step over Bosie and swipe down at Wilde's clothes.

"Now it is my turn to save you, dear Oscar," Ayat shouts as he thrusts the blade through the next man's neck. An elegant twist turns the blade flat and with the slightest flick the steel sweeps away bone and flesh. The head lolls backward and tumbles atop the body that collapses underneath it.

"Oscar, what are you doing? Move!"

Wilde has scrambled back as far as he can go. The Lazari have forgotten him, pivoting to indulge Ayat's fervor. Move, he thinks. He looks for the Webley. It is there—out of immediate reach. His gaze trains on Bosie.

The great coil has sprung inside him. The body twitches with new energy, a scene such as only Mary Shelley could imagine. For the second time in half an hour, Wilde thinks of a scene out of literature and inverts his role inside it. Aesthete, poet, playwright, doomed martyr—all the identities he has created for himself—and in reality he is Bosie's construction entirely. He is the Creature watching his Creator come to life.

He bares his neck for Bosie's teeth.

"Oscar!"

Somehow Ayat has lost his sword. It rattles across the ground with a sound that makes Wilde wince. It is a sound like a perfect gem being dropped on the floor and stepped upon until it powders.

Bosie hisses and sits up.

"Damn it, Wilde, your gun! Shoot something!"

Ayat is breathless again. His French is so hard to understand. Wilde takes a deep inhale, wondering if he'll miss it—breathing. Not here, perhaps. The air is wonderfully poisonous in Paris. He much prefers England where they show their toxins with more discretion, in the heart.

Bosie's eyes are pale blue cataracts that fix on Wilde's slumped body. He crawls, still hissing, his body so lithe and exotic and *seductive* that Wilde's erection actually hurts in his pants. *Take me, consume me*, he thinks. There seems so little remaining to him that Bosie has not already devoured, why shouldn't the flesh yield too? Wilde begins to undo his shirt.

Ayat meanwhile dodges one clumsy blow and throws himself along the ground, rolling to escape being surrounded. He rolls all the way to his fallen sword and takes it up. Wilde's attention flickers a moment at him. Beautiful, daring Ayat—so much more worthy than Bosie in nearly everything, a man of hard effort and harder employment, not the bratty, untalented poet son of a crazed aristocrat, himself possessed of terrible poetic pretensions and sensibilities. *When I am dead cremate me.*

He looks at Ayat and then back at Bosie and wipes away a tear with the back of his hand. Poor boy, raised by such a tyrant and likely touched by inherited madness. It excuses everything. It *must*.

Ayat beheads the remaining Lazari. The last one he toys with, dancing just out of reach as leisured swipes sever the right hand and then the left, followed by both arms at their shoulders by making an exaggerated, cleaving swing. He whittles away the Lazarus man, clipping extremities as a tailor might break off an excess of buttons. It is an unexpectedly cruel performance only Bosie could appreciate.

"Do you know what sword this is, Oscar? It is the Austerlitz Blade—the personal sword of Emperor Napoleon, forged by the great Biennais! How I longed to hold it as a boy every time I saw it at the Army Museum. I am a God with this weapon. I am—who is it to you British?"

"I am not British, dear boy."

"I remember now—yes, I am St. George!"

He delivers the decisive blow and then waxes on, addressing his enthusiasms to the blade at such lengths that it takes a minute to realize Wilde's silence. He turns—and shouts something Wilde cannot understand. Gibberish is gibberish in any language, though he wonders how it must look, with Bosie nearly on top of him and Wilde shirtless, waiting for the dry teeth, imaging how his own blood will warm his lover's cold mouth.

"Oscar!"

Ayat rushes toward them. Wilde realizes his intent and something in Bosie realizes it too. His muscles still have strength and quickness to them. He turns in to Ayat's charge, dodges at the last moment and bites into the Frenchman's leg. The Austerlitz Blade strikes the building a mere inch from Wilde left ear and again falls abandoned. "No, Bosie," Wilde cries. His lover smothers over the shrieking fencer, whose arms flail in impotence without a weapon.

"No!"

Wilde staggers up, a walrus in his movements. He seizes Bosie by the waist and literally throws him to the side. He finds Ayat on the ground, coughing up blood. Bosie had started to bite his throat open.

"Not like this," Ayat manages. "Kill me, Oscar. I don't want to…come back."

All men kill the thing they love.

Bosie rolls over. The cataract gaze locks onto them as he hisses.

"I—I can't, Ayat."

"If you love me," Ayat says.

The brave man with a sword.

"But I am not brave, Ayat," Wilde says, his melodious voice cracking. "I'm not like you, I cannot use the sword." The fencer has no idea what he's talking about. "I cannot even give you a kiss. But here," he says, forcing the Webley into the Frenchman's hand as Bosie manages to stand and shuffle toward them.

"Oscar."

"We'll do it together. I shall help you, if you lend me your strength. Oh, I am a fool. What strength have you left to lend? I am a pitiless borrower, Ayat. Here, both our fingers on the trigger—"

Ayat's face shatters with the blast.

Wilde does kill Bosie afterwards, but not straight away. He takes up Ayat's stolen blade and breaks into the nearest building and climbs the stairs. From the second floor window, he watches Bosie walk about in what appears to be stunned circles for twenty minutes before he suddenly decides on a direction. From his vantage point, Wilde detects the reason for this sea change—a child, lost and terrified, is standing in the middle of the road a block over. Bosie has caught the scent. Wilde's breath hitches and he knows what must come next. He cannot permit such an outrage.

The memory of the deed lingers and refuses to stale. What's so horrifying is the freedom each sunrise brings since Bosie's beheading. He is at first philosophical about it, telling himself that he now realizes death is merely the state in which the striving mind finally perceives the Nothingness it has always suspected was there. He is a delight among the refugees fleeing across France to the Channel, an absurd entertainer, a legend, a perfect Christ. "The best way to conquer death is by not dying," he says, and somehow to the people who have lost their friends and families, their very future, to the Lazarus plague, this statement proves the very essence of cheer.

There are rumors everywhere. The horrors that infected France have moved across Europe and there are reported outbreaks in England itself. This news makes the Channel crossing very tense, as someone announces the British military will either sink the vessel before it docks or else execute them all as soon as they got off. This image is so vivid to mad minds that several men and women jump overboard at the halfway point and are soon out of sight, swimming, swimming.

Wilde however hopes the outbreak *has* happened in England. He counts on it, for Bosie's death troubles him with freedom. He senses his past life with Bosie no longer counts and that he can now live unfettered—almost. One chain remains about his neck, and perhaps around

Bosie's too, if his spirit lingers. But Wilde knows how to break it, and so he crosses back to the country that persecuted him.

All of Western Europe seems to be accompanying him, and nothing staunches the invasion. Wilde encounters no Customs clerk to whom he can declare his genius or Ayat's sword or the more precious thing he carries in a black satchel. Wilde steps onto English soil three years after vowing to never return. In a way, he has not broken his pledge. The Wilde who made it no longer exists.

When I am dead cremate me.

Months ago Wilde heard—and delighted in—a rumor that Bosie's father, despite the wishes stated in his absurd poem, was not cremated but instead buried vertically with his head pointing down, his gaze directed at more eternal fires. If true, his plan may work. Queensberry's body is still far away, on the estates of Kinmount House in Scotland. It will be an arduous affair getting there, especially if every city in England and its countryside teem with Lazari. He already knows this must be the case. The wind is tinted with a familiar chill and scent, even this close to the sea. Survivors call it the Lazari's Breath and it is a combination of mass, mobile decomposition and a sweating terror.

Wilde watches the refugees flock west—thousands of them with thousands more on the way. They are heading for larger ports with ships they will storm, if necessary, to seek shelter in America. Wilde remembers his own trip there decades ago as he stalks northward, stopping just once to set the satchel down so he can grasp Ayat's sword with both hands. It did belong to Napoleon, after all—who is Wilde to deny anyone a thwarted dream? (*And perhaps the Emperor too has risen and even now stumbles and slouches through the Arc de Triomphe in an abandoned Paris, his hand still famously tucked into his shirt, disconnected from any arm.*) With a cry, he takes the sword and plunges it into the ground, releasing it to quiver like a living thing reveling in territorial conquest and triumph. Wilde admires the weapon's grace and beauty, forged from steel and silver, shining with gold gilt but bronzed with dried blood.

Taking up the sword again as he retrieves the satchel, he says, "Bosie, we are on our way."

The journey takes weeks. The sword conquers armies of Lazari. Wilde lacks Ayat's skill but his stamina and ruthlessness, powered by a monomaniacal fixation, keeps him moving. It is more exciting, more electrifying, to dispatch British Lazari. He no longer even sees the business as gruesome—each is a small revenge and freedom leading to the greater one ahead.

If doubts possess him, he need only sleep to have all confidence restored. Each night his dream is exactly the same. He stands in Reading prison watching a young man's execution. He cannot remember the man's name, only that Wilde has sworn eternal love to him. The youth is hanged until death and then his body is lowered to the ground. Almost at once the body resurrects and becomes vibrant. Shocked, the prison officials hang him again. The body thrashes on its rope endlessly and the warden and all the guards flee in terror. The gates are left open and everyone escapes except Wilde, who stands pressing his forehead against the man's bound legs and weeping.

"We are here, Bosie."

The grave of Bosie's father, John Sholto Douglas, Marquess of Queensberry. *When I am dead cremate me.* Perhaps the monster's wishes were carried out after all—perhaps digging will reveal a vessel of ashes where the body should be. Wilde strikes his spade into the earth, snarling at the labor of it, willing the dirt to yield.

A half hour later he finds signs of—O wonderful paradox!—*life*.

The rumors are true. Bosie's father has been buried vertically upside down. There is no coffin at all, just a body jammed into the earth. Wilde's spade finds the feet and the feet are—*moving*. A thin layer of dirt pulses like a beating heart and Wilde clears it to reveal two worn and filthy soles. He gasps, falls back and hastens to the satchel.

He pulls Bosie's head from within and sets it atop the tombstone. "Now at last I understand Salome," Wilde says, considering the head. The desiccated blue cataracts leer straight ahead at Wilde as he resumes digging. Queensberry's legs kick in greater strides as Wilde disencumbers them. It takes almost three hours before he can drag the body out of its hole.

The Marquess is clearly ravenous and Wilde recognizes a hunger that is unchanged by death. Had he been buried like a normal person, he would have clawed his way to the surface weeks ago. Wilde swallows, angered by his fear of the familiar, rotting face. He did not come all this way to indulge fear. Queensberry suddenly lunges stiffly at him and Wilde shrieks and bashes his head with a powerful backhand. The fear goes, replaced with a long nourished rage that seizes all of his being. He will use the sword.

There is no God, Wilde thinks. And if there is a God, what he does next is perhaps not technically a sacrilege, an immorality so vile that even the most decadent of men would turn from the very idea in horror. It is not necrophilia if the body is resurrected, after all, and he pins Queensberry into the dirt before the grave and shames the father in front of the son.

When it is finished, he takes Ayat's sword and beheads the Marquess and puts it on the tombstone next to Bosie's. The air around Kinmount House fills with laughter and the echo of heavy footfalls. It is Wilde, his long arms swaying in the air as his body writhes, a man veiled with life, and he is dancing, dancing, dancing.

THE CONTRIBUTORS

MATTHEW CHENEY's work has been published by *English Journal, One Story, Unstuck, Weird Tales, Web Conjunctions, Strange Horizons, Failbetter.com, Ideomancer, Pindeldyboz, Weird Fiction Review, Rain Taxi, Locus,* and *SF Site,* among other places. He is the former series editor for *Best American Fantasy* and the co-editor, with Eric Schaller, of the occasional online magazine *The Revelator.*

JOHN CHU designs microprocessors by day and writes by night. His fiction has been published in *Boston Review, Asimov's Science Fiction Magazine* and Tor.com, among others.

R. W. CLINGER is a resident of Pittsburgh. His work includes the novels *Nebraska Close, Just a Boy, Skin Tours,* and *The Last Pile of Leaves. The Boyfriend Season,* his first short story collection, was published by JMS Books. He is currently at work on a new gay mystery. For more information, visit rwclinger.com.

SEAN EADS is a writer living in Denver, CO. He's originally from Kentucky and currently makes his living as a reference librarian. His first novel, *The Survivors,* was a finalist for the 2013 Lambda Literary Award in the science fiction category. His writing has appeared in a variety of publications, including *Shock Totem, Waylines Magazine,* and the *Journal of Popular Culture.* His favorite writers include Ray Bradbury and Herman Melville, his favorite sports are basketball and golf, and his favorite beer is Gulden Draak.

Having been, at various times, and under different names, a minister's daughter, a computer programmer, the author of metaphysical thrillers, an organic farmer and a profound sleeper, ELI EASTON is happily embarking on yet another incarnation as a gay romance author

CASEY HANNAN lives and writes in Kansas City. His debut collection of stories, *Mother Ghost*, is available from Tiny Hardcore Press. He can be found at casey-hannan.com.

CLAYTON LITTLEWOOD was born in Skegness, England, in 1963 and grew up in Weston-super-Mare. He has an MA in Film & Television and writing comedy scripts. In his recent incarnations Clayton has been running the shop Dirty White Boy with his partner, Jorge Betancourt, writing the "Soho stories" column for *The London Paper* and contributing regularly to BBC radio. His first book, *Dirty White Boy: Tales of Soho*, was named the GT book of the year. *Goodbye to Soho* is his follow-up.

SAM J. MILLER is a writer and a community organizer. His fiction has appeared or is forthcoming in *Strange Horizons*, *Electric Velocipede*, *Shimmer*, *Daily Science Fiction*, *Nightmare Magazine*, *Beneath Ceaseless Skies*, *The Minnesota Review*, and *The Rumpus*, among others. He is a graduate of the 2012 Clarion Writer's Workshop and the co-editor of *Horror After 9/11*, an anthology published by the University of Texas Press. Visit him at samjmiller.com.

J. E. ROBINSON received an Illinois Arts Council Literary Award for his essays. His novel *Skip Macalester* was designated a *Paperback Pick* by the American Booksellers Association. An ancient historian, he teaches at the Saint Louis College of Pharmacy.

DAMON SHAW lives in the Canary Islands, fifty miles off the African Coast. He makes stuff; puppets and benches and sculptures and life-sized wooden camels, and other wooden inventions which he sells to the never-ending stream of holiday makers who pass his stall every Sunday. He also writes and his work has been in *The Touch of the Sea*, *The Laven-*

der Menace, and *Daily Science Fiction*, as well as other markets. Damon is threatening to write a novel.

C ORY SKERRY lives in the Northwest U.S. and works at an upscale adult boutique. In his free time, he writes stories, draws comics, copy edits for *Shimmer Magazine*, and goes hiking with his two sweet, goofy pit bulls.. When he grows up, he'd like science to make him into a giant octopus.

R OBERT SMITH lives in Brooklyn. He has been published in *Evergreen Review*, several NYC queer publications, contributed to Lambda Literary Foundation, and read original material in curated events at various literary venues, galleries and spaces, including New Museum. He is currently writing his first novel, titled *Numbskull*.

N GHI Vo lives by an inland sea. Her current interests include old gods, new gods, candymaking, alchemy, puppet theater, and the Ottoman Empire. Her work has appeared in *Crossed Genres*, *Strange Horizons*, and *Unlikely Story*.

K AI ASHANTE WILSON lives in New York City. His first published story can be found in the *Bloodchildren* anthology.

THE EDITOR

S TEVE BERMAN owns a great many books, a great many of which are gay-themed and a great many of those are eerie and fantastical. Well, the stories, not so much the books themselves, but he does possess a book reported to turn any flower pressed between its pages into a cordial (he's never dared try because he fears getting the book wet) and a scandalous memoir penned by Didier de Grandin, the bastard gay son of Seabury Quinn's famous occult detective.

CPSIA information can be obtained at www.ICGtesting.com
Printed in the USA
LVOW06s2054100814

398421LV00006B/465/P